The Creative Di

The Creative Director

The Heart Never Lies

Copyright 2020 All Rights Reserved

Sandra A. Sigfusson

Sandra A. Sigfusson

Library and Archives Canada

Names: Sigfusson, Sandra, Ann

Title: The Creative Director / Sandra A. Sigfusson

Description: Romance

Identifiers: ISBN:

Subjects: Contemporary Romance – fiction | Interpersonal Relationships – fiction | Contemporary Women – fiction | Advertising – fiction | Winery – fiction | Erotica – fiction | New York – fiction | Army - fiction

First Edition

Book Cover Design: Sandra A. Sigfusson

Cover Image: iStock.com / photo ID: 467080815 by miljko

Editor: Matthew Goddin / Thames Valley Wordworks

The Creative Director

Unauthorized use or distribution of this book without express permission is a copyright infringement (abuse of the author's intellectual property). If you would like permission to use material from this book (other than for review purposes), please contact the author directly at sandrasigfusson@shaw.ca

The Creative Director is a work of fiction. Names, characters, places and incidents are the products of the author's imagination or are used fictitiously. Any resemblance to actual events, locales or persons, living or dead, is entirely coincidental.

Acknowledgements:

I'd like to thank my readers for their valued time. As a reader and a writer I can appreciate what it takes to make the decision on which novel to buy and finding the time to enjoy it. Please, if you can spare a moment when you've completed this novel, would you offer a review? It matters not if you liked or disliked this novel. It matters that you shared your experience with other readers.

I'd also like to thank Ava Lucas VO for taking me under her wing when I was struggling to get a foot in the door of the audiobook production world. Her kindness, knowledge, and support in guiding me through this additional form of publication for my work is much appreciated.

Sandra A. Sigfusson

Please visit my website for updates on new releases, audiobook versions of my novels, my newsletter sign-up and promotions relating to my current works of romance fiction at www.sandrasigfusson.com.

Table of Contents:

Chapter 1 - 6	Chapter 2 - 11	Chapter 3 – 15
Chapter 4 - 29	Chapter 5 - 43	Chapter 6 – 55
Chapter 7 - 64	Chapter 8 - 76	Chapter 9 – 82
Chapter 10 - 91	Chapter 11 - 98	Chapter 12 – 105
Chapter 13 - 110	Chapter 14 - 116	Chapter 15 – 145
Chapter 16 - 154	Chapter 17 - 164	Chapter 18 – 180
Chapter 19 - 185	Chapter 20 - 191	Chapter 21 – 199
Chapter 22 - 204	Chapter 23 - 215	Chapter 24 – 223
Chapter 25 - 233	Chapter 26 - 240	Chapter 27 – 246
Chapter 28 - 259	Chapter 29 - 265	Chapter 30 – 274
Chapter 31 - 277	Chapter 32 - 286	Chapter 33 – 296

The Creative Director

Chapter 34 - 310   Chapter 35 - 318   Chapter 36 – 327

Chapter 37 - 329   Chapter 38 - 338   Chapter 39 – 344

Chapter 40 - 354   Chapter 41 - 378   Chapter 42 – 387

Chapter 43 - 399   Chapter 44 - 407   Chapter 45 – 423

Chapter 46 - 431   Chapter 47 - 438

About the Author - 466

Sandra A. Sigfusson

Chapter 1: The Perfect Pitch

My business is advertising, and I live and breathe my work. Advertising, when done correctly, is sexy, humorous and captivating. I liken it to a form of seduction. Today my job is to seduce a room full of stone-faced ad executives from one of the most renowned agencies in New York City into believing I have what it takes to represent their deep-pocketed clients. As one of two Creative Directors in their firm, I would be the new visionary for their clients' products and services. The company where I seek this prestigious role is named Digame (dee-gah-meh), which translates from Spanish as *tell me*. And tell them I shall.

    I affix a bright smile upon my face for the six executives seated around the grand, oval, high-gloss maple boardroom table before me and begin my interview presentation.

    "A few years ago, I was tasked with reviving a deceased dog. She had choked on a piece of a rubber balloon and had stopped breathing. But don't worry – there is a happy ending. I was able to dislodge the balloon from her throat and perform mouth-to-muzzle to get her breathing again."

The Creative Director

My story has managed to widen the eyes in the room, but the chilly air-conditioning in their conference room isn't quelling my body's need to sweat under pressure. I push on in the hope that one of the executives will find me persuasive enough to give me the job.

I continue my pitch with confidence. "That experience got me thinking about what we do as advertisers. We've all been handed a dead product at some point. Advertising is intended to create an air of hope regardless of how alive or dead the client's product is. My objective is to look at the client's product or service, assume that it's already dead, and then perform CPR, which in my world stands for Creative Promotional Revival. As fellow marketing experts, we all understand the client's need to ensure whatever campaign they use to present their product to the public is a home run. I have a reputation for said home runs, and for reviving dead dogs." I pause for effect, then add, "True story, by the way."

At this point, I've officially garnered their attention plus a few raised eyebrows. I inject statistics, humor, visuals, and other samples of the work I've recently completed, along with a list of the four prestigious awards I've earned in my career thus far. My awards are confirmation that I rose to this level because of what I knew, not who I blew. As sad as that statement

Sandra A. Sigfusson

is, the stigma follows women of power everywhere – especially when they are as young as I am.

I continue to smile during my entire pitch and make eye contact with everyone. The only person in the room who seems to be uninterested in my pitch is the current Creative Director, the man I'd be sharing the title with, known only as Brantley.

I am familiar with his work. He acquired a top position with Digame two years ago after spending only five years as an assistant CD with one of the largest advertising firms in the US. The move was a smart one, because he managed to become the youngest man to land a Creative Director position at a prominent ad agency in New York. Now that I recognize my pitch interview isn't exactly tugging at this man's heartstrings, I worry that I've blown the entire presentation. He is the very person in the room from whom I want approval. A simple smile or a nod in appreciation would suffice, but neither comes. I keep my brave smile fixed on my face as I summarize and close the deal in the best way I know how. I ask them how soon I can start as their second Creative Director.

A silence fills the room while I stand with my entrails laying out on the table before them, waiting for an answer. A few of the executives turn to each other, and

The Creative Director

they exchange quietly spoken words. Nods and smiles complete their discreet discussions. Pens click, papers get shoved into briefcases and file folders, and then the President of DIA rises to thank me for my time. My smile threatens to fade, but I pull harder on my lips to ensure they are fixed and stable. My presentation was excellent. I know it, and they know it. The real question is always the same regardless of performance: Is the interviewee right for the company?

"We'll be in touch," Brantley says in a deep, rich English accent that surprises me and catches my attention. He glances briefly at me, expressionless, before he rises from his chair and starts tapping something into his cell phone. He doesn't smile or nod at me before he leaves the room. Is that a British thing, or is he simply unimpressed? Shit. If I didn't know better, I'd be sure he would be the one who would ultimately sway the team into *not* hiring me.

While the last two executives mingle, I close up my briefcase, remove my USB from the boardroom TV monitor, and gather my coat to leave.

"Excellent presentation, Miss James," one of them says. That lifts my spirits a bit.

"Thank you." I smile genuinely and hold my head up high as I leave the conference room to exit the office.

Sandra A. Sigfusson

Inside I want to cry. I've spent countless hours preparing for this job presentation, and I feel like it was all for nothing. Brantley was unimpressed, and the President didn't lay his cards down on the table either. Was I reading their faces and body movements wrong, or do they like to make people sweat?

The Creative Director

Chapter 2: And That's How the Fight Started

It is two full business days after my pitch interview at Digame before I receive a phone call from the President, Grady Maxwell III. His offer is short and sweet: one-hundred-seventy-five-thousand starting salary, a lease car, an expense budget of ten thousand dollars per month, and a benefits package with seventy-five-percent coverage on medical, dental and eye care. I accept without hesitation. I received a seventy-thousand-dollar-a-year raise in one phone call. I nearly wet my pants after hanging up the phone. Once the excitement and shock wear off, I realize I need a new wardrobe and a pair of power shoes in cherry red for my first day.

Day one of my new position as one of two Creative Directors at Digame's offices doesn't go smoothly. The morning meeting's main topic is downsizing the firm's office space. What did I just agree to? If they are downsizing, then why the hell was I hired? In our discussions, they inform me I'll be sharing an office with the other Creative Director, Brantley. It is an executive space, large enough for two desks, with a kitchenette and its own executive washroom, but still – sharing an office at this level? It seems cheap and unacceptable. I smile as politely as I can.

Sandra A. Sigfusson

When the meeting adjourns I follow the receptionist to the ample office space Brantley and I will be sharing. He has already claimed his side of the office next to the kitchenette and washroom. "Lazy much?" I mutter under my breath as I set my briefcase and purse down on the empty desk on the opposite side of the room. He glances up quickly as I scan the space, and thankfully doesn't hear my mumbled comment. Thus far, Brantley and I have yet to exchange one word. I fear this guy is going to be a real hardass to work with, but I'm well versed in dealing with hardasses and grumpy fucks.

"You can have whatever wall space you need on your half of the office," he says curtly.

"Thanks," I reply and fake a pleasant smile. "Whiteboards? Art supplies?"

"Carol is our office manager. You can locate her next to reception and she will be able to give you all the items you'll need. Unless you have a project to discuss, I'd be delighted if you'd pose all your questions to Carol. I don't have time to wean you."

"Wean?" I utter under my breath. Is it okay to kick a co-worker in the ass on the first day? Maybe Mr. Sunshine hasn't had his cup of coffee yet this morning.

The Creative Director

"Coffee?" I ask without looking behind me to pose my question to his face.

"Are you offering to make me one, or do you want someone to teach you how to operate the coffee machine behind me?" he asks, his tone condescending.

I turn slowly to face my new partner in crime and smile. "Well, let's start with a deal. You teach me how to make coffee in that fancy-assed machine, the likes of which I've not seen before," I say, pointing at it like he has no idea where it is, "and I promise to share a cup of the pot I create with you."

A smirk tugs at the corner of his mouth as I lean against my desk casually. "That fancy-assed machine only makes one cup at a time. I don't even need to leave my desk to tell you how to do it," he drones. I cross my arms and pitch one eyebrow nearly as high as my hairline in anticipation of his next patronizing words. "Put a clean coffee mug under the spout just there," he says, pointing. "Stick a flavored coffee pod in the dispenser above. Press the button labeled *start*," he says, using air quotes, "and wait for twenty seconds for your cup to be filled. A talented woman such as yourself is likely to get it right on your first try."

Sandra A. Sigfusson

"Those were very concise instructions. I promise not to mess up," I say, a bit more snidely than I wanted to. "And the washroom is for both of us to share?" I ask.

"Yes. Now can you please direct any further questions to Carol?" His eyes lift to meet mine, but his head stays aimed down at his paperwork.

I don't bother replying – what a pompous ass. I can't believe I left one asshole to work with another. And this asshole is even younger than the last one. But fuck it – whatever – two can play that game. He only wants me to speak to him if it's relative to a client, and that suits me fine. I head out to the primary office space in search of the wise and powerful Miss Carol. Hopefully, she is a little more helpful and a lot less condescending than Brantley.

The Creative Director

Chapter 3: Would the Real Woman Please Stand?

Our first project together is for a feminine hygiene product. As much as I want to smirk, I keep my feelings hidden about how any man could understand the value of a well designed tampon. It's not that I don't think a man shouldn't attempt to market a feminine hygiene product, but I liken the idea to me trying to market cock rings – I'll never use one and I'll never know what it feels like to have one applied to my person. Some things are simply better marketed by the gender they apply to.

When I first start a campaign I'm drawn to color and packaging, and I build my ad campaign around that. The two things I know for certain about the item we're marketing are that it is an all-natural product and targeted to females between the ages of fifteen and thirty-five. Since we will be presenting this project together, I pose my first question about it to Brantley, asking what he thinks of my color choices. This is a way for me to test the waters on how involved he really wants to be in working in this female-dominated category.

"Too girlie," he mumbles. He leans back in his chair, which gives out an annoying squeak as he clicks his pen open and shut while staring me down.

I counter, speaking slowly while I frown. "It is a girl product."

"Women and non-binary individuals are your target," he says.

Dammit. He's right. I know this and I can't believe I've stepped backward in time at this crucial part of my career. There are no boys and girls, men and women anymore. The spectrum of targets is much broader. This should technically make marketing products easier, but the contrary has occurred. "Welcome to a new era of marketing gray," he says slowly, embellishing his accented words with a husky tone, then winks at me.

Should I take that wink as another note of condescension, or is he lightening up on me? I nod reluctantly and shrug. "So, dusty rose and black aren't doing it for you?" I ask.

"Black, yes. Dusty rose, no. In fact, I think you can retire the color dusty rose and not one soul on this planet would fault you for it. We're dealing with an age group that is known for displaying emotional issues, and quite publicly I might add. Black has always signified strength, which will appeal to all those in that age

The Creative Director

category. The contrasting color should be something green, I think. Light green. Teal, maybe," he offers, before going back to clicking his pen open and shut.

I nod. Okay. I like what I'm hearing. The black is synonymous with strength, which is why it has always been used traditionally in all marketing strategies, particularly for text. I turn and sit back down at my desk to pull out two different green markers, using them to color in the mock-up outline logo image I have several photocopies of for doodling on. I hold up my rough drafts and ask him again what he thinks.

"Perfect. You make *my* work look so easy," he muses. "How good are you with stringing words together in a sentence? I have some ideas but I'd like to hear yours."

I smirk at his insult but I'm game to play along. "How about *The strength of nature on your side?*"

"No," he replies instantly without even looking up at me. He's busy inspecting his olive-green silk tie for lack of anything better to do.

"No? Why not?" I ask, being a tad defensive.

"It's a tampon product. How is that nature on your side? Are you even a real woman?" he says, then chuckles.

Sandra A. Sigfusson

Well, if that didn't get my panties in a knot, nothing would. "Jesus," I reply sternly. "I don't mind your comments in a constructive form but insulting me is not appropriate under any circumstances. I'll create my own pitch and you create yours. We'll see who the *real woman* is when the clients' faces drop to their asses at what you have to offer."

I shouldn't have lost it on him like that, and certainly not on my first day on the job, but my stress levels are a bit high with this being the first campaign we're working on together at Digame.

"My apologies for the insult. That wasn't how I meant my words to come out. But, game on, Assistant Creative Director," he chuckles again. He reaches for his coffee mug then rolls his office chair over to the coffee machine behind him and makes himself another cup.

I have to wonder if this is a game to him, seeing how far he can push me before I break. And if so, then I'm up for that challenge. My eyes narrow at him and I have a dagger for a tongue now. "I'm not your fucking assistant, nor am I willing to take your bruised ego and patch it up for you like your mommy used to do when you were eighteen." I wait with bated breath for his snide retort, but instead he acquiesces.

The Creative Director

"You're right. I tend to be harsh as a knee-jerk reaction," he says.

His back is still turned to me while he waits for his coffee mug to fill. Did I just win that war on words? Does he have a problem with women being just as powerful as him? I think he does. In under two hours I've managed to both piss him off and defend my corner of the boxing ring. It must be a new record for him to be rendered speechless by a woman in so short a time span. He's lucky his desk is ten feet away from mine, or I'd have smacked his attitude out of him with the backside of my hand.

I try to calm down, but the mere presence of him in my space draws an ire in me that I can't quell. My only avenue for release is to focus on the project, attempting to mentally block him from my side of the office. I refer to the notes the client emailed about the product's detailed description, the dimensions of the box they've decided to package it in, and their research on its use and effectiveness.

The art department can take my color combinations and work on a full packaging mock-up while I decide on a slogan and ad campaign. I should also introduce myself to the writers in the bullpen down the hall and see what ideas they might have for me.

Sandra A. Sigfusson

I've already come up with two slogans: the one I mentioned to Brantley, and a backup, *Comfort Is in Our Nature*. I'm feeling rather happy with myself for coming up with two solid ideas in only one afternoon. After heading to the art department, I sit down with one of the available crew to discuss font styles and logo placement for packaging. Next I create quick sketches of the commercial ad spaces in a storyboard format.

I'll take this work home with me tonight to tweak more ideas in the silence of my living room. I've discovered sharing an office space with Brantley is quite distracting. Along with his loud telephone conversations in his sexy-as-hell voice and the squeak in his chair as he leans back to ponder ideas, the fact that he is devastatingly handsome makes concentration almost impossible.

Although I attempt to ignore his fine clothes, well-defined, slender physique and incredible blue eyes, I'm acutely aware of his movements across from me. It would be better if my desk were spun around to face the wall instead of directly at him. I may have to get maintenance to reposition my desk.

The Creative Director

On the Friday afternoon of my first week on the job, I am stepping out of our private office washroom when Brantley is attempting to come inside. I startle with a short, loud squeal as we nearly collide into each other. Jumping back I lose my balance but grip the door jamb to save my ass from unceremoniously hitting the floor.

A playful grin eases over his full lips as I place my hand over my chest while catching my breath. He towers over me by at least three inches even with my high heels on. I've not stood so close to him until this moment, and his cologne is heavenly. A deep, rich scent with hints of cedar and bergamot fills my senses. There cannot be a more masculine scent than this.

"You startle too easily," he says. "My sister did as well, and I enjoyed every opportunity to make her scream when we were young."

"Please don't do that to me again," I mutter and frown at his beautiful face. "I have a weak heart and I can't take being startled very well. It takes me some time to recover," I add.

Brantley's grin fades. I think he may be considering apologizing to me. No apology comes. "Are you done with the loo?" he asks.

I squeeze past his broad, silk-suit-jacketed shoulder and nudge him as I do. "The *loo* is all yours," I say. My stride back to my desk is full of confidence and purpose. He won't scare the daylights out of me and get away with it. Sadly, I admitted being a target for his pranks. Hopefully he doesn't make it a habit to rattle my composure. Although I wouldn't mind standing that close to him again. I hear myself say, "Snap out of it," in Cher's voice from the movie *Moonstruck,* and chuckle. I need an edge on him and soon.

The following Monday is our first dual-pitch session with Parish, Inc. Brantley has been a tad more respectful of me since our standoff on my first day, and I appreciate this gesture.

      As I follow Brantley into the conference room I get another subtle whiff of his cologne. I somehow can't prevent myself from commenting on how nice he smells as we lay our presentation materials at the end of the massive table. There's a long pause before he acknowledges my utterance, but when it comes it is genuine. "Thank you," he murmurs. "Do you like woodsy-scented colognes?"

The Creative Director

I raise my head up and glance at his profile. "Some, yes. Yours is different. Perhaps it's your skin chemistry that makes it right for you," I reply.

"Have you worked with a perfumer before?" he continues.

"Yes, two years ago. What is it about the scent you're wearing that *you* like?" I ask.

"It drives women mad," he muses as a cocky smirk eases to a full-on smile.

I nod and smile back. "I'm taking you down with this client today. Just giving you a heads-up that whatever you have to present will be blown away by what I have."

He doesn't reply with words, only a quick nod. In a way I feel like I had him just then, but I don't trust him not to pull a rabbit out of a top hat at the last second. Brantley is shrewd. I'll need to remind myself of that every time we're challenged to present ideas to the same client. I am thankful this is not a common situation. He has his list of clients and I have mine. We collaborate when necessary.

This client is pleased with our presentations. It is unknown which of our ideas they like most. A short deliberation with fresh coffee, water and a fruit tray follows our pitch, and we've been inside the conference room closing on two hours. I escape briefly to use the washroom and return to refill my water glass and pinch a chunk of pineapple from the fruit tray.

I can feel Brantley's eyes on me as I suck the sweet juices from the large chunk of pineapple between my fingers. A little bit of the juice dribbles on my lips and chin. I reach for a napkin to dry my hand and mouth before swallowing the whole chunk as elegantly as I can. Why the caterer made the chunks so large is beyond me, but I've never been able to pass on fresh pineapple. I glance sidelong at Brantley, who is eyeing me.

"Shall I get you a bib?" he teases.

I narrow my eyes at him and his cheeky comment. *Yes, I want a bib so I can choke you with it*, I say to myself. "No, thank you. The napkin is sufficient," I reply calmly.

When our ten-minute break is over the client's executive staff reconvene to their chairs and open up the discussion. The chairperson of their marketing division goes first. "We loved both of your ideas. Thankfully you are colleagues and not competitors so when we tell you our decision there won't be any broken hearts," he chuckles.

The Creative Director

Come on, come on, I say to myself. *Which one did you prefer? Please say me. I worked my ass off for this. And little do they know that Brantley and I are indeed competitors.*

"We'd like to go with *Comfort is in our nature,* for the slogan. How soon can we get the commercials produced?"

My smile threatens to break my face. They liked my idea better than Brantley's. I'm so happy I could pass out. *In your face you arrogant asshole, Brantley.* "We have an in-house studio for photo and video shoots," I reply. "I'll get my staff working on the project immediately. Can I have two weeks until the next presentation?"

"Yes. We want to launch as soon as possible. The product is a complete redesign of our earlier one, and none of the competitors in feminine hygiene products have marketed anything this innovative in the past five years. This is big and we're counting on you both to make the launch a massive success for us."

I nod and smile brightly again. "We'll start immediately. I've already secured three models to do three versions of the commercial for you," I state.

Everyone nods and applause fills the room. I could not be happier than I am now. Brantley pats me on the back and offers that smile of his, the one he knows is dampening the panties of every woman here.

"Congratulations," he says as we gather up our presentation materials. When only Brantley and I remain he says, "Just to be clear, I don't plan on letting you win over every client. I gave you that one to boost your confidence. Did I succeed?" he asks with a cheeky smile.

I place the papers in my hand down on the table and push a stray hair away from my eyes. My hands find my hips and I press my tongue hard into my cheek before replying. "Um, I'll have you know that I won the client over because my idea was better than yours, Brantley." I shake my head and go back to fitting my papers into my briefcase.

"Okay. See it the way you want to." He's still smiling as if he won when he clearly bombed. Jesus, he's cocky. I don't give him the satisfaction of another look. I can't look in his eyes any more today without completely losing my cool.

"Do you even hear yourself when you speak?" I chide.

The Creative Director

"Yes, of course. But if you can't handle the truth I'm willing to candy-coat my thoughts for you, moving forward," he chuckles.

"Fucker," I say under my breath, and I'm certain he heard me. In fact, I'm glad he heard me.

During the drive back to the office we remain predominantly silent. Other than listening to Brantley order lunch from Carol on his cell phone, we don't address each other or make any verbal noises. I organize the papers inside my briefcase and sip from my water bottle to pass the time. The scent of his cologne invades my space, and I have to try hard not to waver in my anger when he smells so heavenly.

We're caged inside the taxi for an hour before reaching the office again. It amazes me how long an hour is when nobody is speaking. The cab driver didn't talk after he asked us where to go. No music or podcast played either. Only the crackle and spark of intermittent voices over the cabbie's dispatcher radio filled the interior space.

Brantley seemed to be sleeping for most of our ride. How can he rest when I have a thousand thoughts racing through my head about shooting the commercial and firming up the packaging details within the next two weeks? The client wants to go into production and distribution mode in six weeks. This is going to be so tight my head spins.

When the cab stops in front of our office building I push my credit card through to the front seat. "I'll make you a deal," I say to Brantley. "I'll pay for the cab fare every time I win a client when we do dual presentations, if you'll agree to stop being such an arrogant asshole to me."

Brantley's eyes widen and then a broad smile flashes at me. "Deal, Miss James." Brantley exits the cab and rounds the back of it to my side of the cab. "I'll start now by holding the door for you," he chuckles again. I think he's finding our little private game of war on words amusing.

I want to smile, but I don't want him to know I like this side of him. "Thank you," I offer curtly. He nods and then follows behind me as we enter the building.

The Creative Director

Chapter 4: Pangs of Inadequacy

A week after our joint pitch to Parish Inc., I am shooting the commercials. It goes quite smoothly. All three of the models I chose do an amazing job of reading the lines and making the product look like it's the only one their generation should use. I am beaming inside and out. Giving the client three actor-model options for the commercial sounds frivolous, but it's cheaper to shoot three spots in one shoot than to revisit the studio multiple times.

When I return to my desk later in the afternoon I find Brantley scouring over some design sketches the art department provided him for one of his clients. "Everything going well?" I ask, breaking his concentration.

"Yes. I'm fairly happy with the mock-ups. How did your shoot go?" he asks. I watch as he leisurely stretches his arms up over his head and then cracks his knuckles when his arms come back down to desk level.

"Good to hear. The shoot went well. I'm pleased with all the models," I reply.

"When are you planning on hiring an assistant?" he asks.

I glance over to him and shake my head. "I've never had an assistant and I manage my clients fine without one. Why don't you have an assistant?" I ask.

"Nadia is on maternity leave and I haven't gotten round to replacing her," he says. "You're going to need an assistant, Jess. I split the client list evenly – twenty each. Trust me when I tell you that some of those clients are quite demanding and you'll need another set of hands to help you meet their expectations." Brantley grabs his coffee mug and examines the contents before rising to rinse the cup in the sink. "I suggest you hire internally, or at least interview internally before looking elsewhere. Ask Carol to give you a list of the potentials here." He sets his rinsed mug upside down on a tea towel and dries his hands while he continues. "I know you've not met everyone in the office, and this might be a good time to introduce yourself to the full staff while eyeing up who would make a good sidekick for you," he adds.

I nod and wonder how he managed all forty clients on his own before I was hired. "Why did the management want to hire a second Creative Director?" I ask.

His eyes reach mine as he sits back down at his desk. "I wanted a second Creative Director. And I

The Creative Director

specifically wanted a woman in the role because I think with our diverse client list having a male/female dynamic is most advantageous."

"*You* wanted to share your client list?" I scoff. "I find that hard to believe."

He offers a light chuckle at my disbelief before smiling. "Nadia was overloaded with my projects while I was training her to be an Assistant CD. When she got knocked up, as you Americans put it, by her boyfriend and decided to keep the baby, I knew I was going to have to look elsewhere for someone to fill in for her. That's when I realized that our client base was far too large for me to handle on my own, although I was handling it well until Nadia had to leave," he says, puffing out his chest a bit. "Having said that, I was the one who decided you were the right fit for the job, Jess."

Brantley pauses his story and I reflex a quick smile at him. I'm shocked that he chose me for the job as his equal. Now I can't figure out why he's been so cutting and sharp with his comments to me thus far. In his head this has to be a game to see if I crack under pressure. Does he treat everyone the same way or is it just me? I'm as confused as ever.

I set aside my thoughts on why Brantley decided to hire me and consider what he said about hiring an assistant. He's right. I can't handle twenty clients on my own. Based on the stats I reviewed in my client portfolio, half of them have multiple product lines and we're working with them on at least one product every month. I set myself down at my desk and type out a quick interoffice email requesting that anyone in the office who is interested in being my assistant forward their resume to me by the end of next week. I hit the send button and let out a long breath.

Brantley has filled a glass with ice water and raises his glass to his lips before telling me, "When the resumes come in, let me see them. I can tell you which of the applicants are worth your time interviewing and which ones are complete flakes."

"Thanks," I say before inserting the thumb drive of today's commercial shoot into my laptop to review the images one more time.

By five-thirty in the afternoon most of the secretarial staff have left for the day. Only the creative department has a few people still working past five, and I take note of who puts in the extra time. If any of those people apply to work as my assistant, I'll know ahead of time who is willing to go the extra mile for me.

The Creative Director

"Are you staying much longer?" I hear Brantley ask while he rearranges a few papers and folders on his desk.

"Yes. I'm going to go over the packaging with a fine-toothed comb and a magnifying loupe before I leave."

"Are you blind?" he asks, teasingly.

"No." *Jesus, he's incorrigible. Or is it that I'm being overly defensive?* "I see things in so much more detail that way and it makes me feel assured that the team didn't miss something important. I learned that from the art department years ago when they reviewed photo shoots of models, so I do the same thing with their artwork." I place my loupe back down on the finished packaging I'm reviewing and wait for some other snide remark to fall from Mr. Sunshine's lips. I glance up briefly to see if he's still watching me, and I find that he is. "What?" I ask.

"Are you hungry?" he asks. "Can I add to my order of sushi for you before I make the call for delivery?"

"Oh. Okay. Yes, please. A dynamite roll and a bowl of miso soup should tide me over."

Sandra A. Sigfusson

Brantley picks up his phone and presses one number. I'm assuming he has the sushi restaurant on speed dial. He orders our meals and then promptly goes back to his computer screen. He scrolls and scrolls and scrolls for the longest time.

"What are you looking at?" I ask, since my curiosity is killing me.

"Pornography," he says with a straight face, not looking over to me.

"Male or female?" I quiz, in hopes it will make his resting asshole face crack a smile.

"Male. I like to compare my cock size with other gentlemen's when I'm feeling the pangs of inadequacy. It never ceases to amaze me how few men have large penises," he adds, still expressionless.

That comment makes me giggle. He has to be pulling my leg. I don't know what to make of this very bizarre conversation we've managed to jump into. Sometimes I wonder if Brantley suffers from a split personality disorder. I don't even know if I have a comedic retort to throw at him. Maybe he's just trying to mess with my head again. I have to see what it is that he's looking at, and I rise from my desk to walk over to him.

The Creative Director

As I round his desk with my empty coffee mug, intending to refill it, I lean over his shoulder to review his screen. His arousing cologne arrests me and my heart skips a beat while I adjust to being so near someone who smells so sexy. I really shouldn't stand behind him like this. Surprisingly, he isn't completely lying about what he's looking at. Brantley is scrolling through images of beefcake men in underwear and swimwear from one of the modeling agencies we use. "Those aren't nude men," I remark.

"You can still see how big their cock is," he muses. "Truthfully, I'm looking for a model for one of my newest clients. Underwear manufacturer. In their previous ads they used animated mannequins. Don't ask me why. They thought the ads were amusing." Brantley stops scrolling for a moment and looks up at me as I stand next to his left shoulder. "Two male mannequins wearing their latest designs suddenly come to life and start modeling publicly in shop windows as people stroll by. It had its artistic merit, but it didn't appeal to the right audience. Women found the ads amusing, but men thought the ads were stupid. As much as we know women do eighty percent of household shopping, these ads were meant to target a younger male audience, those who were not married. Massive failure."

Sandra A. Sigfusson

I step away from him, needing to create space between us. "Ah. Well, I can see how that wouldn't have won anyone in the eighteen-to-thirty age group. So what's your plan?" I ask while I start the coffee machine.

"Men are equally as envious over cock size as women are about breast size. If I find the right models for the ads with the perfect-sized cocks then I may have something to work with." I can't help but giggle over the way he says the word cocks. Brantley slips his bottom desk drawer open and pulls out a bottle of bourbon. "Fetch me a glass from the cupboard, will you?" he asks.

Fetch? Is he kidding me right now? My body heats with a hint of anger at his assumption that I'd fetch anything for him, but I shut it back down. "Sure. Do you want me to put ice in the glass for you since I'm up?" I ask, attempting to be rhetorical.

"If you wouldn't mind," he replies, not looking back at me. His eyes are glued to a blond model with eight-pack abs, tanned skin and a rather large penis modeling a pair of swim trunks while standing next to a palm tree on the beach. I'm more enamored with the quality of the shot than I am with the model, his cock size or his attire. I drop three large ice cubes inside a crystal tumbler and close the freezer door.

The Creative Director

"Are you looking to make the ads a lifestyle statement or a product quality statement?" I ask as I pass him his ice-filled glass.

"Thanks, love," he says softly. "I'm shooting for both. Grab them with the lifestyle angle and make them buy the product because the quality ensures long-lasting wear. The humor angle didn't work for them last time, and I'm not so sure I can make buying men's underwear funny." Brantley thinks for a moment, then offers up an idea while I lean my hip against his desk.

"Unless we take the angle of the woman in the man's role in a shopping scenario. He's trying on clothes and she waits next to the changeroom. He comes out, a little nervous about how he looks in them, and the woman gives either a thumbs up or a thumbs down, adding comments like, 'Babe, you look amazing in those underwear. And stop fussing with your hair or checking out your ass three times in each pair. You have a fantastic ass,'" he jokes. Then he goes into the guy's reply with, "Really, honey. You think my ass is amazing?"

I crack up. "That would be a hilarious ad idea, but sadly it would only appeal to women and gay men which is where the client's ads ended up last time. Mind you, girlfriends buy stuff for boyfriends too. And, some women prefer men's underwear to women's underwear. You should get someone to research those stats. If the client prefers humor for marketing, this could be the ticket if it's presented properly," I add.

I sit myself down in the tufted black leather armchair in front of his desk. He pours three fingers of bourbon into his glass and swirls the amber liquid gently until it's chilled enough for his liking. Watching him tip the glass to his lips with his large, elegant hand and swallow a healthy-sized gulp makes my throat silently mimic his swallowing action. He's very seductive in his mannerisms.

I'm not certain he knows he has a masculine elegance, but it's damned sexy. I cross my legs and watch him intently as his Adam's apple moves when the drink slips down his throat. It's playing out in my head like it were in slow motion. I reach for my coffee mug and sip the steaming liquid while Cher's voice tells me to snap out of it again. It's official. I need a man. The one in front of me is highly appealing visually, but his inflated ego is a turn-off. Even his sensual accent can't make up for that flaw. If he never opened his mouth I could get into him. Jesus. Where the fuck is that delivery guy with the sushi?

I rise from the guest chair and stride back to my desk to continue my inspection of the artwork. My loupe is still hanging from my neck, so I may as well put it to

The Creative Director

further use even though I'm done what I was doing. But I have nothing else to occupy my mind in lieu of thinking sexy thoughts about my colleague. I feel my center getting aroused. My clit pulses. I have to remember not to bring up the subject of anything sexual with Brantley because he does something to me. Why the hell is that happening here? I tolerate him because I have to. On occasion he's fine, but as a general rule he's frustrating. Then it dawns on me. It's his damned cologne. I've just figured it out. His fucking cologne is what is making me horny. It literally reminds me of sex.

"The sushi should be here momentarily," he says, breaking my mind out of its rumination. "Security will ring the delivery bloke up and text me when he's been cleared downstairs."

I nod and keep my eyes down on my artwork. Another sip of my coffee and a rummage through my desk for my highlighter pen help me get back into focusing on my work. I highlight a small spot on the artwork then paste a sticky-note on it to remind myself to give it back to the art department for adjustment. For some odd reason my ex-fiancé enters my mind. I've dated so many guys since Anson and I broke up, and none of them were worth staying with for more than a couple of weeks. I shake my head free of the good times we shared and remind myself that Anson is ancient history, no matter how fond the memories are.

Brantley's phone pings and he rises from his chair to go to the front door of the office. I remove the loupe from around my neck and watch through the large glass-paneled walls as he strides with such confidence toward the front door to pay for the sushi then relocks the door when the exchange is complete. My eyes don't leave him when he returns to our office. He catches a glimpse of me staring, but I don't think he knows my loins are aching for him. A quick smile from his luscious lips flashes at me.

"Are you hungry? You're looking at me like you could eat me as well as the sushi," he teases.

"The sushi, yes. You, not so much," I quip back and scoff. Hopefully that little acting job just now has taken him off my scent.

"Are you planning on sitting over there to eat, or do you want to join me at my desk?" he asks. He's opening the bags with a knife from the kitchen drawer and separating the Styrofoam containers, chopsticks and soya sauce packets neatly on the counter in the kitchenette.

The Creative Director

"I'll join you, but I have to go straight home after we eat," I reply.

"Where do you live?" he asks. He mixes a bit of wasabi in with his soya sauce in a small bowl with the chopsticks before dunking his first piece in the concoction.

"The building is called Wildwood Heights," I say, approaching the kitchenette. I touch my miso soup bowl and find it's piping hot; I need to let it cool a bit before I can eat it. "How much do I owe you for the sushi?"

"I'll add it to my expense report. Don't fret about it," he says. I nod and inspect a piece of my dynamite roll before popping it into my mouth.

"Do you want to share a taxi home? I'm familiar with your building and I don't live far from you." Brantley's eyes meet mine and I'm not sure how to respond. I decide to be cheeky about it.

"I'm not feeling the idea of spending another full hour in complete silence with you beside me in a dirty cab. I drove here today in my new lease car, so no thank you." I try not to smirk but I fail.

"You were pissed at me in the taxi. I didn't want to fan the flames so I kept my mouth shut."

"Yes. I was pissed at you. You have a mouth that doesn't always connect with your brain before it opens up and spews condescension. I felt insulted by your snide comments after that presentation. Please don't do that again."

His eyes stay focused on mine for a few seconds before he responds. "Fine. My apologies," he murmurs. I take his apology and smile inside. It's good to know he appreciates my boundaries and we have a set of ground rules. I've never had to work so hard to get a man's respect. I haven't yet decided if this is a game to Brantley or if he's just an ass to everyone. But I seem to be breaking down his wall, one small, heavy clay brick at a time.

The Creative Director

Chapter 5: The Assistant

My email inbox has twelve resumes for me to review this morning. I'm surprised to see that only two applicants are female. The dynamic of men versus women in the advertising field has changed so much in the past few years, and I like seeing more women in executive roles.

I've spent most of my morning reviewing the resumes and narrowed it down to three applicants I think are worth interviewing. I don't bother to ask Brantley which ones he thinks are best for the job because they aren't going to be working for him. Whom I choose is my business. I send off the reply emails to the applicants, telling the three candidates what time and date their interviews will be.

Brantley, having seen me sorting through resumes I'd printed out earlier, takes it upon himself to have a peek at the ones on my desk while I'm in the washroom. As I exit the washroom I clear my throat. "Something you need?" I ask in a light voice.

He turns and seems unfazed about being caught looking at papers on my desk. "I'm interested in who applied for your assistant job. I wouldn't go with Jason," he says, waving Jason's resume in his hand flippantly.

Sandra A. Sigfusson

Brantley leans his bum on the edge of my desk and folds his arms over his chest. Does he really need to look that sexy in his silk suit? And why doesn't he relax a little and take that damned jacket off every once in a while?

"Why not?"

"He's a bit dim. Jason's been here for years, but I'd never consider him assistant ready." Brantley reaches over to the other resumes and scans which ones I decided not to interview. "What's wrong with Jasmine? She's a solid contender." He looks genuinely confused.

"She hasn't completed her degree. I only want to interview those who have finished their college courses," I reply. "This is an assistant for me, not you."

"I think you'd be remiss to not at least consider interviewing her," he adds before setting Jason's resume back down and readjusting the papers on my desk into a neat pile. "She's only down a few credits and she'd pass those remaining classes in her sleep."

"Again, not your assistant to hire," I remind him as I shoo him away from the edge of my desk and sit down in my chair. "Go away. You have your own desk to lean on if that's all you're going to do all afternoon," I

The Creative Director

say. "And if you're so hot for Jasmine, then let her be your replacement for Nadia."

He eases his behind off the edge of my desk and scrubs a hand over his chin. "Go ahead and pick Jason. I've been looking for a reason to toss him for a while now. If he botches up on one of your accounts then he's gone," Brantley chirps as he reaches his desk. A confident smirk is thrown back at me before he sits back down in his chair. I don't bother replying. I get what he's saying, but this is my call.

Thursday afternoon at one o'clock is the time I have secured to use the smaller meeting room for the interviews. I arranged them back to back to be as efficient with my time as possible. Kevin first, Jason second, and Cameron third. I have a good idea who is going to come out the winner, but the interview process is important. Sometimes you see and hear something during an interview with an applicant that the others don't have and that you didn't expect to find.

My first instinct about Kevin was right. He's a tad too egotistical for my liking and I already have an egomaniac to deal with. I could see him going rogue on me at some point, thinking he's better than I am. I'm deciding that he's a no.

Sandra A. Sigfusson

Jason comes in and sits perfectly erect in the chair across from me at the table. His smile is genuine, but he's nervous. "Did your mom poke you in the back a lot when you were little?" I muse, trying to make him relax.

"No, why do you ask?" he says, appearing confused.

"Your posture is perfect. Not many people stand as straight as you do," I reply. He smiles brightly and I smile back. I don't know why I like this guy, but I do. He seems eager to learn, eager to please and finishes his tasks in a timely fashion, so why Brantley calls him dim is unclear to me. This is the kind of personality I want for an assistant. We chat about my expectations and he seems clear on what I need, and I don't think what I expect is overly demanding. I want efficiency, a yes ma'am attitude and a willingness to learn. I close the interview with a good feeling about Jason. The thing that really tugged at my heart was his experience in the Market Research division. I need someone who knows that part of our business well, because it is time consuming and tedious, and not my favorite part of the job. And Brantley's comment about Jason's stress concerns carried no weight during the interview.

The Creative Director

In my conversation with candidate number three, Cameron, I find I'm pleased at his experience level and his overall attitude. He speaks three languages fluently, which could be a real asset for our international clients. He's bright and equally as qualified as Jason, but I don't think he'll make me as happy as Jason will. I thank Cameron for his time. I've made my decision.

Once I confirm with Jason that he's got the job, he can start next week. I'll inform HR of his new assignment so they can find a replacement for him in Market Research.

Come Monday morning, when Jason happily steps into the office awaiting my first set of instructions, I hear Brantley chuckle from across the room.

"Do you have something you'd like to share?" I ask Brantley, in my *teacher's not happy* tone.

"No. Nothing at all," he says firmly.

I fix my gaze on Jason and smile. "We need some ideas for the Mason Mills Tea Company print campaign and I'd like you to brainstorm on that this morning. I'll have a few other things that need attention this afternoon. I've printed up a copy of my schedule for this week. Please make sure you arrange any meeting you need with me on current projects between the ones already scheduled. I'll share my link to my computer calendar with you and we'll manage it together. I like to leave the office before six o'clock but that isn't always the case. As long as you've got what you were working on under control, you are welcome to leave at five o'clock each night. If I need you last-minute to stay, I'll expect you to oblige and I'll keep track of your extra hours for HR to compensate your salary. Is that understood?" I ask.

Jason nods and smiles. "I'll be at my desk if you need me," he adds and quickly exits the room to work on the tea print ads. I pick up my phone and arrange to have Jason's desk stationed outside the door to our office so he's not traipsing through the building all day long for me.

Brantley and I have been working together for over two months. Although he's getting better at behaving like a commoner compared to his initial kingly stance toward me, he's still a tad pompous, and harsh with his remarks. However, I've discovered his sense of humor is wickedly dry and I no longer take offense to his brand of teasing.

I imagine his parents were upper-crust sorts. Maybe his dad was someone working in a highbrow profession – lawyer or surgeon – and he was raised in a house with servants. I think on that for a minute and

The Creative Director

decide that I'm profiling his background based solely on his attitude rather than the facts. One day he'll loosen up and fill me in on his family. He's not asked me anything personal as yet, though, so I don't think it's likely he'll spill his guts on a personal level anytime soon.

Brantley's movements are meticulous as he unwraps a French baguette filled with deli meats and cheese from the deli across the street from our office building. He's very methodical about everything he does. I see hints of tomato slices, cheese and spinach pieces peeking out the sides of the bread. My mouth waters. "Is it as good as it looks?" I ask.

"Yes, quite," he says after completely finishing his mouthful. I could learn a thing or two from his manners. I have been known to talk through my mouthful of food. I may look fine and couth on the surface, but I'm a tomboy with bad manners in my own personal space. Brantley dabs the sides of his mouth with a cloth napkin after each bite. I could learn a lot from him and about him just watching the way he moves.

"Did your servants at home teach you to not talk with your mouth full?" I tease as I turn my back to him and jot an idea down on my notepad.

I hear him chuckle and I turn to see him. He is laughing through the crumbs tumbling from his lips and I

Sandra A. Sigfusson

can't help but laugh as well. I didn't expect to ever see him do anything but chew while he's eating. Once he's swallowed his latest bite and wipes his lips again, he smiles wide. "You have preconceived notions about my upbringing. I have not at any time in my life been so fortunate as to have a servant. What made you think I'd been brought up wealthy?" he asks.

I shrug and tilt my head to the side before replying. "You have elegant manners. Your speech indicates that you were raised in an upper-class setting, as do your general mannerisms."

"You can thank my grandmother. She insisted that good manners were expected regardless of where you came from. If we didn't behave as she deemed appropriate, we were rapped on our hands with a wooden spoon. Not hard, but the gesture and her scowling face were enough to make us take note and not repeat it," he says before taking another bite of his baguette.

"Ah. So your grandmother had an upper-class life. That makes sense," I say.

"Wrong again, love. We were as common as scones." Brantley's face turns inquisitive. "Shall I take a

The Creative Director

stab at your childhood, since you clearly want to know about mine?"

"Sure," I say. "Why not. Take your best shot, Mr. Manners." I lean back in my office chair and cross my legs. I dust off a bit of paper lint on my right sleeve and place my hands neatly upon my lap.

"Your father was an accountant," he says assuredly.

My mouth opens to say something, but I stop and wait for his next thought. I can't believe he nailed my dad's job off the bat, but I don't want him thinking he has me pegged before he's finished.

Brantley taps his chin with his pointer finger, pretending to be in deep thought while gazing up at the perforated ceiling tiles. "Your mother … hmm, let's see. Your mother worked for a drycleaner and had a passion for shoes. She likely spent most of her salary on shoe shopping and fine-quality clothes. She believed that if she walked and talked the part then she'd have the part." Brantley pauses for a moment to narrow his eyes in my direction. "Correct me where I'm wrong. I wouldn't want to drone on for much longer if I'm completely off the mark," he adds.

"You had me and my family researched before I applied for the job!" I say, resetting my chair and unfolding my legs. I want to stand up, storm over to his desk and glare at him so hard my eyes are like laser beams burning out his retinas. "What right do you have to investigate me?"

"Cool your heels, Jess. We have every potential employee screened to be sure we're not entertaining hiring someone who is clearly not of good standing. And the bulk of what I offered was gleaned from your Facebook page. Do you honestly believe that your previous employer didn't do the same before they hired you?" Brantley's eyebrow arches and his expression fades to disbelief as he shakes his head at me. "Tsk, tsk, Miss James. I assumed after working three years in this industry at an executive level that you'd know this was common practice." Brantley goes back to consuming the balance of his sandwich as I remain shocked.

My tone and posture turn indignant. "You are wrong about my mother. She never cared what others thought of her and that attitude was passed on to me. Proudly, I don't give a shit what you think of me or my family," I say, still oddly very pissed off at this information. The truth is, both of my parents haven't worked for many years due to illness and their inability to stay sober for more than twenty-four hours. I don't talk

The Creative Director

about them to anyone because I'm not proud of what they've become.

"Yes, well I did elaborate to make it seem like I was purely guessing. I should practice that more before attempting it again," he muses, then sips his coffee before dabbing his lips with the napkin for the fifteenth time. Actually, I've lost count, but whatever.

"Have you always been one to take delight in putting people down?" I ask with a dry, condescending tone like his – but I don't think I'm pulling it off as well as he does.

"Is that what you think of me? That I take pleasure in putting everyone down?"

"Yes! You do. It's cold and very unattractive," I reply, scowling at him.

Brantley laughs at me. "You are so easy to get a rise out of, Jess. You shouldn't be constantly on the defensive. It's very childish and unattractive." The squeak in his chair makes another appearance and I cringe. Feeling as defensive as Brantley noted, I realize I've let him under my skin yet again. When will I learn?

"Okay," I say. "From now on you'll not need to bother addressing me unless it's related to a project. I

Sandra A. Sigfusson

don't have time to wean you on the merits of not being an asshole to your co-workers."

    Silence fills the space between our desks. At first it bothers me, but before long I begin to find the silence refreshing. My desk is overloaded with multiple projects that have all been waiting for my direct attention since yesterday. I don't care if I've pissed Brantley off or not. I'm just happy to have been able to throw the first snide comment he had for me on day one back in his smug face. Dammit. I have to pee, which means I'll need to walk past his desk to reach the washroom. Fuck it. I'll use the main office washroom while I grab some graphic work from the art department. I swear if I have to be within two feet of that jackass I'll kick him where the sun don't shine with the business end of my cherry-red stilettos. "Deep breath," I murmur to myself. I'm making a mountain out of a mole hill.

The Creative Director

Chapter 6: Enter the BFF

In all the excitement of getting a new job and trying to impress everyone around me at the office I've forgotten to tell Karmyn about any of it. She's been away to France for the past three months on what she calls a soul-searching expedition, and so our conversations have been sporadic and brief since she left. The last thing I heard from her via email was that she was visiting her aunt in Arles, France. Lucky girl.

I've missed our regular Friday-night bitch sessions along with their copious glasses of wine from her father's vineyards. Hopefully, she comes back home soon, as I'm feeling out of sorts without her as my sounding board. I pick up my cell and dial her number. Checking my watch, which isn't keeping time as well as it used to, I realize it may be too late to call her. Arles, France is six hours ahead of here, which means it's well past two o'clock in the morning there. I end my call and decide to text her instead.

Me: *I miss you. Are you coming home soon?*

Me: *Lots to tell you. Call me tomorrow, please.*

I tuck my phone back inside my pocket and get back to working on some promotional materials I brought

Sandra A. Sigfusson

home with me to keep me on track. My mind is not working as well as it should be on these materials, and I decide to open up a bag of potato chips and a can of ginger ale. Plunking myself down on my couch, I turn on my TV and look for something to watch on Netflix. While I'm scanning my options my phone pings with a reply text from Karmyn, and I'm shocked she's awake.

 Karmyn: *Miss you too, Hun. Back Tuesday on the redeye. Lunch Wednesday? xox*

 Me: *Why are you awake, and yes to lunch!*

 Karmyn: *It's too hot to sleep. But I guess I should try. À bientôt Jess.*

 Now all I can think about are French films, so I put that query into my Netflix search. I settle on the 2017 film *Lolo*. For whatever reason I'm not able to keep my eyes open long enough to finish the film. I awaken to a series of movie trailers displaying on my TV screen at three AM. Shutting the TV off, I decide the couch is far too comfortable and warm to leave it and go back to sleep in peace.

The Creative Director

When my lunch date with Karmyn arrives on Wednesday afternoon, we could not be more excited to see each other after so long apart. Our favorite restaurant on Moore Street in Brooklyn serves the best pizza I've ever tasted, and we agree to meet there.

We greet each other with the warmest of hugs and cheek kisses. "So, tell me all about your visit to France. Did you see most of your extended family? How is your aunt doing?" My questions for Karmyn roll off my tongue in rapid succession. Her eyes bulge at me before she breaks out into a fit of laughter.

"Did your doctor put you on some meds recently? You are absolutely wired, Jess," she says as she leans back from our hug, still holding me by my shoulders.

"No, no. Shit, I'm just so happy you're back home. So much has happened since you left."

We seat ourselves at the little bistro-style table and flip open our menus.

"Okay, so spill it. What happened?" she asks, peering at me over the top of her open menu.

"I started a new job. I'm a Creative Director at Digame Advertising International," I say proudly.

Karmyn drops her menu and widens her eyes at me. "What? Holy crap! Way to go, Jess! I'm so proud of you. How did it happen?"

My smile at her excitement over my new job nearly cracks my face. "Regina at my old office plunked a magazine article on my desk about Digame and I decided to see if they were hiring. By sheer coincidence they were, and I got the job."

"Did they fire their old CD?"

"Nope. I share the role with him. Brantley," I say.

Karmyn's eyes narrow as she asks, "Brantley what?"

I chuckle. "To be fair, I don't know what his last name is."

"That's ridiculous. How could you work with a person and not know their last name?" she replies, shaking her head at me.

I reach for my water glass and spot the waiter coming over to our table to take our orders. Her comment makes me think long and hard as to why I've never been told what Brantley's last name is. Now that I've been

The Creative Director

working there for two months it would be crazy to ask him what it is now. I'll check his business cards when he's out of the office this afternoon. "I don't know, Karmyn. I've never asked, and nobody has ever called him anything but Brantley. But never mind that pompous ass." Our waiter stands beside us with a pen and paper in hand.

"What can I get you ladies? A cocktail first, or would you like to order your meal at the same time?" he asks.

I glance at Karmyn, and we agree to split a meat lover's special pizza. We order two cokes to drink. Our waiter nods and carries on to serve other patrons.

"So tell me about this Brantley guy?" she says.

I put my water glass back down and smirk. "He's a Brit with a sharp tongue. It bothered me at first, but I think I may have him figured out now," I say.

"Is he an old guy or a young guy?"

"He's thirty-four," I say as I move my cell phone over to the other side of my plate and unfold my cloth napkin.

"Good looking or no?" she asks.

Sandra A. Sigfusson

"Handsome. Very handsome. Too handsome," I say and sigh.

"So, does that mean you have the hots for him?" she teases.

"No. I could probably get into him if he never opened his mouth, but aside from that we're peers and I don't think it's a good idea to date someone you work with. Especially when we're side by side every day."

"Yeah. I can agree on that," she says, nodding.

Our pizza arrives and my nose fills with the scent of all the fabulous toppings and the melted cheese. My stomach growls as I slip my first piece onto my plate. Karmyn follows suit and we both dive into our meal like we are starving. I giggle at her as I point out a giant smudge of tomato sauce rimming the left corner of her mouth. "Stay like that. I want to post your messy tomato face on my Instagram account," I tease.

"Fuck, no," she replies and swipes the sauce away with her fingers. "If you do I'll have to remind you of all the compromising pictures I have of you on my phone."

"You do not have compromising images of me. I never do anything compromising."

The Creative Director

She cracks up with that infectious laugh of hers. "Oh, hun," she says, fanning her hand at me. "I have taken tons of pics of you when you were drunk at my place."

"Why would you do that?" I ask, feeling a tad violated.

"Because I love you and you are too funny when you're wasted. That's why."

"Show me the pictures," I ask, reaching across the table to snatch up Karmyn's phone.

Her reflexes are quicker than mine and she manages to retrieve her phone before I can get my greasy pizza fingers on it. "No! You'll erase them. I haven't uploaded them to my computer yet," she mumbles through a mouthful of pizza. Karmyn gulps down her latest bite and takes a long sip of her soda then winks. She's pulling my leg and trying to get a rise out of me.

"Well, whatever," I say, then blow out a long breath. "At least somebody finds me charming enough to take pics of me in compromising positions."

"Now, now. What are you moaning about? Haven't you gotten laid lately?"

"Nope. I've been partying solo with that rabbit thing you bought me for a joke birthday present," I say and giggle.

"Hun, that wasn't a joke gift." Karmyn knits her brows together at me while she takes a second slice of pizza off the tray.

I can't help but smile. I know it wasn't a joke gift, but I like to tease her about buying me a sex toy. "Okay. I agree. It's not a joke and a lot more fun than I anticipated."

Karmyn nods at me and smiles. "I have a confession to make."

"Oh, yeah. What would that be?" I ask. She has my full attention now as I bite down on my second slice of pizza.

"I'll tell you Friday night. Dinner at my place. Okay?"

My eyes narrow at her while chewing, and I begin to speak. I'm talking with my mouth full again and it reminds me of Brantley and his sandwich the other day. Thankfully, Karmyn doesn't call me out on my bad

The Creative Director

manners. I crumple up my napkin in my hand and ask, "Why can't you tell me now?"

"Trust me. It can wait. Are you good for Friday night?"

I swallow and nod. "Yes. But I don't have much time left for our little lunch date today. I have far too many open projects that need my attention. I'll call an Uber to take me back to the office."

"I can drive you," she says, surprised that I didn't assume she would.

"No. It's okay, Karmyn. Stay here and enjoy the rest of the pizza. I'll see you Friday at your place. Say, seven o'clock?"

"Sure, hun."

I lean forward and kiss her cheek before grabbing my purse and exiting the restaurant. I can only imagine what scandalous thing she's going to tell me on Friday night. But I can't think about it now. My work needs all my focus.

Chapter 7: The Overshare

Karmyn has outdone herself yet again. Her dinners are always fantastic. The table is set with flickering candles, fine china plates, four different types of wine and a stunning display of delicate pink roses in the center of the table. One would think she was expecting her lover for dinner and not her best friend. "Am I interrupting a date?" I tease as I gesture to her beautiful table setting with my arm sweeping through the air like Vanna White showcasing a new puzzle board.

"We are each other's date tonight, Jess. I even wrote you an erotic poem that I'll read to you later," she says, tugging down on the low neckline of her top and shaking her ample cleavage at me before cracking up at her own silly antics.

My eyebrows pitch high. "And, I see you've already sampled all four bottles of wine too. I never would have thought you'd be *that* happy to see me," I say as I kick off my shoes and toss my coat over the nearest chair.

The Creative Director

"It's our little secret, Jess. Anyway, I hope you're starving because I made enough food for eight people. Plan on taking a doggy bag home with you."

It surprises me how much we have to discuss over dinner. So much has occurred in the three months she and I have been apart from each other. My mouth is filled with the sumptuous flavors of Karmyn's expertly prepared meal and the excellent wine her father's vineyards produce. I wish I had a tenth of her talent in the kitchen. "You know, it takes every ounce of energy in me to not orgasm over your dinners, Karmyn. I swear no matter what you throw on my plate I'm in love with it."

"Oh, Jessica Adeline James. Are you trying to get into my panties?" she asks in a sultry low tone.

"Well, it *has* been a bit of a dry spell for me," I say, coughing like I'm parched before I crack up. Karmyn cracks up with me and we laugh so hard we're nearly in tears.

"Stop, Jess. You're killing me," she says after her laughter subsides. I see her smile to herself and then let out a heavy sigh. She downs the balance of her third glass of red wine and then tops her glass back up, draining one of the red wine bottles. I'm sipping my third glass, as I know I'm much more of a lightweight than she is when it comes to drinking wine.

Sandra A. Sigfusson

We agree to pass on dessert since we ate so much of her cordon bleu chicken dinner, complete with scalloped potatoes, steamed French-cut beans and baked cauliflower au gratin. I'll have leftovers for two days based on how much food is left in the serving dishes on the counter. Together we tidy up the kitchen and pack two Tupperware containers of leftovers for me to take home.

We saunter over to the living room after refilling our wine glasses yet again. Karmyn wants to dance to a few of her favorite songs and lip sync to the lyrics with her pretend microphone. She's a closet lip sync queen. One of these days I'll get her up on a stage in a local bar, but tonight isn't that night. She makes me smile for so many reasons. It seems crazy that we've been such close friends since we were eleven years old. "Hey, so, why don't we go to a karaoke bar one night?" I ask, folding my legs underneath my bum on the couch.

"Not on your life, sugar. I can't sing my way out of a paper bag and you know it," she says while her hips sway to a blues tune that we both love.

"Okay, well then how about a lip sync competition? You'd rock it out of the park. I'm sure you'd win a prize."

The Creative Director

"Oh, yeah. And what would a bar give as a prize? More booze?" she giggles. "I don't need free booze. My freaking dad is a winemaker of outstanding standing. Wait. Did that make sense?" she says, then giggles again.

"Yes!" I say, raising my wine glass in the air as a toast. "To your dad being in outstanding standing!"

Karmyn decides to take a break from dancing and plops down beside me on the couch. She pours more wine into her glass and takes a long sip. "So, hey. Do you remember when we were like fourteen or something and we were starting to date guys?" Karmyn leans back into the cushions of her couch and kicks her feet up on top of her coffee table a bit clumsily.

When I started dating I never thought that her brother, Anson, would be on my list of options, but he was. "How is Anson these days?" I ask out of the blue.

Karmyn shrugs and gulps again from her wine glass. "He's good. I told you he's getting a doctorate, hey?"

"Yeah. That's so impressive. Who'd have thunk a hunk of a man like Anson would turn that direction in his lifetime? I mean, I know he's always been the guy everyone goes to for advice, but a psychology doctorate? That surprises even me. I'll bet every time a new patient

Sandra A. Sigfusson

meets him they glance around the room and wonder if they're in the wrong place," I say and giggle.

"Do you really think that?" she asks, puzzled by my comment.

"Wouldn't you? I mean, he looks more like a linebacker than a doctor, even if he wore a lab coat and a pair of Clark Kent glasses on his chiseled face!"

"I get your point," she nods. "I really wish you two hadn't broken up. He misses you, you know."

I nod and offer Karmyn a soft smile. "I miss him too, sweetie. We had it all planned out until he dropped the joining-the-army bomb on all of us. Maybe I shouldn't have been so hasty to kybosh the whole idea of being an army wife. I don't honestly know if it was the shock of his enlisting without discussing it with anyone first that had me too scared to stay engaged to him, or if it was the thought of losing him in some random accident while deployed. It's too long ago now to remember for sure." I mirror Karmyn by putting my feet up on her coffee table and then slide my body down a bit within the cushions of her overstuffed couch.

Karmyn nods. "Do you remember that time he and Davis were passing the football around in the back

The Creative Director

yard and as Anson leapt in the air to catch it, he missed and landed in the center of the pool while the football smashed through Mom's kitchen window? I wish I'd had a video camera then. It was too perfect. The ball hit the window at the exact time Anson hit the water. God, he was such a clown."

"I do remember that. I think that was about the same time he started showing interest in me. I'm pretty sure he was showing off to get my attention that day. And, it wouldn't surprise me if he missed on purpose so I'd see him do something silly. Guys are so damned predictable. And holy fuck was your mom pissed about the window," I add and laugh at the vivid memory. "How old were we then? Fifteen?"

"That sounds about right. How long did you two date before he proposed?" Karmyn starts scrolling through her phone pics looking for something while I try to recall the date.

"I think it was the week after my twenty-first birthday, so that would mean about six years. He wanted to wait until New Year's Eve to propose but couldn't keep the secret to himself and gave me the ring after that big birthday bash he put on for me at your place. Your parents were away in San Francisco for their anniversary that weekend, do you remember that?" I ask. As I turn my head and look at her, waiting for an answer, she puts her

Sandra A. Sigfusson

phone screen only a few inches from my face to show me an image.

"When was that taken?" I ask.

"Two weeks ago. He was at the base and took a quick selfie for me. He looks pretty awesome, hey?" she asks and nods at me, smiling wide.

"Anson always looked awesome. That's why I couldn't keep my hands off him," I say and smirk. "Do you have any idea how big your brother's cock is?" I ask, and then half-heartedly regret asking the question. The wine is going to my head and now I can't keep my more intimate thoughts about Anson from escaping my lips.

"I *am* unfortunately quite aware of how endowed he is. He and his friends swam naked in Mom's pool all the time. Trust me, I know how big all of them are. I didn't mind seeing his buddies buck naked, but seeing Anson that way is something I truly wish I could erase from my memory," she says, frowning at me. "Why the hell did you have to bring *that* memory to the surface?"

I can't help myself and crack up. I buckle over myself on the couch and have to draw my knees up to my chest to stop myself from peeing in my pants. "Oh my god, that's too funny, Karmyn." She fights hard not to

The Creative Director

succumb to a fit of giggles along with me and loses. By the time we finish laughing I have tears in my eyes thinking about how badly she must want that image to disappear.

A few quiet moments pass as we sip more wine and reset ourselves on the couch. "Do you ever think that you and Anson could try again? I just think that maybe since so much time has passed, and you are both still single, that you should reconnect to see what happens."

"Karmyn. I'm begging you. Do *not* go there. I'll love your brother forever, but too much time has passed now. If he showed up one night randomly and needed to get laid I'd give in, but a relationship is out of the question. He lives in a completely different world than me now. Oil and water is what we are," I say, trying to be firm with my words but not really meaning any of it. Only true love could make me hurt as much as I did when we broke it off. I've never loved anyone as much as Anson, but I don't want to let Karmyn in on just how often I secretly pine for him. As cliché as it sounds, if I give her an inch she will take a mile, and before I know it Anson will be on my doorstep confused as to why Karmyn lied to him about me wanting to get back together.

"So, never mind Anson. Let's just agree that boys suck," I say and snort-laugh over the bowl of my glass.

Sandra A. Sigfusson

"Why did you bring up the subject of the first time we started dating boys?"

Karmyn sighs heavily before turning her gaze to me while I snuggle a bit deeper into the cushions beside her. "Do you remember us practicing kissing on each other so we could be sure we knew what we were doing when we did finally kiss a boy?"

I burst out into laughter again and smile wide at her. "Sadly, yes I do. And to be clear, your brother is a way better kisser than you were," I say jokingly. "What brought on that memory?" I get the feeling that Karmyn is getting serious with me now. This is phase two of her three stages of drunkenness. Phase one is dancing and singing, and phase two is curious questions that she wants answers to but won't bring them up when sober. Phase three is when she passes out.

"I had an experience in France that made me think of you and me practice-kissing," she says quietly.

"An experience? What kind of experience?" Now my interest is piqued.

"I made love to a woman," she says slowly and in a near whisper.

The Creative Director

I blink twice at her and smile. "You're a funny one, Karmyn. Since when do you have lesbian tendencies?" I scoff. I set my wine glass down on the table and focus all my attention on her. If she really did make love to a woman, then this is big news and she's struggling to wrap her brain around it.

"Okay, fine. If you don't believe me, then I don't care. It was only once anyway and I'll never speak of it again." She looks wounded that I don't believe her.

"Hey. I'm sorry. I was sure you were joking. Tell me about it if you want to. I promise I'll listen and won't judge. I love you, Karmyn," I say and reach to stroke her arm in comfort.

Karmyn's eyes meet mine. She flashes me a smile then the smile fades away. "I did make love to a woman. She was, how do you say, so seductive. I may have been a little drunk but I wasn't off-my-ass drunk when I let her take me to bed with her. She was hypnotic to me. Her body was so beautiful. I had been explaining to her about how much time and energy I'd put into my relationship with Lloyd before we broke up, and she listened so intently to me. Like you do," she says.

My heart swells a little. We've always been each other's sounding boards and kept each other's secrets secured deep within ourselves, and nothing would make either of us break our code. This is another secret of Karmyn's that I'm sure she'll want me to keep under lock and key. I reach for my wine glass to take a long sip. "Go on, sweetie. You know whatever you have to tell me is strictly between you and me."

She nods and holds my gaze in hers. "Hun, even though I know you know how much I love you, you may be shocked to know that the entire time I was getting it on with this amazingly beautiful French woman, I –" Karmyn pauses and takes in a deep breath. "The entire time I was thinking of you."

My silence and my shock blanket the room for a few beats before I can manage to address her last words. "Me?"

"Yes you. I've loved you forever, Jess, and I think you and I are strong enough to talk about this without it wrecking who we are to each other."

I nod in agreement, but I'm still in a mild state of shock. I need to be as honest with her as she is with me. "I'll admit to wondering what it would be like to make love to a woman, but I've never ventured to seduce one. I guess the curiosity isn't as strong as it is for those who

The Creative Director

play regularly for both teams," I add cautiously. "Do you think of yourself as a lesbian?"

"No. And for the life of me I don't know why I let what happened happen. It was crazy but in that moment it made sense," she says. Karmyn downs the balance of the wine in her glass before she looks back at me. "Did I scare you?"

"Yes. A little. But I understand what you're telling me. The question I have in my head now is, do you want to make love to another woman, or was it a one-time thing?"

Karmyn offers me a slow-widening smile and holds her eyes in mine once more. "Jess, I'd like to make love to you."

Sandra A. Sigfusson

Chapter 8: Blame It on The Wine

"Okay," I say, my words laden with caution. Suddenly I'm frantically waving my hands in front of my face and correcting the situation. "I mean, okay I heard you – not, okay I'll let you make love to me." Shit. What the hell is going on here? I'm confused and worried that I'm insulting the most important person in my life.

"I've totally freaked you out. Fuck. I knew this would freak you out," she mumbles before rising from the couch and placing her hands on her face to rub her cheeks. "I'm sorry, Jess. I'm drunk and stupid. Pretend I never said what I said."

"Karmyn, please sit back down," I plead. "We have to talk about this. Obviously this is really important to you and I don't want you thinking that I'm rejecting you. I'm just not sure this is something I'm as ready to embark on as you are."

Karmyn turns to face me then agrees to sit down on the couch. She cocks her head a little as she analyzes my face. "So, you've thought about what it would be like

The Creative Director

to pleasure a woman but never acted on that impulse?" she asks.

"Well, yeah. But that was a long time ago."

"What was the situation you were in that made you think about it?"

"I don't know. Shit. That was years ago." I try to recall that moment in time but I'm drawing a blank. I've had too much wine and have been shocked out of my drunkenness by her proposal. I answer her question with another question. "Does it matter when I had that inclination?"

Karmyn thinks for a few seconds. "No, I guess not. Do you think many women wonder about having sex with a woman who are traditionally not lesbian?" she asks curiously.

My mind is racing around in circles trying to decide if the way I feel about sex is as open as Karmyn's is. The decision is swift. Yes. I do feel as open about sex as she does. But do I want to experiment sexually with Karmyn, or would I rather do it with someone I don't know?

"I think that if you're going to lean that way you'd likely be thinking about it at a younger age," I say. "Like when you are becoming sexually aware at thirteen or fourteen. But for some people sex isn't about being male or female. It's just about the sex. We all know men and women don't need each other to get off, and when they do get together for sexual gratification it really shouldn't matter if their partner is a man or a woman."

"Hun," she says, maintaining her soft tone. "I don't want to pressure you into anything. I wanted you to know that the experience I had was surreal. And I also wanted you to know that I was thinking of you while I did it. I'm sorry if I've freaked you out. I'm sorry if this puts our friendship in a weird place, but I had to tell you. It was too big of an experience not to share it with you."

I nod in agreement. This is what we do. We share everything even if it's completely out there, funny, stupid or embarrassing. I reach for Karmyn's hand and give it a good solid squeeze. "Pour me another glass of wine and I'll spend the night here with you. I may not end up being with you in that way, but if that's what you need from me then we can take it one step at a time. But to be very clear, I am not now and will never be a lesbian or even consider myself bisexual," I say and bust out into a fit of giggles.

Karmyn's eyes sparkle as she joins me in laughing at ourselves and this odd little predicament we're in. She

The Creative Director

pours me another glass of wine as I asked, and curls up next to me on the couch. In all the years I've known Karmyn she has shocked me many times, but this is the biggest shock of all. I put my arm around her shoulder. We begin to giggle again, for no apparent reason this time. There were many moments in our lives as best friends when I wished Karmyn were a guy. We are so deeply connected. We get each other in ways that a heterosexual couple might, yet I've never thought of making love with her. Maybe that's why I fell for her brother, Anson.

Other questions fill my mind now, and I have to ask her what she thinks. "Do you think God would forgive us for pleasuring each other? Do you think it's an automatic ticket to hell if you go against the rules of traditional man-to-woman coupling? I mean, the reason men and women are supposed to couple is for the purposes of conception and not just pleasuring. That being said, why would who you give and receive sexual pleasure from matter? Between consenting adults, of course."

"If I had his number I'd call him and ask him that question for you. For me it's too late. I'm most certainly going to hell for the multiple infractions I've made in this lifetime," she muses. "And you know me. I'd lie on a witness stand in heaven for you any second of the day, so if I did get a meeting with God, and he's accused you of sinning without asking for forgiveness, I'll have your back one hundred percent," she says.

That makes me laugh. "Well, the bible does say do to others as you would have them do to you. We know that means being kind, thoughtful and respectful, but it could also mean that loving someone in a physical way is a kindness," I say. A rapid nod from Karmyn's head against my shoulder tells me she wholeheartedly agrees.

We stay on the couch holding each other for a long while. Intermittent questions and observations come from both of us in the relative silence of her apartment before I realize I'm quite tired. "Do you want to go to bed? I'm having a hard time keeping my eyes open," I say.

"Yes. Are you sleeping here on the couch or in my bed with me?"

"In your bed. I would like to hold you in my arms tonight. I'm not promising I'll let you seduce me while I'm there, but I do want to be close to you tonight."

In complete agreement we rise from the couch and head to Karmyn's bedroom. Karmyn passes me a nightgown from her wardrobe while I undress. "Thanks,"

The Creative Director

I say as I slip my naked body into it and crawl inside her bedsheets. Karmyn has rarely slept with a nightgown on, and I didn't expect she would tonight either. We've slept together a thousand times since we were young and being naked has never bothered her or me. Until tonight. I wanted to say something to her about slipping on a nightgown or even a simple t-shirt, but this is her house and her rules. I was offered the option to sleep on her couch and I chose not to.

    I sigh audibly after we are both settled in between the sheets. I spoon my body in behind hers and drape my left arm over her naked form. My hand finds the pillowy-soft skin of her breast – purely by accident – but I don't freak out about it. I stroke the silky skin of her breast with my thumb and close my eyes. I can see why a man would find the touch of a woman's breast so arousing. It is a beautiful thing to caress and to hold. If I can find great pleasure in fondling my own breasts, then why should I feel odd about fondling someone else's?

    "Thank you," I hear Karmyn whisper. I kiss the back of her head and fall asleep feeling more loved than I've felt in quite some time.

Chapter 9: Loving Me, Loving You

Karmyn is awake before I am this morning. I can hear the shower water running in her ensuite bathroom. A good long stretch in Karmyn's massive king-sized bed eases the sleep fog out of my bones. As I sit up on my elbows I can see the curves of Karmyn's slim, shapely figure reflected in the bathroom mirror. As she turns to face the vanity counter from inside the glass shower enclosure I find surprising pleasure in watching her wash her body with a bar of soap. Her eyes are closed as her hands glide over her shoulders, her belly and her ample breasts. She's not in a hurry to cleanse herself and is enjoying the dual shower heads cascading water over her soapy body. I realize I'm being a peeping Tom but I can't stop watching her.

She doesn't likely know I'm awake and have a clear view of her, because she begins to wash her breasts again with both hands. She focuses on the fullness of her chest, squeezing and kneading them within her palms. Then one hand eases down her belly as her fingers find her sex. She tips her head forward when she begins to pleasure herself. I decide to let her do what she needs to

The Creative Director

do in privacy and flop myself back down on the bed, cutting off my view of her. Without warning my center feels the beginnings of arousal. Looking up at the ceiling I have to ask myself, *Why the hell am I so aroused by watching my best friend pleasure herself in her shower?*

The truth is, the answer is inside of me. I do want to touch her that way, but I'm afraid of what would become of us if I did. The only solution to my immediate desires is to masturbate here in her bed while she does the same in the shower only a few steps away. Karmyn has always been sensual in the way her body moves and the way she speaks, and I often admired that about her.

I prop three pillows up behind my shoulders and close my eyes. When I open my eyes I once again have a full view of Karmyn in her shower via the vanity mirror. Her fingers are rubbing vigorously over her clit with one hand while the other hand continues to massage a breast. Her head is tipped back now, letting the cascading water fall upon her face and neck as she finds her much-needed release. Did I force this desire in her through our discussion last night, or is this something she does in her private shower setting frequently?

I can't help myself from being overwhelmed by the scene playing out before me. I replicate Karmyn's movements by finding my clit and massaging it between my fingers in circular movements. The sensation of my sexual desires building up into waves of pleasure makes me close my eyes again and focus directly on the movements of my hand between my legs. My nipples peak to rock-hard nibs while I envision a man, any man readying to suck and tug on them with his mouth. I begin to pant in this full state of arousal before I hear Karmyn's sweet voice speak from above me.

"Let me do that for you," she murmurs. She is still damp from her shower and I didn't hear the water shutting off while I was so self-absorbed. My eyes pop open to see her hovering over me, her body glistening with beads of moisture. I search her eyes while the shock of being caught masturbating in her bed settles in. I nervously nod at her. The prettiest smile I've ever seen graces her lips as she sits on the edge of the bed.

"You're wet," I whisper.

"In more ways than one," she whispers back.

This makes me crack a bashful smile. Karmyn slides deeper into her bed to lie beside me as I scoot over to let her ease in. "It's a lot better when someone does this for you," she says, then leans over and kisses my lips sweetly. I reciprocate her kiss. I know she loves me more than any other person on this planet and the feeling is

The Creative Director

mutual. As curious as I am at this moment, I almost feel like this is more of a dream than reality. Am I awake?

Something about her touch relaxes me and I don't feel as uneasy as I thought I would. "Close your eyes, Jess," she says.

I do as instructed and focus on the warmth of her body as she positions herself over me. As she dapples kisses along my chest and lightly teases one of my nipples with her lips and tongue, her long damp hair lies upon my shoulder, feeling cool against my skin. I'm not sure if I should touch her while she explores me, but I feel the need to caress her body in the same way she is mine.

Opening my eyes I see this beautiful, amazing woman pleasuring me. She smells clean and fresh like spring rain from the scent of her shampoo. Her legs are spread wide over my hips while more kisses trail along my body. Breasts, full and pert, nipples rigid and puckered, their color a deep pink, beg me to touch them. I slip my thumbs over her hard nipples while I palm beneath her breasts. It surprises me how heavy a breast can feel when you hold it in your hand, and Karmyn's are impressive in both size and firmness. A random thought skips across my mind: Why can't breasts stay this lovely as we age? Why can't we reach our prime and stay that way until the day we die?

Sandra A. Sigfusson

As Karmyn's tongue reaches the ticklish spaces between my hips, my palms skim over her shoulders as I quiver at her touch. I rise up on my elbows to watch her as I feel and see her nipples tickling the tops of my thighs while her lips near my throbbing clit.

"Lay back down," she says without looking up at me. "You need to relax."

I obey her again and lay my arms over my head on the pillow, taking in a deep breath while I lie in anticipation. Karmyn slides her knees between my thighs, nudging me to open my legs to let her in. She moves slowly to spread my legs while I try to remain relaxed and keep my eyes closed. I'm compelled to watch her when she flips her wet hair over to one side and nests her face near my entrance, but I promised to keep my eyes shut. A sweep of her fingers across my sex from top to bottom adds to my anticipation. When her tongue parts my lips I shiver. Her touch, be it her hand or her tongue, is so gentle, so sweet, so endearing. "No man has ever touched me as gently as you," I murmur.

"Now you understand why I wanted to share this with you," she replies. A second later her tongue is swirling gently around my clit. It throbs and yearns for her continued attention. Her lips suck at my clit and my

The Creative Director

body responds instantly. The intensity of pleasure is sublime as I feel the rush of my imminent orgasm arriving more quickly than I expected. My shoulders curl back and I let out a whimper as my chest pushes upward. And there it is. Swift glory.

"Oh, my god, Karmyn," I say as my orgasm rushes through me.

But before I have the chance to calm from it, her fingers enter me in quick but gentle plunges. "Sweet Jesus," I murmur. My entire body relaxes while my pleasure senses rise to new heights. Just when I thought her sucking my clit would be the end of her tease, she fingers me repeatedly until I reach a second swift orgasm. How she got me to respond so easily I can't say. I do wish the tease had lasted a bit longer, but I'll not fault her for giving me what I needed in such a beautiful way.

I am spent, tingling all over and a little short on breath. Karmyn crawls back over me and slips a wet finger inside my mouth. "Taste yourself, Jess," she says in a near whisper while a satisfied smile forms on her pretty, pouted lips. It has never crossed my mind to taste myself after an orgasm. The flavor, subtle as it is, has hints of saltiness and sweetness. But, having unabashedly been made love to by her, and now tasting her finger inside my mouth, I feel freed somehow. This is not at all what I expected.

I lift my head to kiss her mouth. I want to show her how much I appreciate what she did for me. How loving it was. "Can I do the same for you?" I ask while my lips are still pressed against hers.

"Yes, please," she whispers, and then she slips her tongue in my mouth to twist with mine.

Afterward we shower, dress and reconvene in the kitchen to make breakfast together. The most pressing issue haunting me is, how does this change our relationship? Based on Karmyn's smile and lighthearted attitude while she scrambles eggs and pops fresh bread in the toaster, I'm guessing she's happier than she's been in a while. But that doesn't answer my question.

I wait until we are seated at the table and have begun eating before I pose my query. "What does what we did this morning mean to you?"

Karmyn stops mid-chew of her toast and fixes a long stare upon me. "I'm not sure what you're asking."

"I'm saying that I'm not going to do that with you again. It was a one-time thing. I was aroused by watching you in the shower without intending to join you. I let you

The Creative Director

and I pleasure each other only because I knew it was important to you. Having said that, I also want you to know that I don't regret it. You made me feel truly special. Loved."

"I know, but if I didn't take that opportunity when it arose you'd likely never have agreed to let me have you that way."

I nod. "Yes. You're right." I exhale a long breath while I look anywhere in the room but at her.

"Are you angry with me?" she asks as her brows knit together. She is worried and I'm mad at myself for letting her think I'd ever be angry with her for making love to me.

"No. It was beautiful, Karmyn. But it's not my thing. I love men and I want to make love with men."

"I know, Jess." Karmyn sighs heavily over her breakfast plate before taking a quick sip of her tea. "Me too. I think we've both established that we have curiosities and desires. We gave in to each other in a way that satisfies a curiosity, but I hope it doesn't change us."

In this moment we both begin to tear up. I don't want to cry but the emotion is swift to build inside me. I'd not realized how much this affected me until now. "This doesn't change who you are to me, Karmyn. This

Sandra A. Sigfusson

experience just makes us closer." My hand reaches across the table at the same time hers does. Tears soak our cheeks while we squeeze each other's hands tight.

"I'm good if you're good," she says as she wipes her delicate fingers over her cheek.

"Yes. We are better than good. We're fantastic. I love you more than life itself," I say and raise her hand to my lips to kiss it. "We'll check this off our bucket list and never look back, okay?"

Karmyn breaks out in a full belly laugh and I can't help but join her. We are most definitely good.

It takes all of Sunday for me to stop questioning what Karmyn and I did in her bed Saturday morning. It is pure craziness that I let her seduce me, but it was so beautiful. During our encounter, I wondered if she was going to bring out one or more of the many sex toys in her side table, but what we shared was about pleasing each other in a way that only a woman could truly understand about another woman. I'd never explored a woman's body like that and I somehow instinctively knew how to make her happy. And although performing cunnilingus was not something I thought I'd *ever* do it was surprisingly enjoyable to pleasure her that way.

The Creative Director

Chapter 10: Batteries Not Included

Arriving to the office at my regular time of eight o'clock, I discover that Brantley has beat me to the punch. He's often in just after eight carrying his specialty coffee, his briefcase and his resting asshole face. I'm guessing he has pressing issues with one or more of his accounts that made him want to get an early start on today.

"Good morning," he says as I rest my briefcase on my desk.

"Good morning, Brantley. I see you're in earlier than usual. Are you worried about not reaching a deadline?"

"Yes, but I'm back on track now. I've been in since six this morning. Early bird catches the worm and all that," he says and chuckles. "And how was your weekend? Did you do anything worthy of sharing?" he says then winks at me.

Jesus. Did he sense something in me that prompted him to ask that question and follow it up with a bloody wink? "Yes. My weekend was fantastic." I pause for a moment and turn my back to Brantley while I say, "I got laid. How was your weekend?" Inside I'm killing myself laughing. I can only imagine the look on Brantley's face at this moment, so I slowly turn back to face him but maintain a calm expression, like what I said and did wasn't any big deal. *If he only knew!*

"Did you? How wonderful. I didn't get so lucky this weekend, but I'm giddy with the thought of you sharing all the sordid details of your encounter."

I burst out laughing. "In your dreams, Mr. Sunshine."

His smile is wry as he prepares to say his next thought. "Would it please you to note that we acquired a new client Friday afternoon?" he asks before sipping his Grande latte.

"A client for you or me?"

"Both, if you're interested."

"Who is the new client?"

"Masterson, Inc.," he says confidently.

"Hmm, I've never heard of them. What is their business?"

The Creative Director

"Sex toys," he says slowly and succinctly. "A perfect little segue to your arousing weekend," he muses.

I nervously cough into my fist and attempt without much success to hide a blush that dances over my cheeks, neck and chest.

"You are blushing. Does the topic of sex toys make you flush?" he teases.

"Apparently," I mutter.

"They sent a package of product samples last Friday afternoon. I've not opened the box yet. Do you care to help me do the honors?" he says then chuckles.

"Sure. Why not. Should I close the office door and drop the blinds so the staff don't catch us fondling pink dildos and various other questionable paraphernalia?" I ask while arching a brow.

"Yes. Good plan."

While I close the door and drop the blinds, Brantley is taking out a pair of scissors to cut the packing tape off the top of the large box beside his desk. Plastic pillowed packing bags are tossed aside while Brantley digs out the various boxes of product samples and sets them neatly on his desk.

Sandra A. Sigfusson

"You pick one and I'll pick one," he suggests. I nod and grab the box closest to me. I review the item with keen interest in the style of the packaging, the quality of the printing on it, and the detailed description of the box's content on the back side. Brantley is doing the same with the box in his hands.

"Mine appears to be some sort of titillating lotion," he says. "What have you got?"

"A vibrator."

"Batteries included or not?" he asks and smiles wide at me.

"Pervert," I muse. "Batteries not included. I'll get Jason to grab some for me." I pick up Brantley's desk phone and press #522 for Jason's desk. He's not there yet, but he'll get my message and bring us the batteries when he's in at nine.

We explore each box in the same manner by analyzing the quality and other details of the exterior packaging. I note that some of the packages have print that's so small it would be difficult to read for someone with 20/20 vision, let alone someone without perfect eyesight. That is one of the first things I would change.

The Creative Director

By eleven in the morning we've managed to evaluate every box in the sample collection, made a substantive list of changes we'd like to make and created a spreadsheet in Excel to keep track of each item. Later we'll open up the products to inspect quality and see if they do exactly what the packaging touts. "Is this their entire collection of products or only the ones they want us to work with?" I ask.

"No. There are several other items in their collection, but I think you and I would rather view them on their company's premises."

"Why?" I ask.

Brantley smirks. "They also import and distribute very detailed companion dolls," he says. "I highly doubt Grady would be too impressed at having our office filled with life-sized dolls." For a moment Brantley's brows knit together and I wonder if playtime is over. He's like a light switch. On, off. On, off. I'm not sure how to read him sometimes. One thing is certain, though. When I see him clicking his pen open and shut and his lips are pressed to a hard line, I know he's better off being left alone.

"Well, then. How about you arrange for a time for us to meet with the client at their office so we can review their other products up close and personal?" I say, trying to be light and airy since a dark cloud is now clearly hanging over Mr. Sunshine's head.

"Right. Get Jason to arrange that, will you?" Brantley doesn't look up at me when he replies. Whatever he's staring at on his phone has sucked the life right out of him.

"Is something wrong?" I ask.

"Yes, but nothing to do with our work here. It seems my mother has taken a turn again in her health. I may need to fly back to London before the week is through. You'd be fine to deal with my clients in my absence?" His eyes flick up briefly to see if I'll mind holding down the fort for him.

"Yes, of course I'll field your calls from your clients. How long do you think you'll be away?" I ask as I approach him to lean my hip on the edge of his desk.

"It is hard to say. I may need to book off short notice for a fortnight holiday to go there. It makes more sense for me to go for that long in case something happens. I'd hate to have flown back here only to turn round again."

The Creative Director

"Okay. Well, you arrange it any way you deem necessary. I'm certain our team of creatives will be able to band together and keep things running smoothly while you're away," I say assuredly.

"Right. Thanks," he says.

I head back over to my desk. "I sincerely hope your mother recovers from whatever it is she's dealing with health-wise," I say.

"Thank you, Jess."

Chapter 11: Sex on The Brain

Come Wednesday morning, Brantley is off on his flight to London for a two-week stay with his parents.

Before his flight, he and I organized the projects he was in the midst of to ensure we didn't miss any deadlines in his absence. I'm sure Jason and I will be run off our feet by the time Brantley returns; however, he has agreed to check in with me each evening so I can give him a rundown of what has transpired with his client base. This is a big step for me. I'll be in charge of every client we have on contract. If I mess this up, it will be a black mark on my resume – so I'm resolved to working many late nights on Brantley's behalf. Jason is also up for the challenge, agreeing to stay until eight each evening. This is all-or-nothing time for my career. I'd not expected to be put in this position after only two months on the job, but I'll take it and run with it the best I can.

I don't receive a call from Brantley until late Friday afternoon. London is five hours ahead of New York, so it must be nearing midnight there. I'm sure he's exhausted while he adjusts to their time zone, even if five hours is not that much of a difference. He's mentioned to

The Creative Director

me before in casual conversation that he's a bit of a night owl, and getting up in the morning to be in the office before eight o'clock is a daily struggle. I'm the same.

Our first conversation from London is short-lived, and he seems rather curt with me, but that isn't a surprise. He is rarely casual with me, but when he is, it's engaging. His wickedly dry sense of humor took me a while to appreciate, but now I love it. I think I finally have him figured out. He's swift to measure those he's meeting for the first time, priding himself on being a good judge of character – something I wish I were better at – and often pulls me aside to rank each new acquaintance on a scale of one to ten. Ten is brilliant, and one, of course, is dreadful. His words, not mine.

Karmyn and I are together for dinner tonight, and she listens to my telephone conversation with Brantley while on speakerphone. Her eyes pop when she hears his sultry accent and deep tone, but she quickly gets the same first impression from that short phone conversation that I got on my first day at the office.

"He's a real piece of work," Karmyn says after I disconnect from the call.

"He rubs many the wrong way at first," I say, "but now that I've worked with him for a few months, I think I've got him figured out. His gestures and facial expressions are very telling – which is helpful – but there have been many times when I expected him to apologize for being an asshole, and he didn't pick up on his poor behavior. Either that or he didn't give a crap about how his words would be so cutting. Maybe I'm too easily insulted."

I slip my bum over one of Karmyn's bar stools at her kitchen island and fill my wine glass with a new wine her father's vineyard is producing in small quantities.

I take my first sip, and I'm in heaven. "This is excellent!" I say.

"Yes. Dad has outdone himself on this one. I don't typically like the sweeter wines he produces, but this one has my name written all over it. So yummy," she says and licks her lips.

While I savor the sweet bouquet of the wine on my palate, I admire how lovely Karmyn looks tonight. She's done something a bit different with her hair and changed her makeup as well. "Are you dating someone new?" I ask lightheartedly.

"Yes. What made you ask me that?"

The Creative Director

"I know you, sweetie. You've made some subtle changes to your look, and that usually means you're trying to impress someone."

"You do know me well. A little better after last weekend," she adds, fluttering her eyelashes at me.

"Yup. Every sexy inch of you. And, if this new guy you've got your radar on hasn't already seen every sexy inch of you, then he's in for a delightful surprise," I say. It seems so odd for us to be talking like this to each other, but we both crack up at the same time and clink our wine glasses together. If Karmyn is as talented with a cock as she was with her tongue on my pussy, I can't imagine why any man would break up with her.

"Lloyd fucked up, you know," I say. I spin my napkin around the marble countertop while I shake my head at his stupidity.

"You think?" she says snidely.

"Why would anyone cheat on a catch like you?"

"Men cheat because no matter how hot or perfect their current girlfriend or wife is, they can't keep their peckers in their pants. Word to the wise: don't date guys who are clearly addicted to sex. You'll recognize them by the amount of porn they watch or how many dirty magazines they have stashed under their bed, or by the

Sandra A. Sigfusson

mega-sized packs of condoms in the bedside table. Guys are far too obvious when they have sex-on-the-brain syndrome," she says matter-of-factly.

I giggle uncontrollably again. She's right, and we've both dated a sex addict at least once. "Sadly, you only find out about them after you've been with them for a while. The first red flag is when they don't want to take you to their place. Sex is at your apartment because there's always some lame excuse like 'my apartment is a mess,' or 'I have a buddy staying with me and we won't have any privacy.' Goddamned liars. All of them," I say, pounding my fist on the counter, pretending to be righteous.

I crack up again, sending Karmyn into giggles with me.

"So, do you think this new guy potentially has sex-on-the-brain syndrome?" I ask.

"Hard to say," she says. "He seems really sweet and genuine. He was raised on a farm in Oklahoma. I got hung up on his accent when we met during a wine tour on the Seneca Lake Wine Trail last Tuesday. Dad sent me out to grab sample wines from the competition for

The Creative Director

analysis and report on their tasting rooms. I think we were at the White Springs Winery when we met.

"Anyway, we got to chatting and decided to follow each other to the next two wineries to compare our tastes. The next thing I knew, I was being asked to go out for dinner with him. When I got back into town on Thursday, we met up for dinner and continued to build a connection," she says.

"Wow. That sounds like you two hit it off pretty good!"

"Yeah, I think we did." Karmyn's eyes drift over to her living room as she ponders her new potential boyfriend.

"So, when are you seeing him again? I mean, why aren't you two out on a date tonight?"

Karmyn slides over the bottle of wine and nods at me to refill my glass. "I'm seeing him again tomorrow afternoon. We're going on a drive via the Palisades Parkway to Bear Mountain. I've never been out that way, so I hope the weather holds out for the scenic drive," she says.

"Nice. I wish I could go with you, but I have work to do at home for Mr. Sunshine's newest client," I say and sigh. I slump against the backrest of the barstool and sport a pouty face. "How the hell did I get so drunk so fast?"

"You didn't eat before you started drinking. Hang on a second, and I'll make a cheese and cracker plate for you. Maybe it will suck up some of that alcohol you've got swishing around in your belly before dinner is ready," she teases.

"Right," I say and giggle lightly at myself. "I'm a bit overwhelmed by my responsibilities at the office, but I don't want anyone to see me sweat. I've held my chin up for three days straight while I was internally pulling my hair out. I just needed a good couple of drinks to decompress. Thanks, Karmyn."

"Anything for you, hun."

Karmyn places the platter of cheese and crackers in front of me and feeds me my first bite like I'm her little bird. "Eat," she says before kissing my cheek and giving my shoulders a quick hug. "So, what is this new client selling?"

I crack up again while bits of cracker crumbs spray from my lips. "Sex toys," I blurt out. "Fucking sex toys!"

The Creative Director

Chapter 12: The Ship Is Not Sinking

The last few conversations Brantley had with me from the makeshift desk in his parents' London kitchen were far more relaxed than the previous ones. I can only assume his mother is doing better than when he first arrived. This is good news for all of us. I'm spent after almost two weeks of handling the additional workload of Brantley's client list as well as my own. But I promised myself that I'd pull through.

"So, Mr. Sunshine, what date is your flight back to New York scheduled for?" I ask, hoping he doesn't hear the desperation in my voice.

"I'll back in New York on Saturday afternoon at four o'clock. Do you think you can continue to keep things moving smoothly until then?" he asks, far more politely than I expected.

"Yes. Yes, of course. Jason and the other team members have our full client list under control, Brantley. You don't need to worry," I say in the happiest and most confident voice I can manage. "And your mother – how is she now?"

Sandra A. Sigfusson

"Better. But only by a small margin. I'm afraid the chemotherapy has been exceedingly hard on her this time round. We're thankful that she's pulled through so far. Now we have the excruciating wait for the tests in the coming weeks to indicate if the cancerous mass is shrinking. We don't want it spreading any further than it already has," he states somberly.

"I can't imagine what she's going through. I know cancer has touched so many lives but I haven't had anyone in my family suffer from it, and I cross my fingers that they never will. You must feel gutted to watch her go through such a painful treatment protocol," I say with much sympathy for his mother's situation.

"She's a fighter like the rest of us. I'm confident she'll beat the devil out of her cancer, if not by chemotherapy then by sheer will. She puts the S in stubborn if you catch my meaning," he says then follows his comment with a chuckle. I liked hearing that chuckle. It means he's feeling less worried about her condition and will be in good spirits when he returns to the office. But then his switch flips and he's all business again.

"I received a distressing message from the Faraday Travel Agency. Mark Faraday said the ad copy he received was not for his campaign. Who is in charge of

The Creative Director

his ad copy, and why did they not send the right materials to my client?" he asks sternly.

I could picture his resting asshole face in full detail inside my head as he posed that question. "It's been corrected, Brantley. Mark jumped the gun on directing his concern to you. We sent the correct ad copy to him only ten minutes after the incorrect copy was emailed. He's a very impatient man," I say.

"All our clients are impatient and like to think they are our only clients," he replies. "Yes, well, thank you for getting that sorted out quickly. Mark didn't send a second message to indicate the situation was corrected. I only knew of the error."

"You can rest assured that the ship is not sinking, Brantley. I'll admit to being exhausted by trying to manage everyone at once, but I'm proud of our team pulling through. Grady will be happy to see you return as well. As much as he trusts me to keep things intact in your absence, I think he's anxious to know when you're coming back. It has been stressful here without you," I say, then mildly regret telling him it's been tough without him here.

"It's nice to hear I'm so dearly missed and loved. Kiss and hug everyone for me, will you?" he says dryly before breaking out in the loudest fit of laughter I've heard from him yet.

"Are you being facetious?" I ask, knowing full well he is.

"Yes, of course I'm joking. Do you not know me by now, Jess?" he muses.

"You're a hard one to pin down, Brantley," I muse back.

I hear a soft chuckle from him before he states he's got other pressing things to work on before heading to bed. "Right then. Good night, Jess. We'll chat again tomorrow, unless you need me prior."

I hear the phone click without exchanging goodbyes, and I frown as I stare at my cell phone screen. "Good night, Brantley. I hope the bedbugs bite and you itch all night long," I say to my blank screen. "Geez, he's so abrupt. What if I had another question for him?"

I toss my phone toward my bed and cringe as I watch it bounce off the edge of the mattress and land face down on my tiled bedroom floor.

The Creative Director

"Shit!" I mutter, reaching to pick it up. I turn it over to look at the screen and am thankful there isn't a spiderweb crack across the surface. I'm so tired that I'm doing stupid stuff like not paying attention to where I'm walking or how inaccurate I am when tossing my cell phone. That phone is my lifeline to every aspect of my world.

Reaching inside the drawer of my side table, I pull out my sleeping aid tablets. I pop one capsule in my mouth and wash it down with the glass of water on the table. I need a good seven hours of quality sleep.

The balance of my week tending to the herd of clients on Brantley's behalf goes a little sideways on me, but after I let Brantley in on my situation he swoops in and makes a few key phone calls to soothe those savage beasts beating down my office door. I'll have to treat him to a fine bottle of whiskey upon his return.

Chapter 13: Patterns

At last the Monday of Brantley's return arrives and I feel a huge weight being lifted from my shoulders. I didn't screw up as much as I worried I would, and Brantley isn't too out of sorts about the few minor things that had me shaking a little in my red stilettos.

As I arrive to the office Monday morning I'm not surprised to see him already hip deep in his work. "Good morning Mr. Sunshine," I say, then breathe out a heavy sigh. "I can't tell you how happy I am to have you back. How was your return flight?"

"Good. But if you don't mind saving the chitchat for later this afternoon, I'd be grateful," he says.

I nod. It's obvious he's very focused now, and I should know better than to interrupt his genius when he's clicking his pen open and shut and his lips are pressed to a hard line. I chuckle a bit to myself and settle in on my workload.

By noon Jason has placed seven more files on my desk. I'm happy that he's being so efficient, but I'm still frowning at the thought I'll likely be here tonight until

The Creative Director

well past eight to catch up on the most urgent of my projects. As I'm rising from my desk to refill my coffee mug for the umpteenth time, Brantley finally lifts his head from his paperwork and addresses me more kindly than he did first thing this morning.

"My mum is doing much better. Thank you for your kind interest in her well-being and for doing a great job of handling my clients and yours for the fortnight I was away. I fully imagined there would be more issues than there were." Brantley flits his tangerine silk tie between his fingers then tugs at his neck to adjust the tension in the knot.

"That's a great color on you," I say as I slip behind him to reach the coffee machine.

"Thank you. I have far too many orange and green ties in my collection, but I gravitate to those colors when I shop for new ties. Funny how we fall into patterns without recognizing it."

"Yes, that's so true," I say. The groaning sound of the coffee machine tells me that my cup is full. I slip a blip of cream in the mug and stir gently while I analyze in my head the patterns of my own shopping habits. That thought makes me wonder if our human natures would make for a good ad campaign for one of my clothing clients. I tap my spoon gently on the edge of my coffee mug and then sip cautiously at the hot liquid.

"What would you think of turning patterns in shopping into an ad campaign? I have a clothing supplier who's looking for a way to give his new line of garments a boost. I'm thinking along the lines of *Get out of your rut and change it up*, as an angle," I say.

Brantley spins his chair to face me at the kitchenette counter I'm leaning on. "You might have something there. A play on the word patterns might also work. Something like, *We've all got patterns, but have you seen these yet?* Okay, maybe that isn't quite right, but you catch my drift," he says. Brantley offers me a small smile while I catch a fleeting waft of his sensual cologne. Oh, how I missed that scent in the office. Patterns. There's another one. Getting used to certain scents and associating them with people, places and objects is another thing we humans do without noticing we're doing it.

"Hey," I say as I stand up from my lean on the counter's edge. "What if we used pattern thinking to work up a new slogan for the Masterson sex toys line?"

The Creative Director

Brantley chuckles and that delicious smile of his returns. I'm feeling very aroused by him at this moment. I attempt to will my nipples away from hardening beneath my blouse, but fail. Is it the sex toys comment or his damned cologne doing this to me? I need to go on a proper date with a horny guy. Maybe Karmyn's new boyfriend has a hard-up pal he can hook me up with.

Shaking those thoughts from my brain, I return Brantley's delicious smile and nod. "What are you smiling about? You never smile. You must have something truly brilliant rambling around in that handsome brain of yours," I muse.

"You think my brain is handsome? How lovely," he teases, smirking. "Never mind. Yes, I agree. However, it is difficult to convince people to change their set patterns even if they don't recognize that there are patterns in the way they think, shop, and" – he chuckles – "make love." Brantley's eyebrows wriggle and his eyes sparkle at me and I feel a flush of heat wash over my face. Fuck. I'm blushing.

"I've made you flush with heat yet again!"

"Shut up," I groan and walk back to my desk. Damn him anyway. I'm in desperate need to find something to tease him about. The bugger doesn't fight fair, having so much ammunition on me when I'm completely bullet-less. I wonder if he's this lighthearted in bed, or if his Mr. Sunshine alter ego is his go-to mood between the sheets. Cher's voice inside my head reminds me once again to snap out of it.

"Listen," he says, catching my attention again before I've seated myself back in my chair. "I've got two clients in the L.A. area who I'd like to meet with later this week. One is the Watson Accessory Company. They hand-make fine leather gloves and felt and wool hats and scarves. Their client base is seventy-percent female and thirty-percent male. The second client produces a carbonated drink called Rasta, which is infused with marijuana oil. Their logo is Bob Marley's face," he adds, rolling his eyes.

I nod while Brantley rattles off information about his two L.A. clients. "So, you'll need me to hold the fort down again while you do a road trip?" I ask, feeling overwhelmed by that thought.

"No. I'd like you to join me in presenting to them. Can I steal you away for two, maybe three days to assist me?" he asks. I watch him flit his tie again and I wonder if this is a pattern of his that I should pay more attention to.

The Creative Director

"Yes. I could do that. Jason is fine to leave alone for a couple of days. He's taken on his role as my assistant exceptionally well. I'm confident all will be fine here while we're away."

"Splendid," Brantley says, exaggerating his accent for what I can only assume is comedic effect. "I'll book our tickets now. Be ready to fly Wednesday evening. Our first meeting is Thursday morning at eleven o'clock with Rasta."

This changes my entire plan of attack when it comes to managing my workload for the balance of this week. I start to rearrange everything and call Jason to my desk so we can sort out what he needs to attend to while I'm in L.A. with Brantley.

Chapter 14: We Shouldn't

After two hours of sharing stories about shitty bosses and shitty employees, my face begins to hurt from smiling so much and laughing too often. I've had three very dirty martinis at the bar with Brantley after drinking four six-ounce glasses of wine at our earlier dinner with a contact of Brantley's in town. I should have slowed down on the drinking, but before I could put my hand up to decline my latest refill the glass was already placed in front of me by the bartender, courtesy of Brantley's generosity. Who am I to pass up free drinks when they're twenty-five dollars each?

My finger taps gently on the side of my cheek as I hold my chin within my palm, elbow firmly planted on the edge of the bar, and continue to be entertained by Brantley's stories. His accounts of people I know and don't know are amusing. A storyteller such as he I have not met before. It makes me jealous in some ways, since we both share a similar title within the agency. I hated to admit it for quite some time, how much I enjoy his wicked sense of humor and his talent for putting the perfect words together. It comes to him with such ease.

The Creative Director

He's without a doubt in his perfect element as an advertising executive.

I have no idea what the time is, but I feel like it's the right moment to part ways before reconvening in the morning for our second set of presentations. I ease my face away from my hand and reach for my clutch purse beside my nearly-empty martini glass. "Should we call it a night, Brantley?" I say in a calm but surprisingly sexy voice. I don't know where that tone came from. Must be the alcohol.

For the life of me I can't recall ever being told his first name. Even the employees and upper management call him Brantley. I looked at his business cards on his desk once after my chat with Karmyn about his last name, but his cards just read "Brantley." I have to assume Brantley is his last name. His first name is likely something funky like Casper or pompous like Jamison the Third. "So, you only use one name, hey?" I say, prodding him to fess up. "Is it a branding thing, like Madonna or Cher?" I tease, smirking behind the rim of my martini glass.

"No, nothing so brilliant as that," he chuckles.

"So, what is it then?"

"What is what?" he replies, pretending he isn't following me.

"Your first name? It's your last name that's Brantley, right? Is it so odd or pretentious that you've chosen to not add it to your business cards?"

"That secret dies with me," he mumbles.

"Nah. You are not getting off that easy. Tell me the story and I'll swear on a stack of bibles that I'll never speak of it again," I say.

"The story is rather amusing," he says. There is a long pause, but he doesn't say anything further.

"And?" I prod, waving my hand in circles in front of me.

"And I'm not telling you the story. It dies with me," he says, imitating my ridiculous hand gesture. "What is this hand thing you're doing? Are you about to upswallow dinner?"

"No," I giggle. "I was gesturing for *you* to cough it up. Your first name. I'll get it out of you somehow," I murmur as I ease myself off the bar stool. My balance is not as steady as I assumed it would be, and I place my hand upon his shoulder for balance before my five-inch spike heels hit the marble floor. Brantley surprises me by placing his warm, strong hand over mine as I step down

The Creative Director

to solid ground. I'd like to pretend I wasn't taken aback by his gentle touch or the fact that my face is directly in front of his, inches away from his lips with his fixed gaze on mine. And that woodsy cologne of his is going to drive me insane. His hand lets go and the moment fades.

He nods and smirks before downing the last sip of his bourbon on the rocks. "I have something in my room that I'd like you to look at before you retire to your suite," he says. I watch as his elegant hand places the tumbler gently down on the coaster on the highly polished black granite of the bar. The bartender swiftly removes the empty tumbler and my martini glass while nodding at Brantley.

"On your room tab, sir?" the bartender confirms.

"Yes, of course," Brantley agrees. His beautifully timbred English voice fills the space between us when he replies. He didn't look at the bartender just then, but at me. I smile and thank the bartender for his perfect service, then realize Brantley's gaze is still hanging over me while he sets a cash tip for the bartender upon the bar. Why is he looking at me like that? His eyes seem a bit glazed.

"Are you feeling your drinks as much as I am?" I ask. Brantley nods. I try not to fix my eyes upon his, as he's doing something to me with those blue pools of

Sandra A. Sigfusson

heaven that I don't want them to do. If I didn't know better I'd say they were undressing me. We can't do this. He can't undress me any more than I can undress him. We are colleagues. Not two strangers hooking up in an elegant bar in a high-class hotel.

    He realizes that he's somehow made me feel uncomfortable and waits for me to move aside so he can also step down from his bar stool. Brantley removes his blazer from the back of the stool and drapes it over his shoulder like he's getting ready to pose for a magazine cover. Dangerous. I swear every single thing this man does screams sex appeal.

    He gestures with his hand for me to lead the way to the elevators and I take my first unsteady steps in my ridiculous heels. I find my rhythm as my clicking heels echo within the cavernous space leading down the marble hallway. I clear my throat as I fuss with the position of my handbag under my arm. I am surprised that Brantley's hand isn't gently nested into the small of my back as we stroll toward the lobby. Strangely, I wanted to feel his warm hand on my back, but I know better than to expect him to touch me again. That simple touch of my hand on his shoulder was not intended to mean anything, but for some strange reason it did.

The Creative Director

"Will you be telling me your first name when we get to your suite?" I continue to ask, since I'm lost for any other topic of conversation.

"Why does it interest you so much?" he asks. I glance back over my shoulder and see his brow is knit slightly at my persistence.

"I don't get why it's such a secret."

"If you agree to come to my suite for a nightcap I will tell you the story. Deal?" he says in a husky voice next to my ear as we step inside the open elevator car.

"Deal," I whisper, doing my best to hold back a grin.

Brantley:

The lift doors open on the seventeenth floor. I wait for Jess to move forward before I do. I'd like to think it is because I'm the consummate gentleman, but in truth I simply love to watch Jess walk ahead of me in those sexy-as-hell cherry red stilettos.

"What room are you in?" she asks.

"1725. Just down the hall on the left."

She nods and follows the numbers on the hallway doors. Her room is directly below mine on the sixteenth. We tried to secure rooms on the same floor for convenience, but the hotel wasn't able to accommodate our request. As I open the suite door Jess comments on how anxious she is to relieve her feet of her shoes and hopes that I won't be offended if she slips them off when we get inside.

"Why would I mind?" I ask. "I can only imagine how much pressure they put on your toes, regardless of how enticing they are to look at while you're in them." Perhaps I should have kept that thought to myself.

I head to the mini bar to prepare a nightcap. "I don't have ingredients for a martini, but can I get you a bourbon on the rocks?"

"No, thank you. A glass of ice water would be fine," she says. Jess eases her way across the room and seats herself in the plush, dark purple, tone-on-tone striped armchair next to the sliding doors to the balcony. Her eyes rise to see me approaching her with a tumbler of ice water. I slip the tumbler into her open palm then swirl the ice in my glass before taking a sip.

The Creative Director

"So, what is this thing you wanted to show me before I go to my room?" she asks.

A smile eases over my lips before I answer. "I made a few more sketches before dinner tonight and I think we should consider changing the color scheme we agreed on earlier for the Bear Creek Estates wine logo. The green and red combination isn't sitting right to my eye, and I wonder if gold and red is a better choice," I say, while eyeing up the recliner chair at the other end of the blond-stained credenza.

While I talk about the logo color choices, Jess twists her bum in the high-backed wing chair to hang her legs over the arm and rest her back against the other arm. Before I can suggest anything further, her left shoe has dropped to the floor and her right shoe is hanging from the tips of her toes precariously. As my ears capture the sound of her shoe dropping to the carpet below, my eyes linger on the shoe that hasn't yet dropped.

"Do you have a thing for red shoes?" she asks, teasingly, then she laughs. She's caught me absorbing the titillating scene in front of me.

She tosses her head back while she cracks up at her innuendo. God, this is delicious. I adore the little things in women's movements. Even if it's something as simple as removing their high heels. "You really shouldn't sit in the chair like that," I say, trying to be stern.

"Why? It's very sturdy."

"No, I mean you're drunk and I don't want you falling out of it," I reply.

"Oh. Well. You obviously have no idea how well balanced I am," she says, then sips her ice water before setting it down on the credenza beside her. Out of the corner of her eye she spies a novel and reaches for it to read the title. It is *The Seductress of Chambourcy* by Rita Redding. Her eyes widen when she realizes it is a sexy romance novel. A smile takes over her face and she darts her eyes sidelong to look at me. "Are you an incurable romantic?" she asks, appearing surprised.

"Put it down, Jess," I urge. I seat myself in the opposing recliner chair and slip off my shoes. I place them neatly beside the chair and adjust my seated position, feeling rather comfortable now, before taking another sip of my cocktail.

"Why do you have a sexy romance novel in your room?" she asks lightheartedly.

The Creative Director

I sigh. "My sister is a romance novelist. This is her latest work that she's self-published. She asked me to help her market her books and recommended I read this one before I embark on a marketing campaign for her."

"Ah. That makes sense. Is she any good?" she asks.

"Brilliant. I'm not saying that because she's my sister. This novel is much better than I expected it to be. Not my preference of subject, of course, but I'm enjoying it nonetheless."

"You'll have to let me read it when you're done," she says enthusiastically. "I love romance novels. How hot is the sex in it?"

I try to hold my manly composure, but I fear she's managed to make me flush a little in the face. "It is an erotic romance set in the eighteen hundreds, so yes, there are some explicit sex scenes," I say under my breath. I'm twisting my cocktail tumbler in circles on the padded arm of the recliner. She's getting under my skin in a way I'd rather she didn't.

She nods and places the book back down on the top of the credenza. Jess closes her eyes briefly as she lays her head back again. Her right shoe is still dangling from her toes while she gently swings it up and down, playing with it while she appears to relax.

Sandra A. Sigfusson

"Please stop that," I say. I've managed to become seriously aroused by her regardless of my attempts otherwise. My hard-as-fuck cock makes me uncomfortable now that it is pressing firmly against my zipper. She is lovely. Especially tonight in the soft light of the suite. I liked the way she relaxed and opened up with me tonight after a few drinks. We needed this casual evening to soften the tension we have in the office, although it has been less tense as of late. I don't want to be harsh with her, but I'm known for my demanding ways and high expectations. That I cannot change, even for her. But why this sudden urge to fuck her into next weekend?

"What?" she asks as her eyes pop open.

I take another sip of my cocktail before replying. "Your body position is exceptionally arousing. I didn't bring you up here for you to seduce me," I say and shake my head. My eyes are now fixed on her while she lifts her head up to look at me directly, appearing to be a tad confused.

"Really? You think I'm trying to seduce you? That's rich, even for you, Sunshine," she says and then sighs. A moment of awkward silence comes between us before we both attempt to speak at the same time.

The Creative Director

"Sorry. You go first," I say.

"No. It's okay. You go first."

I lift my gaze above her head to look out the window at the night lights shimmering through the glass. "I'm a single man with urges, Jess. After this evening with you I've discovered that you are far more interesting and attractive than I first gave you credit for. Having said that, I think you and I should call it a night. I shouldn't have brought you up to my suite. What I had to show you regarding my thoughts on the logo colors could have waited until tomorrow. We are both too drunk to make sensible decisions, and I'm not one for playing in the office pool."

She laughs with full abandon at me. "Playing in the office pool? And, since when do you find me attractive? We've been at each other's throats over clients, creative differences and executive decisions since the day we were thrown together in the same office space. I think you must have me confused with someone else, Brantley. Sexy is not how you think of me, and you are obviously too drunk to remember that," she admonishes.

I chuckle lightly and rise from my position on the recliner. She truly has no idea how beautiful she is or how long it's been since I've had a good shag. I have had many moments of quiet desire for her in the office, but

Sandra A. Sigfusson

what man wouldn't? At this moment I'm dying to taste her slick heat, suck at her tits until her nipples ache and thrust myself inside of her repeatedly until my name is the only thing she wants to scream. She has to go. Now. I rest my tumbler on the credenza then approach her to help her stand from her seat and put her shoes back on. Kneeling before her, I reach for her dropped shoe. It's time to be a gentleman, not a man driven by the mood of his cock.

"I can get out of this chair on my own," she says.

She spins slowly, easing her right leg toward me while her left leg is still slung over the arm of the chair. Her skirt has grabbed the fabric of the chair, and as she twists to sit upright, my eyes become fixed on her display of a perfectly waxed, bare-to-my-eyes pussy. Fuck me, I'm gob smacked. How do I erase that glorious scene from my sex-starved drunk-as-fuck mind? This is a complete disaster. It takes everything I have to not tuck my head between those gorgeous legs and start licking. "Jesus, Jess," I murmur.

The Creative Director

<u>Jess:</u>

His eyes don't leave the clear view up my skirt. They are glued to my sex like he's witnessing a train wreck. His pupils dilate, adjusting to the darker setting between my legs, as I nervously drop my hand down over my skirt to hide my exposure, but the damage is done. I just pulled a fucking Britney Spears limo crotch-flash at my colleague after he just finished admitting to finding me arousing.

I flush with a deep level of embarrassment and swiftly swing my left leg over to try to recoup my composure. I am stone-cold sober after this fiasco of a moment. My face heats to a level I've never felt before and I'm certain my cheeks and neck are a deep red. My eyes widen while I wait for Brantley to stand up and walk away from me in disgust – I'm certain. But he doesn't get up. Instead he clenches his jaw and gently clasps his hands over mine, which are fisted between my legs pressing down on my skirt.

"How long have you been going commando?" he asks in a husky tone. His eyes narrow as he waits for my reply. "Every day, Jess?"

I try to speak but I stammer instead. A moment later when I get my mouth back in working order I assure him it was only today. "I forgot to pack panties," I

Sandra A. Sigfusson

whisper then push his hands away from mine. Our eyes lock on each other and I have no idea what is going through his head. Shock? Disbelief? Disgust?

Brantley slides a hand over his stubbled chin as he stands before me. He uses that same hand to scrub up and down the length of his face, then places both of his hands deep inside his pant pockets with a heavy sigh. He turns his head and looks at the ground as I try as gracefully as possible to rise to my feet. I adjust the length of my skirt over my legs then bend down to grab my wayward shoe from the floor and take the other one off my foot. Holding my cherry-red stilettos close to my chest and slipping past Brantley to grab my purse off the top of the credenza, I'm surprised to feel Brantley's hand clasp my forearm and I'm frozen in place.

"Please," I say. "Don't say anything to anyone about this. This is a huge misunderstanding." My voice is shaky as I try to release myself from his hold and remain calm. "I had no intention of seducing you, Brantley. And I most certainly did not intend for you to know I wasn't wearing panties. Jesus fucking Christ," I mutter between gritted teeth. I'm furious with myself and this situation.

Brantley looks over his shoulder at me. The heat in his eyes is unmistakable. He wants me. I watch as his

The Creative Director

jaw clenches again and he swallows hard while his eyes warn me of what his body is feeling. I search his face in an attempt to read his mind. I lower my gaze down the length of his body and he is clearly aroused by my exposure. The bulge in his pants is huge by any standards, which only makes my cheeks heat with color once again.

I dart my eyes up to meet his. "We can't," I add with my voice still shaky. My gaze betrays my mouth and the words falling from my lips. Brantley's eyes narrow at mine again as he seems to be fighting his own internal battle. My breath hitches while I wait for him to release my arm, but Brantley tugs gently to get me to step closer to him. I hesitate and stand firm in my place – heart pounding, sexual tension at its highest peak. My center begins to pulse and my nipples harden in reaction to his touch. The heat I see in his eyes makes me lick my lips because I'm breathing through my mouth in soft pants like I'm struggling to inhale. As much as I want to break our stare, I can't seem to convince myself to do so. He turns his body to face me and leans forward like he's going to touch his forehead on mine, with his mouth now barely an inch away from my parched lips. I lick them once again just seconds before his mouth hovers so close that I can nearly taste him. I don't know what is seducing me more: the thought that he wants me or the scent of his skin.

Sandra A. Sigfusson

Brantley presses his lips tentatively upon mine and my heart continues pounding heavily in my chest. "We shouldn't," I whisper, since can't is now clearly off the table.

"We shouldn't," he whispers back.

<u>Brantley:</u>

I can't control my need to kiss her with the kind of desire I've not felt for a woman in what seems like a lifetime. But what is fueling this desire? She's groaned and glared at me multiple times a day over my cutting remarks on her suggestions and ideas. I shouldn't have been so harsh with her. But that was all before tonight. Tonight we took the time to learn more about each other. We laughed and smiled freely as if there were never a wedge between us.

Her eyes hold me hostage. In them I see a fire burning. A fire I want to stoke so that it doesn't fade to a flicker before she lets me taste her. I'm so fucked. How did this happen? How did I let myself be so careless with my thoughts in her presence? This could ruin me and give me a reputation. She could take me down with this heady tease between us – use it against me somehow. But in the heat of this moment, I don't care. I need her.

The Creative Director

"Do you want this as much as I do? Be honest, Jess," I murmur against her lips.

She swallows and I can tell her mind is spinning a million miles a minute. Her eyes search left to right over mine. I want to kiss her neck and run my tongue up the length of it. I imagine the silkiness and the light saltiness of her skin upon my taste buds. At the thought of exploring her body this way, my cock grows firmer, fueling its need to be addressed.

She nods. That was all I needed. Confirmation that we're both willing to risk everything we've worked toward. To risk our professional reputations and our careers for a tumble in the sheets with a colleague.

Jess:

Brantley's lips crush against mine. He is devouring me. I feel his strong, broad hand hold the back of my head then his fingers gently tugging on my hair. My shoes drop to the floor at our feet and my purse slips from under my arm to join them on the floor behind me. Brantley's other hand rests on my hip as he presses my body backward with his chest against me, guiding me to the recliner he was in just minutes ago.

Sandra A. Sigfusson

His desire for me is now my drug. I tug upon on his bottom lip while I unbutton his dress shirt, pulling it up from within the band of his dress pants. I loosen his tie and drag my teeth across his lip again. As he lowers himself down on his knees before me as if to submit, gently inching his hands up the length of my thighs, his touch fuels me further. I push his shirt over his shoulders and love the sensation of his warm skin in my palms. Broad shoulders, defined muscles, and pronounced veins running down the length of his arms give me pause. I'd not expected to see him so trim, so fit under his layer of clothes. I lower myself to sit on the edge of the recliner, putting us eye to eye. My fingers trace the length of his arm to his wrist while I admire how impressive his physical form is. His eyes stay locked on mine as I grip my hands around his loosened tie and pull him toward my face to kiss him again. This time our tongues are slow to twist together, exploring. I have an aggressive need for this and for him, more than I could have imagined, yearning for that tongue of his on more than just my mouth. A soft moan escapes when the thought enters my mind.

Strong hands grip my hips when Brantley's tongue meets mine. I reach down to undo his belt buckle without letting his mouth free. I manage the task without

The Creative Director

looking down, then release the top button of his pants and lower the zipper. He clasps both of my hands and places them on his shoulders. Lifting my right hand, I run my fingers through his hair. He has the most incredible hair – glossy, soft, with a subtle wave. I visually explore every little nuance of his face while he unbuttons my blouse. There's a light spray of freckles on his skin that one would never notice unless you were this close to him. His skin bears a light tan, smooth to the touch with nary a wrinkle to be found. I'm admiring the straightness of his nose, the depth of blue in his azure eyes when he catches me analyzing every inch of his features. Our eyes lock on to each other and we crush our lips together again, hungrier than before.

My blouse slips off my shoulders to the cushion behind me. "These beautiful tits of yours have been taunting me for too long," he says in a darkened tone. His lips trace my collarbone momentarily before he bites at the fabric of my lace bra while undoing the front closure clasp. Both his palms sweep over my breasts when he releases them from the black lace. I feel the heat of his breath over one breast – his tongue circling my nipple while his other hand pinches and rolls the other. They were erect and hard before he started his delicious teasing of them. Brantley sucks at each nipple to the point where they hurt, but I'm loving the little sparks of pain. I feel this desire, this need, straight down through to my thumping center as my body temperature rises and my breathing becomes more labored.

    Brantley puts his palms around the back of my hips again and tugs me to slip forward in the recliner. I know what he wants but I feel the urge to make him work for it. I want this moment to slow down a bit while my senses bathe in his scent and the caress of his hands on my skin. He places his palms on my thighs once more, inching up higher and higher beneath my skirt. His tongue still licks and sucks at my nipples, ridding me of any and all previous inhibitions.

    As his fingers draw closer to my center, he presses against my inner thighs, urging me to widen my legs. I oblige him – giving in to both our needs. I think I know how to make this a little easier for him, and now I want to let him have me any way he wants. I slide my backside deeper into the seat of the recliner, then lower the back of the chair. He tries to tug me back to where I was but I stop him. His eyes narrow as if to question my moves. I wriggle my skirt higher to the edges of my hips, then spread my legs wide and drape them over the arms of the recliner.

    Brantley's grin returns. "Oh, how I love a waxed pussy," he murmurs. My eyes close as I lean back and

The Creative Director

wait for him to continue. He growls deep in his throat at the sight of me like this. My center throbs harder now and I don't doubt that the flesh of my exposed sex is a deep pink and engorged. I cup my breasts in my palms and massage them. I lick my lips in anticipation of his fingers finding me wet and so ready – and then I feel his thumb upon my clit, and I hitch a breath at the thought of coming for him like this while he watches.

The circular movement of his thumb sends me into deep pleasure mode. I moan before he speaks to me. "I can't believe how wet you are. Jesus, Jess," he groans. I press my hips upward in appreciation of his further teasing. Seconds later he plunges two fingers inside of me and I nearly explode from the sensation.

"Oh, sweet Jesus," I murmur while I continue to savor each deep pleasuring plunge of his fingers. "I want your mouth on me," I say between heavy breaths. "Lick me. Flick your tongue over my clit while you finger fuck me."

He does exactly as I ask. It only takes a minute more of this sweet torture before I come for him, over his tongue, his lips and his hand. I'm so stimulated I'm seeing stars.

Brantley stands to drop his pants to his feet. I watch him pull a condom from his wallet and hear a wrapper crinkle in his hand. My eyes fixate on him as he sheaths himself with the condom. I press the button on the recliner to lay it back as far as it will go. He climbs over me, hovering his mouth over mine, then plunges himself deep inside of me. His mouth devours mine again while he pulses with long smooth thrusts into me. I want to cry out how incredible he feels inside of me.

"You feel too good. I didn't expect you to feel *this* good," he whispers while I press my hips up to match his rhythm. We keep this pace for a few minutes, rocking together, savoring the friction and the closeness. We kiss again, softer than a moment ago as we fuck our pent-up desires and frustrations out of each other. This connection is crazy, amazing, delicious and so unexpected.

As we pulse faster now, I can feel him getting harder inside of me. He's close to his release, and the thought of him reaching his breaking point inside of me makes me smile. "Come for me, Brantley," I say. "Explode inside me." And within seconds of my request he comes as hard as I knew he would. Brantley shudders and presses himself inside of me slowly twice more before completely relaxing. He gently withdraws as I catch my breath. A trail of chaste kisses upon my lips, my breast, and my belly follow as he rises to his feet.

The Creative Director

Breathing heavy, he removes the condom and tosses it into the waste basket next to the credenza. My eyes are flooded with the nakedness of Brantley's beautiful form. My legs are still spread wide on the arms of the recliner as I wonder how wrecked my skirt is from our little fuck session.

Brantley:

I'm in awe of what just happened. It's been a while since a woman told me flat out how to please her. I love that in a woman. I like a little dirty talk, the kind of precise instructions she gave me. I didn't think my cock could get that hard so quickly, but Jess gave me far more than I ever expected from this unplanned encounter.

"Stay there for a minute," I say before heading to the loo. Turning my head toward the recliner while I walk away, I watch as Jess closes her legs and adjusts her skirt. I bring a warm wet facecloth to her and she stands before me. "Shall I or would you rather?" I ask.

She seems genuinely surprised at my gesture. "What would you prefer?" she asks.

"Let me," I say. Jess undoes the zipper of her skirt and lets it fall to the floor. I smile as I step forward to place the face cloth over her mound to smooth the cloth between her legs, staring deep in her pretty eyes, and then I give her a chaste kiss on her mouth. Her face beams.

"You promised to tell me your first name," she says while reaching to the floor for her skirt.

I chuckle when I reply, "Brantley."

"No. That is your last name."

"No, that is my first name."

"Well then, what the hell is your last name?"

"Brantley," I say again. She's getting a little testy over my riddle. She zips her skirt and adjusts her blouse. I know she's thinking that I'm pulling one over on her.

"Your first and last name are both Brantley?" she muses and looks at me with an expression of pure disbelief.

"Now you're getting it," I smirk.

"What parent names their kid the same first and last name?"

I pause as I place the warm washcloth on the credenza and reach to the floor for my clothes. "My

The Creative Director

mother was drunk when she filled in my birth certificate information. She put our last name on the document twice – once in the first name space and again in the last name space. Nobody at the birth registration office questioned it. Thus I've never been called anything but Brantley."

I don't think she believes my crazy story. It's the same thing I tell everyone who inquires, and now I've told this lie so many times I believe it myself.

"Why didn't you call yourself Brad or something?"

"I don't know. I just didn't. It wasn't my name," I say, a hint of frustration in my tone.

"I'm sorry. I didn't mean to make a big deal about it," she replies, trying to soothe me. "But I don't believe you regardless."

I nod. As I zip up my trousers and twist the button into the buttonhole I ask, "What would you call me if you could pick any name?"

"Colin," she says, without much hesitation.

"Really?" I say, surprised. I stuff my hands in my pockets and pitch one eyebrow high. "And you never thought twice or were teased as a child for being called Jessie James?" I say and grin.

Sandra A. Sigfusson

"Jessica Adeline James," she says, correcting me in the teacher's-not-happy tone she tosses around from time to time. "Nobody calls me Jessie."

"Why do you shorten your first name to Jess? Jessica sounds elegant."

"It sounds prissy," she says, then sighs. "Jess is more casual, easy to remember and spell."

I place my finger upon my lips and start tapping it playfully. "Jessica Jones, Jessica Alba, Jessica Lange – ooh, Jessica Jaymes the porn star – Jessica Capshaw, and we cannot forget the lovely, voluptuous Jessica Rabbit," I growl as I pick up and hold both of her cherry-red stilettos with the fingers of my right hand and grin at her.

"So you'd prefer I used my full name?" she quizzes as she retrieves her shoes from my hand.

"It's not my call to make. I have my own name issues to deal with, and curious women such as yourself hell-bent on knowing why I only use one name." I reach for my tumbler on the credenza and wash back the melted ice flavored with a hint of bourbon in one gulp. Without turning my head to look at her I ask, "Do you want to spend the night, or would you rather sleep in your own

The Creative Director

bed this evening?" When I turn to look at her, her eyes grow wide before she replies.

"I don't know. I got dressed and collected my things, assuming the last thing you wanted was for me to spend a full night with you." Her voice registers her shock at my suggestion. "Do all your dates sleep with you afterward?"

"No, they don't. But I don't offer that every time. And you're not a date, Jess."

"So, why this time?" she asks, gripping her purse tightly against her chest.

"You have a very inquisitive nature, Jessica," I say, broadening my smile.

"And *that* is your reason?" She laughs incredulously at me.

"No. I want you to sleep next to me because I like you more than I should." I stroke my fingers through my hair before stuffing my hand back deep inside my pant pocket.

"No you don't. You tolerate me just as I tolerate you." Jess begins to search the room as if to locate something else of hers. "This was just drunk sex allowing us to blow off some steam. Nothing more. I know your type and I'm not it. I've seen your dates at various functions and I'm nothing like them. You're still drunk, Brantley. When you sober up in the morning you will have regretted asking this of me."

I swallow hard at her words and speak genuinely when I reply. "Clearly I've left a bad impression of how I feel about working with you. I know I'm hard on everyone, even you, but that is who I am. And, I'm not so drunk as to not understand what I'm asking of you, Jess. It's just one night. Please stay." I reach to touch the side of her arm to assure her.

"Do you want to have a second go-around?" she asks curiously.

I don't know why she thought that was my intention. "You are complicating the invitation, Jess. I want to sleep with you next to me tonight. If you want to have sex again, we can, but that isn't a prerequisite. Please. Stay."

The Creative Director

Chapter 15: The Morning After

It is presentation time. But that isn't where my mind is at. I slipped back down to my suite before Brantley woke so I could compose myself and prepare for today's meeting in my own space. I'm anxious as I shrug on my blazer and dip my toes into more sensible shoes than the ones I wore yesterday. I pull my hair away from where it got tucked in beneath my blazer and shake it out. I decide to plait my hair and drape it over my shoulder to keep it controlled. The clients are conservative and I want to look as polished as possible. This high-necked blush pink silk blouse and my cream linen dress pants will work well in this situation.

My cell phone pings with a text, and I step across the room to the edge of the bed to retrieve my phone.

Brantley: *Are you ready?*

Me: *Yes. Meet me in the lobby.*

My briefcase is standing ready at the entrance to the suite. I adjust my new Cartier watch and smile at how much I love my new accessory. Although I don't make it a habit to spend loads of cash on accessories, my old watch wasn't working as well as it used to. Keeping correct time is important to me. I am driven and diligent in the planning and execution of my tasks. Slipping my room key inside my blazer pocket, I leave the suite and stride down the hall to the elevator. I don't have to wait long for it to arrive at my floor. As the elevator doors open I see Brantley is inside. He's busy looking at his phone screen when I enter, and it isn't until I stand next to him that he realizes it's me.

A smile creeps ever so slowly over his face as he asks, "Did you sleep well?"

"Surprisingly, yes," I say and nod. I shouldn't be standing so close to him this morning. His cologne is tempting me to allow him to suck my face off before the elevator car reaches the lobby. Not that it's safe to assume that is what he would want to do, but I doubt I'd have the backbone to stop him if he did. *Shake it out of your head, girl,* I internally remind myself.

"Good to know. As did I." He bumps my shoulder with his as his way of saying hello, like boys did in high school, and goes back to whatever is holding his attention on his phone screen. "We should be right on time," he mentions. I nod again and suck in a deep breath but I don't think he witnessed my gesture. My hands squeeze a little tighter on the handles of my briefcase in front of me and I roll my shoulders a little in an attempt to relax. "Not

The Creative Director

a morning person?" he asks as the elevator door opens on the lobby floor.

"I need coffee and a pastry," I say with a sigh.

"We have time to stop for that on the way. The rental car is being brought up now," he says. "Have you got all the paperwork I gave you?"

I smile to myself. When do I not have all my paperwork with me? I live, sleep, dream and breathe my job. I'm always prepared and not easily distracted – until last night, that is. It's bad enough that he's so attractive, but to also discover he is a wonderful lover makes this situation even more confusing. The second time we made love in his bed was completely different than the first round. A lover so tender I'd not had before. I recall telling Karmyn how no man has ever touched me the way she had, but Brantley did. And, for him to be that way was so unexpected. I only regret what we did last night because I know we'll never be able to do that again. What a shame it is to discover the perfect lover and not be able to have him for more than one night.

I've worked much harder than most men in my industry to get a Creative Director position – albeit a shared one – and I'm not letting this indiscretion destroy my career under any circumstances. I keep telling myself it was a round of drunk sex with my colleague in a moment of mutual weaknesses, but that lie sits heavy in my heart.

"I'm ready to assist you with the presentation, and all paperwork accounted for," I say, with a hint of indignation. "The storyboards are in the trunk of the rental car."

"Hmm. Maybe I'll save my questions until after you've had that coffee and pastry," he mumbles.

We reach the client's office with ten minutes to spare before our set meeting time. I seat myself in the client's lobby, rest my briefcase at my side and cross my legs.

"Not feeling the cherry-red spikes today?" he muses.

"How about we keep last night in the past, where it belongs," I scold under my breath.

Brantley sighs rather loudly and nods. "You're right. My apologies. Business and pleasure don't mix."

The receptionist approaches us and we stand. "Follow me," she says.

The Creative Director

Brantley allows me to lead the walk to the conference room. I will present the graphics and Brantley will present the pitch.

All goes according to plan with our conservative clients. They like the ideas we present and the new CEO, a woman, seems taken by Brantley's sultry English accent and charm. The charm specifically reserved for his clients, that is. I can't blame her. If she only knew how arousing it was when he talked dirty to me last night in our second round of drunk sex. I feel heat flushing my cheeks, and I turn, pretending I need to adjust something with the storyboard beside me. I have to get thoughts of Brantley's amazing body and touch out of my head this instant. I can't believe how unprofessional I'm being by letting my sex rule my emotions. I've not been laid by a man like that in years. I thought he'd be selfish and rough, but instead I saw a part of him that I'd truly not expected. One would never suspect he was so – fuck, what is the word – thoughtful? No. Kind? No, that isn't right either. *Loving?* My eyes widen in shock at the fact that I settled on the word loving to describe how I felt in the arms of Brantley last night. Was it an act? Does he do this with every woman to make her feel at ease?

Brantley gently nudges me with his shoulder to catch my attention. I place a confident smile on my lips before turning to face the room again. "If you have any concerns," Brantley says, "while my colleague and I are firming up the ad space materials for next month's launch, please call either of us directly." He reaches across the front of my body to shake the hand of the Marketing Manager, and then goes around the room to shake the other executives' hands before they exit the conference room. I follow behind Brantley and do the same.

As we gather up our presentation materials Brantley whispers in my ear, "We should enjoy a nightcap every night before a presentation like this. I think it put both of us at ease."

I try not to laugh, but a small chuckle escapes before I take in a deep breath. Is he kidding me right now? He could not be more wrong about our little nightcap last night putting me at ease. It made me tense and unsure of myself today. I was busy scolding myself for being scattered in the head while Brantley was on cloud nine and flying high. How do men do that? How do they take a serious situation like fucking a work peer and pretend there are no lingering questions, feelings or repercussions afterward? "Yeah, sure. That was a breeze," I say, as I don't want to dampen his happy mood.

The Creative Director

I remain quiet during our drive back to the hotel. I want to address what happened last night but I'm not sure how to package my words. Brantley seems aware that I haven't uttered more than two sentences since the presentation ended, and begins to talk freely about the ad campaign we'll be creating when we return to the office tomorrow. I nod in agreement at all his observations but don't offer to add to his attempt to make conversation.

"Are you pissed at me again?" he asks softly.

"No. God, no. You wrangled the new CEO in with such ease. It was a pleasure to watch," I reply. I adjust the seatbelt over my jacket and pull my braid over my shoulder.

"Glad you feel that way. However, I sense something isn't quite right. Do you care to enlighten me?" he asks.

"We can't do what we did last night ever again, Brantley. As lovely as it was to have a warm touch and amazing sex with you, I feel that doing so again should be out of the question." There. I said it in as plain a way as I can. No point mincing words or dancing around the issue. He likes it direct and up front, and that is how I handed my thoughts to him.

Brantley continues to drive silently. He flips the turn signal on to turn left at the intersection and doesn't respond even after we've cleared the light and begun heading west toward our hotel. As he arrives at the circular drive that leads to the underground parkade, I can feel the tension in him rise. He has some thoughts on the matter too, and I'm not so sure I want to hear them. Once he's parked the rental car, he shuts the engine off and reaches for my hand across the console. A gentle squeeze from his warm broad hand melts me and I close my eyes.

"If you'd rather not do that again I'll understand. Although I should, I won't ever regret taking you to bed with me, Jess. I've not done that before with someone I work with, and for good reason." He takes a deep breath as he touches my chin to make me look him in the eyes. "You really are a lovely woman, a talented woman, and an impressive associate that the firm and myself think highly of. We won't speak of this again if that is what you'd prefer."

As he unfastens his seatbelt to exit the car, I speak. "I think of you as a mentor. I look up to you and your opinions, even when they are spoken in a cutting way. I don't want to jeopardize what I have with the firm by letting myself become emotionally involved with you, or any other member of the staff. I'm glad that you and I can agree not to repeat or think of our indiscretion again.

The Creative Director

And thank you for your kind words about me and my work."

Brantley grins and nods at me in acceptance of a sex truce between us. I'm certain it won't happen again and we'll both forget it even transpired within a few days.

Sandra A. Sigfusson

Chapter 16: Yes, Dammit.

The last three weeks have flown by since our presentation to Parish, Inc. We've both been consumed by ad space preparation and other smaller projects from our own client lists.

To Brantley's amazement, Jason continues to be stellar as my assistant. Jason has even set aside time to help Brantley out here and there when things were getting out of hand on our respective desks.

Brantley and I have spent countless nights working late, sharing sushi orders and pizza after Jason and the rest of the floor staff have headed home for the evening. He is kinder to me since our trip to L.A., and that has eased the typical tension in our shared office space. He is more than a colleague now. He is a friend.

I lean back in my chair to release the braid in my hair and shake my head to untangle the strands. As I reach for my empty coffee mug I decide I'm done for the night. It's time to rinse out my coffee mug in the sink of the kitchenette and head to the washroom for a quick pee before I head home. Brantley's eyes follow my

The Creative Director

movements before he stretches his arms above his head and tries to stifle a yawn. "Are you done for today?" he asks.

"Yes. My eyes are going blurry from reviewing ad copy materials. To be honest, I'm exhausted."

"I am as well," he replies.

I head to the washroom and close the door behind me. I have a quick pee, re-dress and begin washing my hands in the marble pedestal basin. For an office washroom, this one is quite opulent, and I take a minute to appreciate the fine details of the tile floor pattern, the ornate accessories and hardware, and the crystal wall sconces on either side of the silver-framed mirror. As I turn to dry my hands I notice the door to the washroom ease open.

"I'm almost done," I say. "Just another minute." Brantley enters, regardless of my comment, and closes the door behind him. He leans his body against the closed door and gazes upon me.

"Is something the matter?" I ask as a sense of confusion sets in.

"Yes," he says, and then pauses. "Jess, I can't get you out of my head."

Sandra A. Sigfusson

His eyes stay fixed on me as I finish drying my hands on the plush white hand towel. I hang the towel on the bar next to the basin and say, "Oh." Brantley steps closer to me as the room suddenly fills with the scent of his sexy cologne. "I thought we agreed to not get involved again," I whisper, even though I know we are the only two people left in the office.

Brantley steps closer once more as my eyes widen. "Are you certain we can't make love to each other ever again?" he asks. His eyes are fixed upon mine as he waits patiently, and far too close to me, for my answer. I'm at a loss for words. I swallow hard while I wait for my lips and tongue to respond with the words I know I have to say. But the words don't come. I'm silenced by his closeness to me. I want him to take me. The thought of his mouth and hands on me again have filled my head every night as I lie alone in my bed in my lonely condo.

"Are you going commando again today?" he asks as a grin forms over his luscious lips. I wonder if he's attempting to lighten this heavy mood he brought into the room.

I laugh nervously and shake my head to indicate no. My hands find comfort inside the pockets of my dress pants. I'm desperate to touch him, but I know I cannot.

The Creative Director

"That's too bad," he muses. "It was the sexiest thing I've witnessed in a very long time. In fact, I think of you pantiless daily and it fucking kills my train of thought. I've never had to work this hard to get a woman out of my head before you, Jess."

"I … I, um. I'm not sure how to respond to that," I manage to reply. I clear my throat, pinch my brows and wish desperately that I had a nice cold shot of whiskey in my hand so I could down it for the courage.

"Where are you going when you leave here?" he asks. Brantley steps one more pace forward and now he's only inches from me. I tip my head up to meet his eyes and instinctively place a hand on his chest to stop him from pressing me further.

"I'm going home to rest. You should do the same," I whisper. My hand has somehow been taken over by something other than my brain. I'm slowly fisting Brantley's shirt in my fingers beneath his tie. He searches my eyes while I breathe in his scent and feel the heat of his body radiate toward me. My mind, as it should, is saying this is such a bad idea, but I can't seem to get my body to respond with that level of common sense.

His breaths become louder to me the longer we stand like this. I tip my head down and rest my forehead on his chest next to my hand fisting his shirt. "This is far more difficult than I imagined it would be," I say against his chest. "You know I want you, otherwise you wouldn't be standing here in this office washroom with me with the door closed, after hours."

"Have you ever made love in a corporate washroom?" he murmurs into my right ear. My body suddenly becomes coated in goosebumps as his lips graze the edges of my earlobe after he's posed his seductive question.

"No," I say and shake my head. I realize my breaths are also more noticeable. I'm acutely aware of my chest rising and falling as I take deepened breaths in from my mouth. I lick my dry lips and tug on Brantley's shirt. Without any further words I find his head dipping down to caress my lips with his. The first touch of his lips only serves to further fuel my desires. He did these same moves to me in the hotel room – lingering, gently tasting, and teasing my arousal out of its hiding place. "I think we need to stop this before it goes further. We shouldn't," I murmur.

Brantley kisses me harder now, preventing me from finishing the sentence that was on both of our minds. "We have, and we will again," he says with his lips against mine. "Say it, Jess. Say it," he taunts.

The Creative Director

"That I want you to make love to me again?" I reply with my lips still touching his.

"Yes, dammit," he says, but the word dammit doesn't hold the weight it would if we were arguing. Instead it has an urgency of passion behind it and I feel it flow straight through my chest.

My eyes slowly close. "Yes, dammit. Make love to me," I reply. My fingers release the grip on his shirt so that I can unbutton it and splay my wandering fingers over his chest. I need to tickle my palms with the soft curled hair over his pectoral muscles. He has the perfect amount of body hair – not too much – in light crops of it in all the right places. As I undo the buttons of his shirt, Brantley is unzipping my dress pants and letting them fall down my legs. I step out of the pant legs and hope that the floor is as clean as I think it is. I'm wearing a sweater, and without a second's notice his hands are beneath it attempting to pull it up over my head. I lift my hands up high to ease the sweater's removal and shake my long hair away from my face so my lips can find his again.

The heat from our bodies has changed the typically cool temperature of this washroom substantially. My senses, all of my senses, are on high alert. My nipples pebble beneath my bra in anticipation of his mouth or hands upon them. What is it about sexual arousal that makes people agree to do things they wouldn't normally?

Sandra A. Sigfusson

I feel helpless against his advances like I'm being slowly drawn into a vortex, but I'm not afraid of where I'll end up. I just want to savor the journey, let my senses guide me and my mind be free from obligations, expectations and rational decisions.

The pace of my removing his clothes and kissing his lips has doubled. I feel his lips release themselves from mine and touch above my shoulder, kissing a trail toward my breasts, while his hands find the clasp at my back to release my bra. My goosebumps are gone as my skin begins to prickle with heat in their place. "Fuck me, Brantley," I command, and within seconds of releasing my bra strap, his right hand is inside my panties and I feel two nimble fingers insert themselves inside. The pad of his thumb finds my clit and he rubs it while he pumps his fingers in and out. My increased wetness tells him I'm ready the moment he is, but Brantley keeps pumping his fingers into me. I moan and feel limp, succumbing to his tease. He kisses me hard while I hold back the urge to release around his hand.

"Don't let me come yet," I beg. I reach for him and realize I've not removed his pants. I'm going to come before I've even put my hands around his firm shaft. I want to stroke him while he finger fucks me. I want to

The Creative Director

prime him the way he's priming me so we are nearly ready to explode when he fills me. But it's too late for that. I've come without any ability to control it. A hit of euphoria rises inside of me as my body shakes from the release. All my pent-up desires have driven me to a point where the mere thought of his cock anywhere near my sex is enough to make me wet myself. Until now, I never realized that what I do to him is the same as what he does to me while we sit across from each other, day after day, silent about our internal desires, pretending that this heat between us isn't real. Pretending that the night at the hotel was a moment for each of us to let off some steam. But the steam is still there.

"I'll make you come again, Jess," he promises as he swiftly removes his pants and underwear. I clasp my hand around his firmness and squeeze as I stroke him. He's unbelievably hard for me. I feel rushed, as if we were on a time limit, but that isn't what is going on here. The rush is because we've waited three weeks since our first encounter to acknowledge that we fuck good together, really good, too good.

"Turn round, Jess," he murmurs. "I want to take you from behind. I want to fuck you hard and fast. Is that okay, love?"

While he sheathes himself in a condom I breathe the word yes, but he knew I'd comply without his asking.

Sandra A. Sigfusson

His hands were already on my hips, twisting my body around so I can hold on to the pedestal basin when he's ready to drive into me. Once again I feel his hands working me from the inside. His thumb is pumping in and out of me and I swear I could come again this instant – and then he replaces it quickly with his cock. The first press is slow, as if to test the waters. His moan in my ear over my shoulder is so hot that I can't help but echo his sentiment. His warm hands cup my breasts and he holds them firm while he thrusts inside me, a little harder this time.

"Tell me you want me as much as I want you, Jess," he breathes in my ear.

"Yes," is all I can manage to utter in reply. He pulls out slowly and throws his weight into plunging back into me, squeezing my breasts with every pulse. I pant and hitch my breaths with each thrust as they become faster and firmer. "Yes, I want you."

He's claiming me, like he has to prove that I belong to him. This feels like more than just a need to get laid; he needed to lay me. But I also have a need to be claimed by him, and this moment feels like a long-awaited victory that I hadn't realized I was vying for until now.

The Creative Director

His panting grows heavier until he stops breathing, holding his last breath inside while he comes, as hard as he was fucking me. I feel his forehead resting upon the back of my shoulder as he collects himself.

My skin is damp from the intensity of the passion we shared. At one point I worried I was going to rip the basin away from the wall, but thankfully our momentary bliss didn't end up destroying company property. The thought makes me laugh to myself at first, and in an instant I'm laughing out loud. I turn myself around and face Brantley while trying to prevent myself from completely losing out to a long fit of giggles. He smiles wide at me and strokes the back of his hand over my cheek before joining in on the laughing.

Chapter 17: Unwell

The following morning I wake to the familiar sounds of the street noise below my open bedroom window. Some find that the sounds of the city are too much, that they interfere with their ability to rest, but I've lived in the city all my adult life and thus they are part of me. These sounds are a rhythm, like a heartbeat. It's only when I'm on holiday or visiting some sleepy little town in the middle of New York State that I realize how loud the city is regardless of the hour. And not surprisingly, in those silent moments I miss it.

I often rise feeling a bit groggy. Neither the length of time I spend at the office nor the shitty food I insist on eating while constantly running at full speed bode well for my quality of sleep. But last night, after Brantley and I banged out our sexual frustrations in the washroom, I slept better than I have in at least three weeks.

That quick realization sends shock waves down my spine – it has been exactly three weeks since he and I first broke the *don't fuck your co-worker* rule. I stop in my tracks on the way to my kitchen to make a pot of coffee and cover my gaping mouth with my hands. Shit!

The Creative Director

It's him. He's the reason I slept like a baby. It was the same blissful rest I got when we slept together in his bed after we made love to each other in the hotel. I sit down at my kitchen table and realize now, fully, just how much impact he has on me. "No, no, no, no, no," I say aloud in a low growl. "That can't be right. It's a mere coincidence. There is no way having sex with Brantley is the reason I slept so well."

I will admit that I'm happy because I got laid, but the sleep thing is in no way related. My fingernails tap quickly on the laminate surface while I force myself to believe my last thought.

After putting on a pot of coffee I wander to my bedroom to take a quick shower and sort through my closet for something to wear. We have a meeting with Grady to review our progress with the top three clients in our portfolios and discuss any new business we've acquired since we last reported in to him.

When I arrive at Grady's office, Brantley is prepared with his reports and is having a lively conversation with Grady about something he did as a kid. Interrupting their lighthearted banter I seat myself down next to Brantley and smile. It appears that, while in the presence of our boss, Brantley and I are able to pretend our corporate washroom romp last night didn't happen. My heart rate settles upon this realization. I feel like I could be a contender for an Academy Award for this morning's acting skills.

It's been three months since the day I started with Digame. I've had a good run with the clients in my portfolio thus far, and I added a small account for a local candy maker last week. Most of our clients are big-name corporations who spend millions every year on marketing their products and services. Many of my clients seemed to welcome my taking over their portfolios from Brantley; however, there are three who are still miffed about Brantley's handing them over to me, the unknown Creative Director. "Should we put those clients back onto Brantley's client list to appease them?" I ask Brantley and Grady.

"I'll contact those clients and reiterate that we work as a team regardless of who is managing which account," Brantley says. I nod in agreement and feel reassured Brantley can appeal to them on the teamwork angle.

Thankfully the meeting with Grady is short. He's a man of few words, liking to keep meetings brief and on task. I'm not certain how to read Grady yet. I'll have to speak to Brantley about him, and see if there's a secret to

The Creative Director

getting the man to open up or if he has some quirks I should be aware of.

Brantley appears to be in good spirits this morning. I don't know if I have anything to do with his perky mood or not. I don't care to assume sex is the only thing that makes a man happy, although I'm sure it occupies a high position on most men's lists.

I set my documents and reports on the corner of my desk for Jason to file later, then glance over my shoulder toward Brantley seated at his desk. He is staring at me like he has something to say. "Do you need something?" I ask.

"No, thank you. I'll be good for a couple of days," he replies with a cheeky grin.

"What is that supposed to mean?" I'm confused. A few seconds later Brantley wriggles his eyebrows at me. Just as I've clued into Brantley's innuendo, Jason approaches me from behind and startles me. I visibly jump in my place while Jason breaks out into laughter. Brantley also seems rather amused, although he doesn't bust his gut like Jason did.

"Not funny!"

"Oh, yes it was, Jess," Brantley replies, trying hard now not to laugh at me.

Jason apologizes, and I nod in acceptance. "I'd appreciate it if you'd announce your entrance if I don't see you first," I tell him. He nods and tries to hold back more laughter. "I swear you two have it out for me. What's next? Someone jumping out from behind my desk so I have a massive heart attack and drop dead?" I say in frustration. "How many times do I have to tell you two jackasses that I have a weak heart?" I slap the papers in my hands down atop my desk and land my hands firmly on my hips. I need something to drink, and I ain't talking 'bout coffee. I strut over to Brantley's desk and stand beside him.

"Something you need?" he asks curiously.

"Yes," I say, flicking my wrist at him twice. "Scooch over. I need inside your booze drawer."

"Are you planning on drinking straight from the bottle, or shall I get you a glass with ice?" he asks, smirking at me.

"Yes, that would be lovely," I say in my imitation English accent.

"My God, that was bloody awful," he muses.

The Creative Director

"My God, that was bloody awful," I repeat and stick my tongue out at him.

"You're pissed off," he says, looking a bit shocked at me.

"Yes, I am. You two turds have perfectly good ears, but you only use them when it pleases you and not when it pleases others. Stop fucking scaring the daylights out of me!"

Brantley holds up his hands and rolls his chair away from my position beside his desk. "Okay, love. Untie your knickers and we'll stop scaring you. I promise," he says, placing his palm over his heart.

I sigh and relax my body posture. "Thank you. Now where is my glass with ice that you promised me?" I ask as I fold my arms across my chest and pitch an eyebrow high.

The balance of the day goes by without a hitch or many words exchanged. I think the boys finally get that I have a breaking point and they hit it earlier today. I know how funny it is to watch someone jump out of their skin when startled, but if they want to see that they can watch the thousands of such YouTube videos, instead of attempting to kill me for their entertainment.

Sandra A. Sigfusson

As I'm packing up for the day and gathering the papers I want to review in peace at home tonight, Brantley asks me what my dinner plans are.

"I'm going home to relax and do some work in a quiet environment," I reply, still being short with him.

"Would you care for some company?" he asks.

"What? You? I don't think so," I mutter and chuckle under my breath.

"Are you really still that angry with me over laughing at Jason scaring you?"

I sigh before I reply. "No. I'm just exhausted. Maybe I'm coming down with something and I just need a good night's sleep." In an unexpected move, Brantley approaches me and presses the back of his hand against my forehead. "What are you doing?" I ask, pinching my brows together and leaning away from his hand.

"You do seem a bit hot, and I don't mean that in a sexual way," he murmurs.

"I don't have a fever. I'm tired. That's all. Now go back to your desk and leave me alone, please."

The Creative Director

"No. I'm coming home with you and we're going to fix that fever and share some chicken soup or some shit to make you feel better. I can't have you off for days on end, ill. I need you here because virtually every client on both our lists is gearing up for their Christmas promotions. Christmas starts in July," he reminds me.

"Fine. But only if you're buying dinner. And I want fish and chips from that place you ordered from last month," I say in a demanding bratty-girlfriend tone.

A grin tugs at Brantley's lips. "Yes, love."

We drive together in my car to the fish and chip place, grab an order of four pieces of halibut and a boatload of fries, and head to my condo. Brantley seems intent on being a doting friend and I'm happy to hand him the reins. He gives my condo a sweeping once-over with his eyes before setting our food bags and his briefcase on the counter in my kitchen.

"Have you been here long?" he asks.

"I guess about five years or so," I say. I'm reaching inside my cupboards for plates and cutlery while Brantley takes it upon himself to search my fridge for ketchup and mayonnaise. I squint my eyes at him about his selections. "What's the mayonnaise for?"

"It's for the chips?"

Sandra A. Sigfusson

"You dip your fries in mayonnaise? Why aren't you grossly overweight?" I ask.

"In England we dip our chips in mayonnaise. Not ketchup as you do here."

"Oh, well, have at it then."

As we settle in to eat at my kitchen table we don't say much of anything other than me asking, "Can you pass the salt?" Or him saying, "Would you have preferred cod? I never bothered to ask."

"No, the halibut is nice. It's more delicate in flavor than the cod and less fishy," I reply.

"Are you sated now?" he asks after wiping his mouth for the twentieth time with his napkin – once after every bite.

I giggle at him while I suck back the last of the soda in my can. "Sated? You English do have very proper ways of saying things. Yes, I am quite sated," I say and grin wide at his lovely face.

"Nice. Some other time I'll give you a proper education on how to speak the Queen's English. In the

The Creative Director

meantime, I promise not to cringe at your heavily slanged version of the English language," he replies dryly.

I laugh for no other reason than the fact that his pompousness is kind of endearing. As much as I hate his typical holier-than-thou attitude, I have become accustomed to his ways without being constantly insulted by them.

"Now then. Shall we test your temperature properly with a thermometer, or are you going to ignore your sweat-coated brow?" His right eyebrow pitches high at me.

"Doctor Sunshine, I'm feeling fine. I need a good-quality sleep." My recent realization about how much better I slept after having sex with Brantley suddenly enters my mind. Dammit. I don't want him to think I let him come to my home with the hopes he'd get his rocks off under the guise of concern for my wellness.

"Vitamin C?" he asks. "Have you got it in a crystallized powder? Ascorbic acid?"

"Vit-amin C?" I say, imitating his unusual pronunciation of the word vitamin.

"Stop making cracks about my way of speaking and just answer the damned question, Jessica," he says, frowning at me.

Sandra A. Sigfusson

"No. I do not have any ascorbic acid. What do you want it for?"

"For you. I think you need a bump-up in it. It is the only thing that works to fight off any infection brewing in you without resorting to antibiotics from a physician," he says.

"That can't be true," I say, in disbelief.

"It is a well-known fact that humans cannot produce their own vitamin C. Neither can bats, oddly enough. Virtually all of God's other creatures produce their own vitamin C," he says.

"Really?"

He nods. "I'm going down the block to find a pharmacy that sells it. I insist you take it as I prescribe or it won't be effective."

I nod and dig my condo keys out of my purse for him. "Take these so you can get back inside the building. I hope you know what you're talking about," I say, feeling a bit unsure of his methods. Brantley grabs my keys, gives me a swift kiss on the cheek and heads out my door without another word.

The Creative Director

Nearly twenty minutes later he's returned with a white paper bag containing the vitamin C. Brantley opens up the brown-tinted plastic vitamin container and hands me a 1,000mg tablet and a glass of warm water. "Take this and in six minutes I'll have you take another. We'll repeat this process until you've had the equivalent of ten thousand milligrams of it. Then we'll see how you are feeling."

"Are you out of your mind?" I say.

"No, not at all. Doing this every six minutes mimics an intravenous vitamin C protocol." Brantley taps his watch to note the minute hand and watches me down my first tablet. "We've been doing this with my mum after each of her chemotherapy rounds and it is very helpful to her healing."

"How do you know this isn't going to be harmful to me?" I ask. "How do you know it won't react to any drugs I may be on?"

"It won't and it can't. Be quiet. I want to watch the local news before the program ends." He takes the remote control for my TV off the coffee table and flicks channels until he finds the station he prefers. It seems he's just as bossy at home as he is in the office. Should I be surprised? I'm not.

Sandra A. Sigfusson

Within two hours of beginning the 1,000mg-every-six-minutes plan he insisted I partake of, I feel much better. My fever has lifted and I have more energy. I'm not jumping up and down like a three-year-old high on a bag of jujubes, but I do feel revitalized compared to how I felt at the office earlier.

"I do feel better now."

"Glad to hear it, love. Get in bed and I'll tuck you in," he chuckles. "And if you happen to be a tad flatulent I won't fault you for it. We'll blame the vitamin C."

"Flatulent? Dear god, I hope not! Do I get a kiss goodnight and a bedtime story too, Sunshine?"

"Why do you insist on addressing me as Sunshine?" he asks. Brantley sits up from his slumped position on my couch to stare me eye to eye.

"Because of your bright and sunny disposition in the office," I say and crack up.

"So, you're mocking me? Is that it? And here I thought you liked me."

"Oh, I like you, Sunshine. But only when you're smiling and laughing, which is all of point zero one

The Creative Director

percent of the time we spend together in our office. I'm sure you have a name you call me under your breath," I say, smirking.

"Oh, yes I do," he says under his breath.

"And?" I ask, patiently waiting for him to divulge my nickname.

"Pet," he says, and a delicious smile eases over his luscious lips.

"Pet? What the hell is that about?" I'm shaking my head in disbelief that he's referred to me as his pet.

"Do you not approve?"

I pivot my head to look him in the eyes. "You call me love sometimes, but I know that is something a lot of Brits say easily to others. Not pet." I flop my head back on the cushion behind me and close my eyes. I'm tired now. I feel better, but I'm still tired.

"Is Pet not endearing enough for you?" he asks, pretending to be wounded.

"No. It is endearing. I don't think of you and me in an endearing way. We like to fuck each other, but the term pet sounds more like we're lovers, not fuck buddies."

Brantley doesn't respond to my observation. He seems to be mulling it over in his head. Rising from the couch, he offers his hand to help me to my feet. I take his hand and he hoists me in one smooth move, then he wraps his left arm around my waist and gives me a gentle tug toward his chest. I resist, frowning at him.

"Don't deny we are more than fuck buddies, Jessica Adeline James. I'm much fonder of you than you realize, or rather, than I should be. Let me take you to bed. If you'll allow me to spend the night, I promise to be on my best behavior." That sexy-as-hell smile is back on his lips and I'm melting inside his arms.

Brantley eases his face closer to mine and plants an unexpected kiss on my lips. "Why are you kissing me when I'm sick?" I ask.

"You're going to be fine. I take vitamin C every day so as not to succumb to whatever bug is going round in public. Now stop arguing with me and let me kiss you, please," he says before I let him plant a firmer kiss on my lips.

When our sweet kiss releases I say, "Fine. You win, Sunshine. Take me to bed and let me get some sleep.

The Creative Director

If you're still here in the morning when I wake, then I'll reward you for your kindness."

Chapter 18: Playing Hooky

"Holy crap! It's eight o'clock. What the hell, Brantley," I bellow when I catch the time on my alarm clock. "Why didn't my alarm go off?"

A warm, strong arm drapes over me and tugs me back down inside the bedsheets. "I turned your alarm off," he mumbles into the space between my shoulder blades. "Now cuddle into me and be quiet," he says.

"But we'll be late for work."

"No. I've already left a message to the office that we have an unscheduled meeting with a client and won't be in until ten-ish."

"Oh." I relax my shoulders and relish the warmth of his body spooning mine. "And who are we supposedly meeting with this morning, in case Jason asks?"

"Masterson, of course. You don't play hooky well, do you?" he chuckles.

I can't help but giggle. "It would help if I was aware of the rules before the game started."

The Creative Director

I feel a warm hand sweep my long hair away from my neck and a sweet kiss send a wave of goosebumps across my arms. "I believe you said I'd get some sort of prize for still being here when you woke," he says between his tender kisses now trailing down my spine.

"I did," I giggle. Another little chill runs through me at the tickling of his lips.

"Did you sleep well, Pet?" he asks and chuckles. "Or should I nickname you C.G.?"

"C.G.? What does that stand for?" I ask, smiling to myself.

"Commando Girl," he growls in a low tone in my ear.

"Well, I'm full-on commando now, so what are you going to do about it?"

Brantley tugs me harder into his body and I feel his firm shaft pressing against my butt cheeks. "I believe I'm owed some level of gratitude for my kindness last night. Are you willing to pay up now?"

"Commando Girl says yes." Rising to my elbow I twist my body to front my British bedmate. His voice and the lingering scent of his cologne in my sheets make me wet without him doing anything but talking and kissing my spine. Rolling over to fully face him, I press my lips to his and let my tongue move in lazy circles inside his mouth, tempting him to reciprocate my French kiss. He's there for me instantly. A soft hand cups the side of my face, holding me while we indulge in this tenderness. My chest begins to ache in the same thumping pattern as my clit, and I press harder with my lips in our already deepening kiss. I'm devouring him now. I'm all in – heart, body, mind and soul. Am I falling for him, or is it simply that he's so delicious that I can't stop myself from diving headlong into his brand of lovemaking?

"I think you might be the death of me," he says when our kiss releases. Brantley raises his shoulders and leans on his elbow while his free hand slides gently between my thighs, searching for my center. Two large fingers find their way inside of my sex, slowly pumping, sometimes wiggling while within my depths. I react instantly to the sensation. My body relaxes while my breath hitches softly with each plunge of his fingers inside me. "Come for me, Pet. I want you soaked before I fuck that sweet, perfect pussy of yours," he growls low onto my lips before biting my bottom lip and tugging at it.

The Creative Director

"Don't stop, Sunshine. I'm almost there, I'm almost ..." I don't finish my sentence. I've released gloriously at the touch of his skillful hand. I don't know how he does it but I've come so fast for him that it's shocking.

"What were you about to say?" he whispers over my lips. I dive back into a deep, tongue-tangling kiss. "Damn you, Sunshine," I moan. I reach between us to find that beautiful cock of his. With a firm grip I pump my hand over him and watch as his eyes roll back inside his head from the pleasure. Sliding my body down deep inside the sheets, I intend to wrap my mouth around his shaft, but Brantley climbs over me. His hips and hard-as-steel cock hover directly above my chest. I take his cock inside my moist lips and press him as deep inside my mouth as I can. Releasing slowly back, I let his crown rub against the fine ridges of the roof of my mouth then suck hard.

Brantley takes the lead as I allow him to methodically penetrate my mouth. The wide O of my lips feels every inch of him as he presses forward and back, his eyes fixated on how deep his cock penetrates with each slow press. "I'm not coming in your mouth, Pet. Unless that is what you want," he says, his panting breaths matching his rhythm.

I suck harder on him, hoping he gets the message. *Do what you want, Sunshine. I'm game if you are.* My signal is received loud and clear. When I sense he's close to climaxing I focus my sucking on his crown, and moments later his cock firms up even tighter and a blast of hot liquid fills my mouth. A swift shudder and a loud exhale of breath from him lets me know his release is complete, and I let him slip away from my lips. I swallow and take in a deep breath as he hovers over me still holding the top of the headboard with his hands. "Did you enjoy that?" I ask, then smile, knowing full well he did.

Brantley nods and smiles as he slides his body back into the sheets to meet me eye to eye. "That was brilliant, Pet," he says. His nose touches mine then rubs in a gentle circle around it before his deep passion-filled kiss arrests my heart. I may be falling in love.

.

The Creative Director

Chapter 19: All Cocked Up

After a good long, warm cuddle we agree to rise and shower. I fully expected Brantley to want to make love to me again in the shower, considering his cock stood at full attention while we washed each other off under the hot cascading water. More kisses graced the edges of my neck and shoulders while he used my sea sponge to cleanse me. He's so tender in his touch, be it his lips or his fingers. His hands gently press my shoulders to indicate he wants me to turn to face him. Another series of soft kisses graces my lips while my heart pounds deep beneath my ribcage. I place his hand over my heart. "Do you feel this?" I whisper.

"I feel everything," he whispers back. "I'm spellbound by you, Jess. How and why I can't say, but we are most definitely no longer simply messing around. I adore you," he says. My heart flutters at the same time my half-hooded eyelids do at his words.

Gripping his cock in my hand I gently stroke him. Our mouths crush against each other in another wave of heat. My bathroom is shrouded in a heavy fog of steam, mirroring my sexually clouded mind as I stroke him and tease his crown with the open palm of my other hand. "Come hard for me," I command.

I increase my fisted thrusts over him a few more times before I lower my face to his rigidness to suck on his crown. Warm soft strokes of his hands sweep over my back while I suck, lick and coax him to build fast in his orgasm. He moans through increased breaths as I continue. "My god, that's it Pet."

Brantley guides my head up with his hands to kiss me and I release him from my mouth. He presses himself against my wet body, his eyes hooded in deep desire, then thrusts himself deep inside of me in one firm stroke.

Our kisses deepen while he presses several times, harder and faster – deeper. His release comes quickly. Brantley rests his forehead on my shoulder as he catches his breath. He'd pulled out of me before he came and I have to wonder if he's worried that I'm not on contraceptives. "You don't have to pull out," I say into his left ear. I stroke his water-soaked hair then hold him tight in my arms while I also relax.

Brantley chuckles nervously and shakes his head at himself. "That was very stupid of me. I was so swept up in the moment and I seem to have little control when I'm near you. I'm sorry, Pet. I never asked if you'd be fine without a condom or if you had other measures in

The Creative Director

place. It was incredibly stupid of me. I'm so, so sorry," he whispers in my ear.

"It's fine. You don't have anything to worry about."

"Oh, thank Christ," he says, as he looks me in the eyes. Brantley pushes my hair across my forehead and kisses my nose. "We're mad, I think."

"Mad? Is that a good thing or a bad thing?" I ask.

He flashes me a swift smile. "Good and bad, I'd say. Good in that we are clearly feeling right about each other, but bad in that we're colleagues and how we're going to manage to keep our hands off each other in the office is unknown." He chuckles and smiles again. "I may have to get more argumentative with you in front of staff. They couldn't possibly assume you and I were together if I'm a complete ass toward you."

"You mean like you already are? Bring it on, Sunshine. I know how to handle your cutting words now. Do you mind if I fight back more often? You know, for the cause," I muse.

Brantley cracks up like I've never seen him do before. His laugh is wonderful. So full-bodied and contagious, and surprisingly loud. He throws his head back as he tries to contain himself, but my outburst of laughter only fuels him to continue cracking up. "For the cause, yes," he manages to reply between chuckles.

"Okay, Sunshine. Get the hell out of my shower and get dressed. You'll need to stop in at your place to get new clothes. Take my car, and when you're ready come back to get me."

"Yes, love," he says.

When we arrive at the office, Brantley only has ten minutes to spare before a quick conference call with one of his clients. I settle myself down at my desk and empty my briefcase of the files I'd brought home last night to work on. I snicker knowing that I did no such thing. *Best-laid plans, as they say?*

As I rise from my desk chair to get my first cup of coffee to go with the breakfast sandwich I picked up on the way in, Jason enters my office with his perfect posture and a bright smile.

"How did things go with Brantley this morning?" he asks while setting two new file folders on the corner of my desk. My eyes pop wide and I'm stumped for a reply. *Does he suspect that we are fucking each other? Have we*

The Creative Director

been that obvious? Jesus, this is a disaster! I twist my head quickly to look at Brantley, hoping he has something to say.

"Brilliant," he chimes in. "We got all cocked up on the way to view the new companion dolls at Masterson's headquarters, but rest assured things worked out for the best." I want to buckle over in a fit of laughter and it takes everything I have not to do it. I contain the bulk of my giggles and wink at Brantley over his choice of words. Two truths and a lie.

Jason tilts his head a smidge before he asks Brantley, "What does cocked up mean?"

"Brit slang for trouble," he says.

"Oh. I'll have to remember that one," he says. Jason looks back at me and I realize I'm completely flushed in the face again. "Are you feeling okay, Jess? Can I get you something?"

"No. I'm fine. The room feels very warm this morning. Brantley texted me over his mom's secret tea recipe for the *unwell*," I say, throwing air quotes on the last word. Jason continues to stare at me, then turns to stare at Brantley, then back at me. A smile curls over his lips as he asks me what we have on the agenda today.

"Let me get my coffee, eat my breakfast sandwich and then I'll call you in to hash out what needs our attention most this morning," I say. Jason nods. He takes another quick look at Brantley, smiles again and leaves our office.

"What the hell was that look for?" Brantley asks.

"I think he likes you. He r-e-a-l-l-y likes you," I tease.

"Bollocks," he replies before leaning back in his squeaking chair and clicking his pen open and shut three times.

The Creative Director

Chapter 20: The Big Snit

Brantley and I have a plan to ensure none of the staff get a whiff of us as a couple. Randomly he'll start in on me in a gruff tone about a client's product or the mess I left in the kitchenette. I play along easily, as I know when he's making legitimately cutting remarks and when he's just playing it up for the show.

"Did you really send that ad copy out to the client before I approved it?" he charges loudly.

"I don't know what you're talking about, Brantley. Which client?" I say sharply. "I'm not working on any client that involves you at the moment."

Another time he rants about office supplies missing from his desk. "Would you please stop taking my supply of post-it notes and highlighters from my desk? Surely you know where the office supplies room is, Jess."

"I wasn't stealing. I was borrowing. And yes, I'm aware of the office supplies room's location, Brantley. Do you really have to act like a child over post-it notes?"

In boardroom meetings we make a point of sitting as far away from each other as possible so it looks like we are constantly at odds. One afternoon we carried on so

Sandra A. Sigfusson

well that Grady was compelled to pull us aside and tell us to keep our arguments down to a lower decibel level. "It's unprofessional for my executives to air out their dirty laundry so openly in front of the other staff," he warned. We nodded and apologized.

As we enter our office space after our chiding by the big boss and close the door behind us, Brantley asks, "Do you think we've overdone our public spats?"

"I think so. If Grady felt the need to intervene, then I guess we should taper it down."

"Agreed," he says as we head to our desks to carry on with the balance of our day.

It doesn't matter if we continue to argue loudly now. It's clear to everyone around us that we are complete opposites. Mission accomplished. Tonight we'll celebrate our win at an out-of-the-way restaurant.

The meals served at Mandolin's on East Road are so delicious that it may become the new go-to place for Karmyn and me. During dinner Brantley shares more hilarious stories with me and even lets me in on a few

The Creative Director

secrets from his past that are delicate in nature. I swear this man surprises me at every turn.

Tit for tat, I share the fact that I once made love with a woman. The moment those words slip from my lips I regret every syllable, since I'd told myself that I'd never, *ever* tell anyone about it. But the pussy is out of the bag now. Why couldn't I just have admitted I was a bedwetter until I was eight or something? Not my lesbian one-night stand with my best friend. Fuck me.

As expected, Brantley's eyes nearly pop from their sockets. But a second later a dirty, sexy smile beams back at me and I have to wonder what is going on inside his gorgeous head.

"What?" I say indignantly. "We were drunk and curious," I add, trying to dumb down the situation.

"Oh, dear God," he says and sighs.

If I didn't know better I'd swear his eyes had a new sparkle in them and he was aroused by the thought of me getting it on with another woman.

I wave my hands frantically, attempting to erase my confession. "Pretend I never said anything," I beg. "I wasn't ever going to tell anyone, but I'm drunk and you shared something raw with me and so I instinctively reciprocated."

Sandra A. Sigfusson

Brantley is trying desperately to accommodate my request, but he can't get the smile off his face regardless of his gallant attempts. "Really," he says. "Well, I'm sorry to inform you that I cannot now and likely never will get that image out of my head."

"Well, try. Try hard," I say in a hushed tone, staring darkly at him.

"Why are you so embarrassed about it?" He leans forward and rests his arms along the edge of the table. "It fascinates me to envision you and another woman together."

"No. It doesn't. Stop thinking about it."

Brantley's face turns serious now. Again I find myself wondering what he's thinking. He solves that query in his next sentence. "Would you do it again and let me watch?" he asks in a hushed voice, raising one eyebrow with curiosity. I can't tell if he's teasing me or being serious.

"No! Why on earth would I do that?" I huff, tossing my napkin on my plate and crossing my arms over my chest.

"Because it's fucking sexy," he says.

The Creative Director

"Are you saying you'd be into a threesome?" I ask, still hushed.

"Probably not, but I'd very much enjoy watching you lick another woman's pussy."

"You're broken," I say, and begin to chuckle at the absurdity of his last comment.

"No. I'm intrigued," he says firmly.

"Well, get your head out of that gutter you're wading in. It is never going to happen."

"Pity, Pet. You had me all excited and then, well, then I wasn't." Brantley sighs again and leans back in his chair. "Shall we call it a night?"

"Sure. I've destroyed the evening with my kinky confession now anyway. Can you drop me off at home?"

"Don't you want to spend the night together, Jess?'

"I assumed that since I messed up our mood you'd rather go home alone." My heart sinks in my chest. Aarrrgh. I'm so mad at myself.

"I'd love you no matter what kinky shit you were into, Pet. Grab your things and I'll pay for dinner. Your flat or mine?" he asks as he wriggles his eyebrows at me.

I can't help it. A blush and a stupid-ass smile cover my face. "That's my girl," he muses. "And you'd better not be wearing panties or I'll be *very* disappointed in you."

By the time we reach Brantley's place I've managed to get over my embarrassment at divulging my deepest, darkest secret. I didn't tell Brantley that it was Karmyn whom I bedded, and I think I'd rather not let him know it was her. And I wonder if I should tell her that I told our secret to him, or forget about the whole thing.

Brantley serves me a tall glass of wine and suggests I relax on the couch. He's going to pull out a snack for us to nibble on and watch a bit of *telly*, as he puts it.

"What do you want to watch?" I ask as I get sorted out on the couch.

"I'm sure there's a film worthy of our next two hours of time," he says.

When he comes to the couch holding a dish of pretzel sticks I smile. "I love pretzel sticks," I say.

The Creative Director

"Brilliant. Perhaps next time we're in bed together I'll dress my cock in a bit of pink Himalayan rock salt for your palate's pleasure," he muses.

"Get that ridiculous smile off your face, pervert. You have some serious explaining to do. And, your liking my girl-on-girl action makes me wonder what other kinky things you have a penchant for. Seriously? Rock-salted cock. That's actually pretty funny," I say. I can't help but smile and giggle a bit.

"Oh, I'm not too adventurous, really. I'm not into BDSM, if that's what you're worried about. I'll only admit that I find a woman's body exceptionally arousing, and if I have to picture two of them rolling around in the sack naked I may as well let my cock explode in my jeans every time the thought crosses my mind. A massive turn-on for me."

"That's good to know. I'm basically as vanilla as you can get, with the exception of my temporary stray from vanilladom during a drunken stupor."

"How about we watch a film I came across the other day on Netflix that I thought might be interesting?" he asks.

"What's it called?"

Sandra A. Sigfusson

"*Bloomington.* Released in 2010. It's a chick-flick and I'm sure you'll love it."

The Creative Director

Chapter 21: Thirty-six, Twenty-six, Thirty-four

The bugger made me watch a movie about a female college student who has a romantic fling with her professor – another woman. Bastard! When I clued in to what he was up to I had to shake my head. He's never going to let my secret fade.

"You did this on purpose," I say, as I stuff my face with more pretzel sticks.

"Of course!"

"I'm never telling you who it was that I had my experience with, Sunshine."

"I'd rather you didn't anyway. It is much more delicious to conjure up in my vivid imagination what your partner looked like."

"Okay, smartass. How would you describe the woman I got it on with?" I'm giggling now because I can only imagine what he's thinking. I'm sure it's a Jessica Rabbit–type woman.

"Hmm. Let me think for a moment," he says, pondering his choices. "Long blonde, silky hair. Pale skin and deep blue eyes. She measures roughly 36-26-34 and is about five-feet-six-inches tall without heels. Oh, yes, heels. Cherry-red stilettos like yours. Her undergarments are black lace. When you two decided to partake in each other's shapely assets, you were pantiless under your dress. You kissed tenderly at first. You wanted to explore each other's mouths to slowly build up the heat between you. Next came a bit of fondling over your clothes." He pauses to look at me, and the smile on his face is soaked in satisfaction.

"Why did you pick a blonde-haired woman as my lover in your vision?"

"Opposites. You are a vivacious brunette with green eyes. Your lover has to be different from you in order for it to work in my sordid mind," he chuckles, and I think a bit of a blush danced across his normally stern face.

"You're getting hard thinking about this, aren't you?" I tease. And damned if he didn't nail what Karmyn looks like nearly to a tee.

"I've been fighting off a hard-on since dinner, Pet. I'm afraid you're right, I'm nearly dying here. Could you help a poor bloke out with that?"

The Creative Director

I nod and climb over Brantley's lap without a second thought. I take off my shirt and bra, releasing my breasts right in his face, and he dives straight in on sucking and fondling them. My eyes roll back inside my head while I relish the feeling of his hard cock nestled between my legs. I undo his pants and lift his shirt over his head. The movie continues to play in the background, but I've tuned it out completely. He flips me over to my back on the couch and slides his pants off while I wait for his cock to spring free from his underwear.

He stands before me fully naked, fully aroused and fully mine.

"I want to fuck you so hard, Pet," he says as he positions himself over me.

"Take me any way you want. I'm all yours." I breathe heavily as I pull his face close to mine and search his eyes. I part my legs wide to let him in, and feel him thrust inside of me just seconds later. All I want to do is devour his lips with mine and feel his girth widen me with every pulse.

"Damn woman, you feel so good. I waited too long to get inside of you tonight," he breathes as he pounds through me into the deepest recesses of my sex. I love watching his expression when he fulfils the need to be inside of me. His desire is written all over his face and it pushes my own desires to a heightened level. He comes so hard after a session like this, and I feel his release almost as much as he does. I know he's had a particularly stressful week, and so did I. We needed this hard-hitting release of pent-up energy to right our worlds again.

As Brantley collapses over me I let out a heavy breath. He starts laughing heartily with his face buried in my long hair, and that prompts me to laugh with him. "I love your laugh," I say.

"You do, do you?"

"Yes. It's strong, warm, infectious and loud. Almost the complete opposite of what people see of you in the real world. You should laugh more often."

"I find myself laughing easily with you around, Jess. Perhaps that is why I call you my pet," he ponders. Brantley rises from the couch and heads to the bathroom. "Stay right there," he calls out from another room.

I wait for only a few minutes, returning my gaze to the movie we were watching. I'm not surprised he has a warm cloth in his hands when he comes back to me. He gently wipes me off and kisses the tip of my nose before stating, "I'm in the mood to mine for liquid gold."

The Creative Director

I can't help but smile. He most certainly knows his way around my cave and he's welcome to mine it with his tongue any day of the week. "You're the first guy I've ever met that does this," I say, pointing at the washcloth.

"Really? Those other guys are assholes. A good woman deserves respect, especially the ones who like to go commando," he says.

Sandra A. Sigfusson

*Chapter 22: The Cat Is Out Of
The Bag*

After a few weeks of not being able to connect up with Karmyn, I finally manage to hook up with her for a Friday night dinner. It turns out she's still into her Oklahoma wine-tasting guy, and I'm happy for her. As it always is when your best friend finds a lover, the times you spend together become fewer and farther between.

I arrive at her apartment at seven o'clock and I cannot wait to see what dinner she has prepared for me. To my surprise, her new boyfriend is joining us. I would have appreciated her telling me he'd be there, but I'm not going to argue the point.

Caleb introduces himself nearly two seconds after I enter Karmyn's place. He's very handsome in a cowboy kind of way. Army-style buzz-cut hair, large deep-set brown eyes and one hell of a sexy smile. He has a thick build with broad shoulders and loads of well-earned muscles. "Pleasure to finally meet you, Caleb. Karmyn has told me a little bit about you, but not much," I say at our introduction.

The Creative Director

Karmyn smiles from behind the island in her kitchen. She is head over heels for Caleb, and I can't help but smile at how happy she is. He reminds me of Karmyn's brother, Anson. Same build, same beautiful smile. I need to know about Caleb, so I don't hesitate to fire a few questions at him while we wait for dinner to be ready. I stand beside Karmyn, stirring the gravy in the pot while she sets the turkey on a serving tray and fills the other dishes with veggies and mashed potatoes.

"How long have you been in New York?" I ask.

"Six years now," Caleb replies.

"And what do you do here? I mean, what brought you to New York from Oklahoma?"

"I came here to get my Sommelier Certificate. My goal is to achieve my CMS." Karmyn hands Caleb a knife to carve the turkey and slides the plated giant bird across the island toward him.

"What is a CMS?" I ask. Karmyn shakes her head at me: after all the years I've been her dearest friend, I should know all these wine terms by heart.

"It is the Court of Master Sommeliers – the highest rank in sommelier training."

Sandra A. Sigfusson

"Oh," I say, now silently chiding myself for not knowing this stuff. "I'm not an expert on wine on any level, so my understanding of the differences in wines is limited to what I've learned from Karmyn and her dad."

I pour the finished gravy into the gravy boat and place it on the table. Picking up a clean wine glass from my usual place setting, I rest the glass on the island and smile at Caleb. I wonder how a country bumpkin from Oklahoma who looks like he should be out riding bulls decided he wanted to be an expert in wines. In fact, his looks are so strikingly like Anson's that I start to reminisce about Anson and wonder what our lives would be like had I not broken our engagement off. Now that Brantley and I have gotten so close I don't think of Anson as much as I used to. Perhaps that's a good thing, since that boy has rattled every relationship since our breakup – to the point where I often wondered if I should contact Anson again to give us a second chance.

This is not the place nor the time to be thinking of my past, though, and so I dive in with more questions for Caleb. "So, the obvious question now is, what wine is best served with turkey, Brussels sprouts and mashed potatoes? A white or a red?"

"White," Karmyn chimes in, and Caleb nods.

The Creative Director

"There are a few reds that would pair nicely with turkey, but the typical go-to is a white. I prefer to serve a dry white with notes of apricot or apple. I like the 2017 Cantelys Blanc – a Bordeaux, in this instance." A quick smile flashes at me from Caleb and I nod.

"I'll take your word for it. Is that what you brought here today?" I ask.

"No," he says. "We're serving one from the Beaumont family stock tonight, since I'm learning about the wines that Karmyn's father's winery produces."

"Damned straight," Karmyn interjects. "If it ain't my daddy's wine, it ain't on my table."

Caleb chuckles and nods. "We'll see about that. She's a bit pig-headed about serving anything that isn't from her dad's winery, and I understand it, but I'd like her to see what else is out there. In the meantime, I'm getting to know George Beaumont and his product so that I can help him widen his current distribution to restaurants and clubs in the state of New York."

"Wow, how exciting!" I'm stoked to hear that Caleb is working with George in this manner. "When did this arrangement come about?"

Karmyn pipes in. "When I took the competitor's bottles to Dad, I introduced Caleb to him. They hit it off immediately, and now they're working together while Caleb works on his sommelier training."

I raise my glass in a toast to Caleb and Karmyn being a seemingly perfect couple. It appears we've both been handed a decent-guy card in recent months. When she meets Brantley, who could not be more different than Caleb, I'm sure the conversation is going to be interesting.

In the following days I speak with Karmyn twice. She continues to fall deeper in love with Caleb, and it makes my heart smile. We tentatively arrange for us to have a foursome dinner on Saturday night. I'm as excited for her new relationship as I am my own, not to mention the prospect of my dearest friend meeting the pompous ass she heard on the phone when Brantley called me from England. I can attest to Brantley not being the best when it comes to first impressions, but once you know him you know he's true gold.

As I go to make myself a fresh cup of coffee after my long chat with Karmyn, I realize the tray of coffee pods is empty. I head to the supply room three doors down the hall to fetch more coffee and a few other

The Creative Director

supplies. Carol and I meet each other in the room and as always, she has a smile for me. Today, though, her smile is a bit different. Almost apprehensive.

"Is everything okay?" I ask.

"Yes. How about you?" she asks.

"Good, great even. Are you sure everything is okay? That isn't the sunny smile you normally give me. What's on your mind?"

Carol closes the supply room door and locks it behind her. She turns to me and smiles quickly. I'm curious now as to what is going on. Is there something she heard around the office about big changes coming, or did I do something wrong that she wants to address privately?

"Did you enjoy your dinner last Friday at Mandolin's?" she asks. Her eyes are fixed on mine as if she is trying to read me.

"How did you know I was there?"

"My uncle owns Mandolin's Restaurant, and I was there last Friday helping them out when one of their cooks called in sick. I don't normally help out in the kitchen but I happened to be there for a visit and just slipped on an apron and threw myself into the mix," she says.

I am no longer wondering what she's thinking. She must have seen Brantley and me together having dinner. Dammit. Our secret is out. The big question is, can I trust Carol to keep it to herself. "Oh. Well, that's nice of you to pitch in to help them out," I say, trying to redirect her and avoid the inevitable. "I didn't know you enjoyed cooking."

Carol hesitates for a moment. "Are you and Brantley seeing each other?"

Thinking fast, I reply, "We've shared a couple of work-related meals together."

"Oh. It's just that when I saw you two at Mandolin's, it looked like there was more going on than dinner out with a peer. You seemed a bit angry with him like you were having a lover's spat," she adds cautiously.

I giggle and rub the end of my nose while I figure out how to explain that one. "Sometimes we act out scenarios of how a commercial might play out. For example, our newest client, Masterson – who as you know is an adult toy manufacturer and distributor – is

The Creative Director

wanting a dramatic-style online ad, so Brantley and I were role-playing," I say.

Carol nods, but I don't think I've fooled her. Shit. Brantley is going to lose it if he knows someone in the office has figured out we're dating.

"Listen, Jess. I'm not stupid or naïve, so if you are having an affair with Brantley I won't say a word. You can trust me, you know."

I mull that over for a few seconds. She's right. She knows I'm lying regardless of how good I've gotten at it as of late. My Academy Award performance in front of Grady a while back appears to be a one-time deal. I've lost my touch.

I tip my head down and stare at my shoes. "Yes. Brantley and I are seeing each other. I expect that you'll keep that knowledge to yourself, as I'm aware that Grady frowns upon staff messing around with each other."

"I like the idea of you two as a couple. He adores you, and you understand him and his hard-edged ways," she says.

"Hard-edged ways? That's perfect," I giggle. "You are very astute, Carol. But what tells you that he adores me?" I have to ask. If she's seeing it, then it's likely others have too.

Sandra A. Sigfusson

"I run this office," she says, smiling, and a twinkle reflects back to me from her eyes.

"I know, Carol. My nickname for you is the Wizard – you know, all-seeing, all-powerful," I admit and chuckle, hoping that wasn't an insult.

"He was smitten with you the day you walked in here in those badass cherry-red stilettos. And every time you wear them he seems to follow you around like a hungry dog. So, there's that," she says, breaking out into a full-bellied laugh.

Suddenly there's a knock on the door and we both jump a little. "Yes," I call out.

"I need office stuff," the male voice says behind the door. "Can you guys have your giggle fest in another room? I'm on a deadline here."

Carol and I bust a gut again as she unlocks the door and fixes the side of her hair. "Sorry, I didn't realize the door locked behind me when I came in," she says, then walks with purpose and confidence back to her station next to reception. I stuff my hands full with coffee pods and slip back to the hallway with a stupid grin plastered over my face. I feel like we're two school girls who were caught smoking in the bathroom.

The Creative Director

I return to my office and refill the coffee pods basket on the counter. I'm still giggling to myself when Brantley returns from his client lunch meeting.

"Are you having fun over there all by yourself?" he asks dryly.

"Yes. It's a private party that grumpy fucks like you would never be invited to," I tease.

"You'd better have that coffee before that potty mouth of yours insults someone other than me in this office," he says.

"I need to talk to you about something, Mr. Sunshine," I say. I lean my bum against the counter edge while my mug fills with a fresh cup from the machine.

"What's this about?" Brantley sets his briefcase on the floor next to his desk before giving me his full attention. "Actually, can it wait for a few? I'd like to make notes on my luncheon today before I forget all the things we discussed."

"Sure. It can wait," I say. I turn to retrieve my fresh cup from the coffee machine and slip a blip of cream in it, stir and return to my side of the office. Brantley gets right into his laptop, tapping away feverishly while he recalls his conversation at lunch. I smile at how driven he is. Then I smile at how I love him driving into me the way he does when he just needs a good old-fashioned shag. As I giggle to myself, he stops his typing and looks over to me.

"What is it that you insist on laughing about?"

"You," I say and giggle again.

"Me? What have I done to make you laugh?"

"You being you," I say. "Never mind me. Go back to what you were doing."

Brantley frowns at me and then goes back to his typing. Hard-edged. Carol nailed that one.

The Creative Director

Chapter 23: Where There's Smoke ...

The weather report on the news this evening sounds rather ominous. It's a long weekend for me, as I needed a break from my schedule to chill out and booked Friday off. Sadly the weather is not great – lightning storms for today, and possible heavy rains tomorrow in the late afternoon. I don't have any outdoor plans, though, and I'm fine to be locked indoors today to clean my house and read a book I've been meaning to start since last month.

Brantley has been busy with two out-of-town guests this week at his apartment, so I haven't been seeing much of him this week after hours. But, we have our foursome dinner with Karmyn and Caleb planned for Saturday night. I decide to take the spare time to evaluate my wardrobe.

I can hear the strong winds pick up through the open window of my bedroom as the expected storm passes through. I like the sound of the leaves on the trees outside my condo rustling briskly in the random gusts. I get an invigorating vibe from windy days, as if they're a form of cleansing.

Sandra A. Sigfusson

I decide to sort through my wardrobe, looking for clothes that I no longer want or need, and find about fifteen garments worth donating. Shoes I will not donate under any circumstances. As I head into my kitchen to find a suitable plastic bag to place the donations in, a news item on TV catches my attention.

"A massive fire caused by lightning strikes is raging out of control southwest of New York City," the newscaster says as a quick inset film clip over his left shoulder shows a blazing fire consuming a large tract of farmland. *"We'll return in a moment."*

Fires like these are hard to control. It has been an exceptionally hot summer here in New York State and everything is tinder dry. As I'm pulling out a clear recycling bag from my cabinet, the news returns.

"The Beaumont Winery has been set ablaze by multiple lightning strikes earlier this afternoon. At present, over fifty percent of the vineyard has been destroyed. Firefighters have been focusing their attention on creating a fire break to protect the remaining crops and the buildings on the property in addition to preventing other nearby crops from being destroyed. No injuries have been reported." The longer version of the video footage of the raging fire over Karmyn's family's

The Creative Director

vineyard plays, and I'm thrown immediately into panic mode.

My eyes widen as I absorb the reality of what I'm hearing and seeing on my television screen. I reach for my phone to call Karmyn and dial her number with shaking hands. The connecting call rings several times but she doesn't answer. "Shit!"

Dropping everything I'm in the midst of, I throw my cell phone in my purse and rush out the door to drive to the Beaumont Vineyards. I'm sure Karmyn is there with the rest of her family and I want to help out any way I can.

The traffic out of the city is crazy on Friday afternoons – worse than any other weekday. I fight the urge to scream at others while I zigzag and force my way through the heavy traffic to reach the freeway. Everything is gridlock now. I should have known better than to attempt to exit the city with any level of efficiency on a summer Friday afternoon.

I start some slow-breathing exercises as I sit in near-standstill traffic. Inch by inch the cars move along until there is finally a break in the crawl on the outskirts of the city. I should be able to reach the vineyards within the next hour now.

Sandra A. Sigfusson

My cell phone rings and connects up through the Bluetooth in my car. "Hello?"

"Hello, Pet. What are you up to? Do you care to come to my flat for a visit with my cousin and his wife tonight?" Brantley asks.

"No! Sorry, I didn't mean to be so abrupt. Have you been watching the news?" I ask frantically.

"What's going on?"

"The Beaumont Vineyard, Karmyn's family vineyard, has been struck by lightning and the entire crop is ablaze. I'm on my way to the vineyard now and I should be there in the next hour," I say quickly.

"Shit! I'm sorry to hear that. Just a moment," he says before he yells across the room to his guests to have them change the channel to a local news station. "Right. You get to the vineyards, and for God's sake be careful. I'll look for the story to hear more about it. Keep me posted, will you?" he asks.

"Yes. I'll call you when I know what's happening. I've heard that everyone is safe, but the fire is bad, really bad. I'll call you later," I say and drop the call. I go back

The Creative Director

to listening to local news updates on my radio while flying down the highway at top speed.

Approaching the side road that leads to the main office and sales center for the vineyard, I'm awestruck by the billowing black plumes of smoke and the wall of flames in the distant field. I'm stopped by local police redirecting traffic away from the fire. I have to get in there, and I begin an argument with the female officer.

"You don't understand," I say anxiously. "This is my best friend's family's vineyards. I need to get in there and help out."

"Miss, you are not getting in there with your car," she tells me. "The road is blocked off. Everyone in the area has been evacuated. The only vehicles traveling down this access are emergency and police vehicles, so you'll have to turn around and head back."

My blood boils. I should have realized everyone would be evacuated. But where the hell did they go? I nod reluctantly at the officer and pull a U-turn with my car. I pull over to the side of the road and try getting in touch with Karmyn again. They've likely gone to the family house. Finally, she answers.

"Jess. Did you hear the news?" she says. Her voice is shaky and my heart breaks to hear her so upset.

"Where are you? I'm at the vineyard now but I've been informed everyone was evacuated."

"I'm at Mom and Dad's place. Come here, will you? I need you."

"I'm on my way, Karmyn. I'll be there in twenty minutes." I'm already back on the road before our conversation ends.

Reaching the sprawling ranch-style house of Karmyn's parents' place in record time, I scramble out of my car and head for the front door. Karmyn is there with open arms as I approach and she begins to cry.

"Is everyone safe?" I ask.

"Yes. Come inside. We have some of the staff who live on the vineyard staying here with us until we can return to the property. I'm so upset right now I can't think straight."

"Do you think the firefighters will be able to save all the buildings? I mean, I know the crop is destroyed, but the buildings," I say before Karmyn's father approaches to hug me.

The Creative Director

"I'm hoping they can get it under control and save the structures," George says. "I'm being updated every hour. We're watching the news reports and that's all we can do."

"What about the inventory?" I ask. "Has anyone organized a transfer of the inventory to another location?"

"Yes. We've got five trucks loaded with as much remaining product as possible. The minute we were aware that the crops were on fire I called in all my distribution trucks and had them load whatever they could. I'm hopeful that we don't lose the buildings. Karmyn packed all the gift shop merchandise and it's being stored here in the garage," he says.

I can see that the situation has taken its rightful toll on George, but he's a positive man and if I know him at all he's not losing hope. Thankfully, this isn't the only vineyard the Beaumont family owns.

As we enter the kitchen I spot Karmyn's mom Gabrielle rushing around her kitchen making pots of coffee and trying to make food for people to eat. She has a nervous energy about her, and I wonder if she's trying to keep busy so her mind doesn't focus on the losses at the vineyard. "Here, let me help with that," I say to Gabrielle. I stand behind her and give her a hug before diving in to help her with the food prep. Karmyn is on the other side of the large kitchen island making a cheese and veggie platter. We work in silence but glance up at each other intermittently from opposite sides of the island.

"I'm so glad you're here," she says.

"Me too," I reply and smile.

The Creative Director

Chapter 24: The Phoenix

It's eight hours before we hear that the fire has been completely extinguished. By then it's ten o'clock at night and we are all sitting outside on the patio beside the pool, feeling relieved that the buildings on the property have been saved. The estimate is that seventy percent of the crop has been destroyed.

"What about insurance?" I ask George.

"There is no insurance coverage for acts of God, Jess. I'm afraid we've lost that crop without any form of compensation. The smoke from the fire over what remains of the crop has likely ruined them as well. It's a complete loss," he says somberly.

I nod and ask why the field sprinklers didn't help to keep the plants from burning.

"The pumphouse is at the spot where the first lightning strike occurred, and it was blown up when it struck," George confirmed. "The main shut-off was where the firefighters hooked up their pump trucks. The lines to the fields were disconnected."

My heart sinks deep inside my chest at how tragic this is for the family. It was the largest vineyard in their portfolio, and the loss will set them back substantially in profits for the coming years. I sip what is left of the fine wine in my glass. The notes are wonderful and fruity. And if I remember correctly, this was the wine that Caleb said he liked the most of the five wines the Beaumont family produces.

"I'll buy the balance of the stock of your Pinot Gris right this minute if you'll let me," I say to George. He smiles. It's the first smile I've seen on his rugged face since I arrived.

"Have you got a couple million burning a hole in your pocket, Jess?" he asks jokingly.

I smile wide and laugh. "No, sadly I don't. How about I take a dozen cases off your hands to start and we'll work out how I'll pay for the rest of them," I say.

"Deal," he says and chuckles. I watch him gently swirl the balance of the red wine in the bowl of his glass before he consumes it. I can only imagine what pressures are clouding his mind now. This is a major financial loss that would slide most people into bankruptcy, but I think they have enough to survive. Every vineyard has had bad years at some point but losing the plants in their entirety is far more devastating than losing just one season's crop.

The Creative Director

I glance across the circle of farm workers and wine-making staff around the patio. Some of the workers that are staying here have fallen asleep in their pool loungers and others are discussing the work needed to rebuild the vineyard when everyone is able to go back on site.

Rising from the ashes like a phoenix, I think to myself. "George," I say, trying to get his attention. "What does the word phoenix mean to you?"

"It's a bird, mythical, that's reborn after it dies, as far as I know. What's on your mind?" His eyes are fixed on me now.

"The phoenix dies in a show of flames and then is reborn," I say, nodding in agreement at his definition. "Are you planning on replanting the vineyard and starting again? Rising from the ashes, as it were?"

"I don't know, Jess," he replies, shaking his head. "It will take more money than we have available and four years after planting to see a crop worthy of making wine from. I don't know if I have it in me to start from scratch. Those vines were over forty years old. My favorite wines we produced came from that vineyard," he says. "Half the vines were red and the other half were white."

Sandra A. Sigfusson

"Can you get me a projection of how much capital you'd need to replant and operate for four years without profit from that vineyard?"

"I guess. What's your plan?" he asks, now visibly more interested in this conversation.

"If you can get those figures to me within the next month I'll work on a plan to raise the capital you need. I'm a marketing wizard, remember?" I say and smile.

"Sure," he says. "I guess I could do that. Anything that can save that vineyard would be great, but I don't have much hope. It might be best to sell off the property and let someone else start from scratch. That way it isn't a complete loss and we can reinvest those profits into the other vineyards we own."

"Don't sell out just yet, George. Let me see what I can do while you salvage what you can of it," I plead.

"Okay, Jess." George stands to approach me and give me a sweet kiss on my cheek. "You have always been our loudest cheerleader."

Karmyn and Caleb were sitting beside me during my conversation with George. Karmyn squeezes my hand and kisses my cheek too. "If there is anything I can do to

The Creative Director

support what you have in mind, you know where to find me," she says.

Since I'm of no use to them at the moment, and it's getting very late, I decide to head home. After our hugs and kisses goodbye, I climb into my car and call Brantley, hoping he's still awake entertaining his cousin.

"Hello, Pet," he answers softly. "How is everything?"

"Not good. The vineyard is a complete write-off and insurance doesn't cover acts of God, so the loss is substantial. The good news is that not all the structures there were affected by the fire. There's a lot to discuss, and I'll need your help in the coming weeks to see if the vineyard is worth replanting and if we can find some financial backing to that end. At the moment I'm too tired to think any further about it. I'm heading home now. Can I see you tomorrow?" I ask, stifling a yawn.

"Yes. Tomorrow then," he says. "Sweet dreams."

I'm awake before the birds are on Saturday morning. I had a restless night's sleep with so many thoughts about the fire and how to save the vineyard short-circuiting my brain. After I've had a quick coffee and some toast, I sit down at my desk next to my kitchen and start making notes on how I will approach this project.

I start with a list of all the potential investors I think may be interested in saving the vineyard. The Beaumont family's wines have been a staple in New York for over twenty years, so it shouldn't be difficult to gather interest.

I make a few sketches, using the shape of a wine bottle as the body of the phoenix and adding flaming wings. I think that if we can get this vineyard replanted we should call the first series of new wines the Beaumont Phoenix line. We might also revamp the existing gift shop to add a small restaurant serving fire-grilled dishes that pair well with the wines in stock.

Two hours pass in what feels like a blink of an eye as my ideas flow like water from a fountain. I'm excited now. I have a plan, some design ideas and a heart filled with hope.

Brantley and his cousins meet up with me at a little bistro down the block from his place. Lillian and Davis are lovely people and I'm enjoying listening to them all chat in their English accents. Our lively luncheon

The Creative Director

conversations and the good food give me reason to put my worries for the Beaumont family out of my mind temporarily.

Lillian and Davis are off tomorrow to tour the east coast before taking part in a cruise to the Caribbean from Miami next week. On Saturday afternoon Brantley and I will be alone again to enjoy each other's company in private. I still haven't had the time to tell him that Carol has figured out we're dating.

That evening Brantley cooks me the one and only meal he knows how to do well – shepherd's pie. After dinner I'll break out my news.

"So, I was going to talk to you about something on Thursday, but we never got around to doing it."

"What's that?" Brantley says as he rises from the table to take our finished dinner plates to the dishwasher.

"Carol knows," I say.

"Knows what, Pet?"

"About us," I say.

Brantley thinks about that tidbit of information for a moment before replying, "How?"

"Her family owns Mandolin's where we had dinner last week. She was there and spotted us at our table. She put two and two together, so to speak," I say.

"Bloody hell. Does nothing get past that woman?"

"No, but she promised to keep it to herself. Honestly, I thought you'd be more pissed off about her figuring it out," I say.

"I am rightly pissed. Don't let my calmness fool you. My concern is if Grady has figured it out. You know how he is about staff dating each other."

"I know, I know," I say then blow out a loud breath. "But as best as I can tell he hasn't yet."

"Right. We'll have to continue to be at each other's throats."

I giggle before I remember something Carol told me. "Carol says she suspected you were highly interested in me a while back. She says that when I wear my red shoes you follow me around like a hungry dog." My giggles are now a full belly laugh. "Maybe that's something you could stop doing."

The Creative Director

"Shit. Really?" he asks. "Damn you and those sexy-assed shoes," he mutters. Brantley tosses a handful of knives and forks in the dishwasher's cutlery basket then wipes his damp hands on a tea towel. "Do you have any idea how amazing your ass looks when you wear them?" A boyish smile eases over his lips. "Your ass gives me a rise on the regular; however, those stilettos, those damned cherry-red stilettos are my weakness."

"Is it just my shoes or any woman wearing red shoes that does it for you?" I ask, but I don't really want his honest answer.

"Just you, Jess. Just you." Brantley approaches to hug me. I believe my shoe talk has somehow aroused him.

"Did you get hard just now thinking about my ass?" I giggle again.

"I get hard thinking about every part of you. You are highly distracting even when I'm frustrated by something you've done or said."

"Is that so? Perhaps we shouldn't be working in the same room together. Shall I put in a request for my own office?" I ask while I tug and play with the collar of his shirt and hover my lips an inch away from his.

"I'd be devastated if I couldn't see your beautiful face every day across the room from me. Separating us is out of the question." His lips find mine by way of a gentle bite on my lower lip. My loins, nipples and heart react to his touch and seductive bite. My eyes dart sidelong to the cleared kitchen table and his lips ease to a devilish smile. "Right. Let me fetch a can of whipped cream so you can serve me dessert. Get your clothes off and lay upon that table, now." Brantley wriggles his eyebrows at me.

My eyes flash wide at his suggestion, before I dive in for a long, sensual kiss. "I'll be ready to eat when you are," I whisper in his ear.

The Creative Director

Chapter 25: Teamwork

Come Sunday morning when we wake nestled in a pile of sheets, a heavy dark-gray duvet cover and pillows scattered across the bed, I feel Brantley's warm hand caressing the length of my spine and the shape of my hip. I love the sensation of having my skin caressed this way, especially first thing in the morning. In the relative silence of his bedroom I am treated to the deepening breaths from his mouth as a trail of kisses adorn my shoulder.

"Are you awake?" he murmurs.

"Yes, but don't stop touching me. I love your touch."

"Is there a limit to where you can be touched, or is every beautiful part of you on offer?" I can feel the smile on his lips at my shoulder and I smile too.

"On offer?" I tease in my pitiful imitation of his glorious accent.

"Up for grabs," he says louder as he attempts to tickle my sides.

I squirm wildly, as I'm exceptionally ticklish. And dammit, now he knows that too. The scaring-me issue has been resolved, but now tickling me is on his radar. I slap madly at his hands grabbing my waist. "Please. Don't tickle me. I'll pee nearly instantly if you do," I say firmly.

"You are entirely no fun, Jess. I can't scare you and I can't tickle you. Should I be advised of other fun things I'm not allowed to do to you?" He groans and rolls over onto his back in an exaggerated display of playful disappointment.

"No. Just a weak heart and bladder. Other than that I'm good," I say a bit defensively.

"Don't be angry with me, love. I am learning things about you as you are about me. I promise to remember not to tickle you unless you're already in the loo. The scaring thing I cannot guarantee I won't do, as I tend to be quiet in my footsteps and often unintentionally startle people. Now, turn yourself round in the sheets and let me have my way with you."

I do as Brantley instructs and rub my nose against his once I'm facing him, then close my eyes. This closeness and his willingness to compromise on even the littlest things is one of the things I love about him. No other lover has ever been so accommodating. When I

The Creative Director

open my eyes his devilish grin has taken over. "I know for certain there *are* parts of you that you don't mind if I tickle," he says, then growls playfully while he crawls down my body under the sheets.

By the time we've had our morning bump and grind, showered and eaten breakfast, we are ready to sit down together and hammer out some ideas about reinventing the Beaumont vineyard. Brantley suggests that we get as many newspapers and online news outlets as we can to pick up this story from a historical level. A true story of the Beaumont family and how the vineyards got started. I love that idea. We can build on a marketing strategy after we've told the story to the public. I'd thought about setting up a GoFundMe page, but I think I'd rather exhaust private investor options before heading in that direction.

While I make more notations, Brantley rises from the dining room table to refill our coffee mugs and grab the box of donuts he has on his counter for a pick-me-up sugar fix. When he turns to the table he reaches for my hand and stills me. "The day you interviewed at Digame, I believe the words you said were, *I have a reputation for reviving dead dogs,*" he says, nodding at me as he reaches to hold my chin in his hand and gazes longingly into my eyes. "We'll revive this dead dog together, you and I," he says.

Sandra A. Sigfusson

I nod before placing a heartfelt kiss on his lips. "This is the most important project I've ever taken on, both personally and professionally. Thank you, Brantley," I say and smile. I ponder my dead dog story for a moment, and then wonder what it was that I did during my interview pitch that got me the job at Digame. "Why did you hire me over the other applicants?" I ask.

Brantley bites into a donut and promptly wipes his mouth with a napkin before speaking. "You had the job before your interview, Jess. The pitch was merely a formality so that the other executive staff could have a chance to meet you." He follows that comment with an inquisitive smile. "And, by the way. How does one give a dog mouth-to-mouth resuscitation, and how do you know how to perform such a feat?"

"I worked with my uncle Charlie at his veterinary clinic on weekends during my college days. He was hoping he could change my mind about going into marketing and becoming a veterinarian instead by teaching me all kinds of techniques, including resuscitating a dog."

"Now it all makes sense." Brantley embraces me and I snuggle up in his warm chest and close my eyes.

The Creative Director

"We have so much work to do," I say, "but I'm driven to make the Beaumont winery property rise from its ashes. Speaking of working on personal projects, how goes it with marketing your sister's romance novel?"

"It's doing well. We found several reputable online book reviewer blogs that post their thoughts on social media as well as on their own sites. Sales numbers are not leaping off the page yet, but the next stage is to generate a following on various platforms. We've bought ad space on several popular social media sites targeting romance readers. She's also interested in getting involved in audiobook format. We'll do a three-month blitz, rest for a month, then hit social media heavily again while she waits for her queries to traditional publishing houses to get replies. It's a long game when you're unknown," he says. I nod, understanding the logic in his pattern of attack.

"You know, for Valentine's Day we could package a Beaumont wine with your sister's romance novel," I suggest.

"That is a brilliant idea. She'll love it. We'll work on that after we sort out our Christmas programs for our clients," he says.

"What do you say to contacting potential investors on our lists tomorrow evening after work?"

Sandra A. Sigfusson

"That is a good plan too, Pet."

Back in the office Monday morning, Brantley and I dive in headfirst, as our clients are itching to get cracking on their Christmas ad-campaign ideas. Brantley is always one step ahead. At the end of each Christmas season, when the sales numbers and client responses to their ads come in, he takes detailed notes and begins to formulate ideas for the following holiday season based on those stats. And, since most of my clients were previously managed by Brantley, I have his last season's sales stats at my fingertips. A blessing, as my previous employer never thought to look that far ahead with their clients' seasonal needs.

As I'm skimming through reports from the clients with a heavy presence in the holiday season, my phone pings with a text from Karmyn.

Karmyn: *Are you free for lunch today?*

Me: *Sure. What time?*

Karmyn: *I'll pick you up at 12:30.*

Me: *Perfect, thanks.*

The Creative Director

I glance at my watch and realize Karmyn will be here in under an hour.

"Brantley, do you have plans for lunch?" I ask. "Do you care to join me and Karmyn?"

He pops his head up from his laptop screen. "No, Jess. I have a meeting in twenty minutes on the ninth floor with Nortex Energy. But thanks. I'll see you back here in the afternoon."

I nod. He'd probably feel like a third wheel in our conversation anyway.

Ten minutes later Brantley is packing up his briefcase and rinsing out his coffee mug in the kitchenette sink. "I'll be back before two, Jess. Enjoy your lunch with Karmyn," he says.

"I will. I've got so much to tell her about our ideas. She'll be quite excited."

Without another word Brantley is out the door of our office and whizzing past Carol in reception to head to the ninth floor.

Chapter 26 - Brantley: Enemy Mine

As I pass through the reception doors I am greeted with the lovely face of a woman I feel like I recognize. Then it dawns on me that this must be Karmyn, based on photographs of Jess and her in Jess's flat. A man slightly older than her, built like a linebacker and dressed in camouflage trousers, a ball cap, army boots, white t-shirt and a necklace of dog tags stands beside her. I'm happy to be finally meeting Karmyn, and I have to wonder who the bloke is standing next to her.

"Karmyn, yes?" I say, offering my hand to shake. She smiles but is unclear as to who I am.

"Oh, English accent! You must be Brantley," she says.

"Yes. I'm just off to a meeting. Good to meet you, love. You are here to take Jess for lunch, yeah?" I ask.

"Yes. I think we're a bit early but I have a surprise for her. I'd like to introduce you to my brother Anson," she says, all smiles.

The Creative Director

I give the man another once-over and smile politely. "Pleasure to meet you. I wasn't aware that Karmyn had a brother, let alone one who's in the army." I reach my hand out to shake Anson's, and the exchange is very firm.

"Pleasure to meet you too," Anson replies, removing his ballcap.

"Right, well I have a meeting on the ninth floor. You two carry on and I'm sure I'll be seeing you again soon, Karmyn. Anson, thank you for your service," I say.

"The pleasure is all mine," Anson replies and I nod.

As I wait for the lift to arrive, I remember that only one of the two building lifts is in operation this morning due to maintenance. I ponder taking the stairs up four flights but then it arrives and the doors open. In my haste I didn't note that it was heading down to the lobby and not up four floors where I need to be. That is when I also noticed that I'd forgotten my cell phone on my desk. "Bollocks," I mumble to myself.

Shaking my head at myself and my scattered mind as of late, I land in the lobby and stay inside the lift until I can go back to the office to retrieve my cell – and then I'll take the damned stairs up to the ninth. Hopefully this will not make me late. If so, I'll blame the broken lift as my tardiness excuse.

The lift fills quickly with several people as I glance at my watch again to check the time. It should be fine. It is just my luck today, though: the lift stops at every floor heading up to the fifth, and I want to growl at the lazy asses who cannot take the stairs up one flight. Now the lift is full to capacity with those going up and down. This is madness.

Pressing my way through the crowded lift on the fifth floor landing I manage to get back to my office floor and barge my way through the reception doors quick as I can. I am stopped in my tracks when I look through the glass walls to my shared office with Jess. She is in an embrace and kissing Anson with surprising passion while Karmyn stands there smiling like a wretched fool at them both.

"What the fuck?" I say loudly. Carol grabs my attention swiftly by stating my name in a low voice as a warning. I know what she's doing. She's trying to protect the office from knowing I'm losing my mind while I watch the woman I've fallen in love with in a passionate kiss with another man.

The Creative Director

Carol rounds the reception desk and stands before me. She grips my arms and turns my body away from the scene playing out before my eyes. "I don't think this is what you think it is, Brantley. What did you come back to the office for?" she asks quietly.

"Nothing, apparently. Absolutely nothing." I charge my way back out of the reception and fly up the stairs in record time. I can't think about what I just witnessed while I'm trying to woo a new client. At the eighth-floor landing I stop to catch my breath. I'm not in poor physical condition but my heart rate is astoundingly high. I'm gutted. Glancing at my watch again I decide that my client is more important than my love life and I must carry on. I take the next flight in slow, steady steps to regain my composure and slow down my breathing. Forcing a smile on my face I walk toward the office door for Nortex Energy, Inc. and enter their suite.

Our meeting carries on for the better part of two hours before I've run out of things to discuss with my new client. They've agreed to let me work on an ad campaign for a series of trade magazines in the energy sector. I'm dreading heading back down to the office and having to look Carol in the eye, let alone seeing Jess after what I witnessed.

I take in a deep breath and agree to let these gentlemen return to their work. I realize I'm starved at this point and should go back to the office and order sushi for delivery. While I make my way back down the stairs to our fifth-floor office it dawns on me that Anson is Karmyn's brother. Did Jess date him before meeting me? And, has she made love with him? That thought guts me even more.

    I resolve to not let earlier events cloud the balance of my afternoon. I have loads of work to do, and as a professional I should be able to keep my personal life and corporate life separated. But I fear that isn't an easy task since I'm already fucking my business associate and I've suffered watching her kiss another man.

    Carol stares at me with a blank face as I enter the reception area. I don't look back at her, marching myself into my office to check my cell phone. A text is there, along with three missed calls. After I've dropped my briefcase on the floor at my desk and filled a glass from the kitchenette with ice and a shot of bourbon from my liquor drawer, I knock the drink back and decide to return the missed calls.

    The first two messages are from clients wanting to book a meeting. The third missed call is from Jess. I hesitate to listen to her message at first but decide it is

The Creative Director

likely something to do with a client and force myself to hear what she has to say.

"Hi Brantley. I won't be coming back to the office today. I'm heading to the Beaumont family home with Karmyn and Anson to discuss some of the ideas you and I came up with for the vineyard. I'll see you tomorrow morning bright and early."

My teeth grind as my jaw cinches tight at the thought she'll be spending the balance of the day with Anson. That kiss was not a peck on the cheek, and the image of it has burned a hole in my head and heart. I'm useless today. I should go home as there is no way I'm going to be able to focus on my work.

By the time my sushi arrives I've lost my appetite. Tossing it aside to the counter of the kitchenette, I reluctantly resume working. I don't know all the facts yet about who this Anson bastard is to Jess. It could be that they haven't seen each other in a very long time. Am I leaping to conclusions?

Sandra A. Sigfusson

Chapter 27: Past Suddenly Present

The sudden appearance of Anson has me a bit shaken. It's been two years since we've been in the same room together, at George and Gabrielle's thirtieth wedding anniversary party, and eight years since we broke off our engagement. He had a girlfriend with him at that party. Anson and I chatted only briefly then but I knew he wanted to say more to me. I still hold his letters in a shoebox in my closet but I haven't read them in a very long time. The mere presence of him floods me with memories I can't and would never want to erase. He was trouble, he was an instigator, he led me down so many bad paths – and I fucking loved every minute of it. Anson had a way of convincing me to do things I would never have done or thought of on my own. Together we broke and bent every rule we came across, and Karmyn was never far behind us in all our crazy antics. I'd never thought much about the past and how much influence Anson had on me until our ten-year high school reunion, where random classmates would dredge up old stories: "Remember the time when you, Anson and Karmyn set fire to your locker so we could all get the afternoon off

The Creative Director

from classes?" Jesus, we were such assholes. I was so glad Anson missed the ten-year reunion because of his army commitments. I'd have never been able to handle seeing him there, and I'm having pretty much the same reaction to him gripping me so tightly in this hug now. I try to release myself from his warm embrace and passionate kiss, but he seems hell-bent on starting our relationship again with no more than a hello and a heady kiss that has me nearly buckling at the knees.

I stand back from Anson and smile quizzically at him. "Wow, that was one hell of a hello," I say as I adjust my clothes and dart a sidelong glance over at Karmyn. I think she's as taken aback as I am at the reception Anson gave me.

"Hi, Babe. You look amazing. How've you been?" he asks, and I'm suddenly a puddle of goo just hearing his words in my ears.

"I ... I'm good, Anson. You look amazing too." I smile a bit nervously at his handsome face while it sinks in that he's standing here in front of me after all this time has passed. "Should we head out for lunch now?" I say, hoping to make everyone less nervous. Actually, it's just me that needs to calm my nerves. Seeing Anson again after so long apart and being kissed like we were still lovers has my mind reeling. My heart twists in my chest when I look in his eyes. This man. This amazing,

Sandra A. Sigfusson

beautiful man was once mine and I let him go. I never expected to be this torn over seeing him again. How is it that so much time has passed, yet my emotional attachment to what we had haunts me like a ghost the minute our eyes meet?

Anson's eyes remain fixed on me and his brilliant bad-boy smile shines back like a beacon on a distant shore. I'll never be over him. I'll never forgive myself for my childish reaction to his decision to join the army just weeks after we became engaged. He, Karmyn, George and Gabrielle are my family. When my parents couldn't be there for me, the Beaumonts were – no questions asked. And everyone was so excited to hear Anson and I announce our engagement. "It is a match made in heaven!" Gabrielle said to me when she heard the news.

Damn him, anyway. As much as I wanted to stay distant, I had been keeping tabs on his life through Karmyn and by using a second stalking account on Twitter to follow his life and career. It is laughable that I've done this. I've kept my stalking indulgence on Anson quiet, like a snake slithering on the sand. I should be embarrassed with myself for tracking him as I do, since it was my decision to end our engagement. I couldn't handle the thought of being an army wife then, and I still

The Creative Director

can't fathom it now no matter how hard it's been to keep my distance from him.

"Sure," Karmyn says. She rubs her hand across Anson's back and nods at him. "You go ahead to the lobby, and Jess and I will get her purse and cell phone and meet you out there."

Once Anson is out of earshot, Karmyn pipes in. "I'm sorry, Jess. I had no idea Anson would be so … so exuberant at seeing you again. I thought what you two had was long over," she whispers as she hands me my cell phone.

I let out a loud sigh. "I don't think what we had can ever be forgotten, Karmyn," I say and then lead the way out to the lobby from my office.

Carol gives me a tentative smile before saying, "I'll need to discuss some things with you when you get back, Jess." I nod and smile before pushing the reception doors open to exit.

The elevator is packed with people since the second car is still out of commission. We squeeze inside and Anson is shoulder to shoulder with me. Those shoulders are unbelievable and, my God, he's still as handsome and ripped as he was the last time we were together. I lick my lips nervously as I try to get the image of his amazing body out of my head.

Sandra A. Sigfusson

"Are you back in town for a while?" I ask quietly.

"I came back because of the fire at the vineyard to help Mom and Dad. My leave from my base is on a family emergency. I'm able to stay as long as I'm needed," Anson says. I nod and lick my lips again. Why is my mouth so parched?

Once we've agreed on a place to have lunch and settled down at our table I begin to feel less anxious. That is, until Anson places his big warm hand on my knee under the table while we're ordering our meals.

Trying to ignore his ease at touching me, I stand to excuse myself to the washroom. I need a minute to figure out what I'm going to do here. Anson is without a doubt thinking that we've still got a thing for each other, and he's dying to have me throw myself at him. And he's not wrong. My heart tugs in two distinct directions while I envision Anson and Brantley in my head simultaneously. I can't do this to myself. I'm with Brantley. Fuck! I stare at my reflection in the bathroom mirror and I look pale. The truth is I still love Anson. He was my first real love. In our early twenties we were inseparable. We made love every day, hung out with all

The Creative Director

our friends, partied until the sun rose and made plans for our future together.

I shake myself out of my rumination and reapply my lipstick. I pinch my cheeks to reinstate some semblance of color and wash my hands. Standing tall I head back to the table, and before sitting down I ease my chair a bit farther away from Anson's wandering hands.

"Are you enjoying your army career?" I ask.

"Yes. Very much," he replies as a wide satisfied grin is sent my way.

"I've missed you," I say before I have a chance to think about those words so easily escaping me.

A glow of warmth washes over Anson's face and his beautiful smile grips my heart. "I can't tell you how much I've missed you too, Jess. It's so good to see you again."

Karmyn interrupts our reminiscing to discuss the situation at the vineyard. She stares directly at Anson. "So, Jess and her partner, Brantley are working on a few exciting things to help get the vineyard back in action. As daddy told you, we're on our own to rebuild." Karmyn sips her cocktail and rearranges her place setting while she looks at me.

Sandra A. Sigfusson

I know that look. That look is saying that she knows Anson and I are still a thing in our hearts. And she has to know how hard this is for me, to see Anson after so many years apart. Not to mention she is well acquainted with my relationship with Brantley. I'm sure there is a long conversation ahead of me and her.

Our lunch continues without much discussed except the vineyard. I mention the plans Brantley and I are putting in place to find investors willing to help with getting the field replanted and the main building renovated to include a restaurant and an updated gift shop and tastings bar.

Anson seems pleased with our ideas. His smile for me has not left his face since the moment our eyes met earlier today. I want to go back to my office to work, but Karmyn and Anson insist that I go back with them to George and Gabrielle's for a family reunion and a deeper discussion of our plans for the vineyard. George and Gabrielle have always treated me like I was their daughter, because I've been best friends with Karmyn most of my life, and also because of my short-lived engagement to Anson. His news about joining the army sent all of us for a loop.

The Creative Director

We arrive at the family home and are greeted with big smiles and warm hugs. I don't think George and Gabrielle have seen Anson in a long while, as his travels and training with the army have taken him all over the world. As I enter the house I can smell the dinner that Gabrielle is preparing in her kitchen and know I'm not getting out of here anytime soon. This visit is going to be an all-nighter.

I call Brantley hoping he won't be too bothered about me not coming back to the office this afternoon. I'm sure he'll understand why I'm here with the Beaumonts, considering how much brainstorming he and I have done in the past few days.

It isn't long before I find myself getting too drunk. I've managed to consume three large glasses of wine before dinner was served and then another three after dinner. I hadn't planned on letting myself get so inebriated, but the conversation and the wine flowed with such ease in the presence of all the people I love.

Gabrielle insists that I not go home this evening, but I have to get back to my condo. And I have to stop drinking if I'm going to be any use to Brantley and my clients tomorrow at the office. I rise from my chair in the dining room, intending to head for the bathroom. I stagger my way toward it, thankfully without my shoes on. The rich terracotta tiles beneath my feet are smooth,

Sandra A. Sigfusson

as are my stockings. I slip a little on the floor when I take the corner too confidently, and nearly fall. Before I can attempt to brace myself against the wall, I feel big hands around my waist assisting me. Anson has followed me down the hall and I have to assume he thinks I'm too drunk to keep my balance.

"Anson. You can let go. I'm fine," I say.

"No you're not, Jess. You're drunk. Let me help you get to the washroom."

I nod reluctantly. I don't want him near me like this. His pull on my heart feels very raw and exaggerated now that I'm drunk. Anson holds his arm around my waist as he guides me to the door to the washroom. I pry his grip from my waist and close the door behind me, leaning on it for balance. Maybe I should force myself to throw up to get all this alcohol out of my system.

My hands follow the length of the vanity counter as I walk cautiously on the tiled floor toward the toilet. I've managed to get myself seated on the toilet without further issue. My eyes close briefly while my body gently sways as I pee. I am really wasted.

After what feels like ten minutes I've completed my washroom mission and re-dressed. That's when the

The Creative Director

door is pried open slightly and Anson's warm-timbred voice asks me if I'm okay. What is it with men wanting to join me in the bathroom lately?

"I'm fine, Anson. Just give me a minute, please," I say. Anson enters the washroom and waits for me to rinse my hands in the basin. "You don't need to help me wash my damned hands, Anson," I say, being short with him.

"No, I suppose not. But you're going to need me to take you home," he says. My eyes meet Anson's and I'm overwhelmed by him being so close to me. I think he feels the same.

"We can't do this, Anson. I'm seeing someone," I murmur and turn my gaze away from his.

"Who is he?"

"A guy I work with. We're not living together or anything, but I'm in love with him," I say.

"No, you're not, Jess. I can take one look in your eyes and know you are still very much in love with me. No matter how much time has passed, you've never been involved with anyone more than a few weeks."

Sandra A. Sigfusson

"And how the hell would you know that?" I ask, shocked by his words. Has he been stalking me like I've been stalking him? Shit.

"Karmyn keeps me posted on how you're doing," he admits. Anson folds his big beautiful muscular arms, covered in tattoos I've never seen on him before, across his chest. I gulp at how attracted I still am to him. This is so fucked up.

"She shouldn't have done that," I say. "It's none of your business what I do in my life. You left to join the army." I'm pissed off now. He has no right to bring this up all over again. He crushed me. I wasn't interested in marrying a man who would rarely be around, or traveling from base to base with him while he advanced in his career and I left mine behind. I had my dreams of being an ad executive, and I wasn't giving up on my dreams to live in army bases worrying about when he'd be back home, or if he was ever coming home.

"Nothing has changed, Anson. I'm still not interested in marrying an army guy."

Anson releases his folded arms and reaches for me. "I got my psychology doctorate in the army. I'm working with veterans suffering from post-traumatic

The Creative Director

stress disorder," he says. Anson holds me by the shoulders and forces me to look at him by guiding my chin up with his hand. "I'm done working on bases at the end of November. After that I can go anywhere I want and set up my clinical practice. We can be together again, Jess."

My eyes search his. I can't believe I didn't know he was planning on leaving the army to work as a civilian. "Karmyn didn't tell me you were leaving the army. I knew about your doctorate degree, which is amazing, by the way, but why would you leave the army?" I ask. My brows are pinched tight together while I fight the urge to kiss him and let him make love to me where we stand. I must be more drunk than I first thought, if these feelings are surfacing for him so readily simply by his touching my chin and forcing me to look at him.

"I don't know, Jess. Karmyn does a lot of shit that doesn't make sense to me. I never kept that part of my decision process secret. Mom and Dad both knew I'd be finished in November."

I'm ashamed of myself and my unintended feelings for him resurfacing. I fall into his arms and hold my face against his chest while the scent of his skin, the scent I'm so familiar with and have missed so much, cloaks me like a warm blanket.

Sandra A. Sigfusson

"I have to go home and you're not taking me. Call me a cab, please."

A warm kiss atop my head and a tight embrace from his big, inked, strong arms grip my heart again before he agrees to my request. "Yes ma'am," he whispers.

The Creative Director

Chapter 28: The Big Chill

My office feels decidedly cold today. Brantley hasn't spoken more than two words to me since I came in this morning, and both of them came coated heavily in salt. By the time ten o'clock arrives I can't take his silence any longer and have to figure out what his problem is. "Are you angry about something?" I ask, knowing full well it is a rhetorical question.

"Yes," he says curtly, but that is the extent of his reply.

I keep my mounting frustration in check before asking, "And is there something I can do to help you not be angry?" I stand to approach his desk but he holds his hand up in the air at me.

"Unless you're using the loo or getting a fresh coffee you'd be best to keep your distance," he says. Brantley's eyes look like they are filled with fire.

My frustrations get the best of me. "What the hell is your problem?" I ask, returning his stern tone. This isn't like him to be so cold and indifferent to me on a personal level. We still argue and throw barbs when it comes to business ideas, but this is different.

Sandra A. Sigfusson

"We'll discuss it later after hours, Jess," he hisses between his teeth.

I chuckle sarcastically at him. "Not unless you can get the devil out of your eyes," I say, sitting back down in my chair and ignoring him. "Jackass," I mutter.

With the exception of Jason popping in and out of our office to discuss projects he's fielding the room remains quiet. I can feel the chill of Brantley in my spine every time I glance over to his desk. What the hell he's so upset about I have no idea, but I'm anxious to get to the bottom of it.

After my lunch break, Carol corners me in the hallway and tells me she needs to talk with me privately. "What's it about?" I ask, now curious.

"Come with me," she says, as she grabs my hand and leads me inside the copy room, closing the door behind her. "Brantley saw you kissing that army guy," she says. She looks pissed at me.

I stare at her blankly before I reply. She blurted that out so quickly, and those were not the words I was expecting to come out of her mouth. "He's my ex-fiancé who I've not seen in a long time, Carol. He's also my best friend's brother."

The Creative Director

"Well, I guess Brantley doesn't know all of this, and I think you need to sort that out before he strips every employee in this office bare of their confidence. He's an absolute animal today because of seeing you kissing your ex."

"Carol," I say, slumping my shoulders. "I appreciate you telling me this, but it really isn't your business. Please stay out of my relationship with Brantley. Yes, he is a bit of a bear today but he's not that bad."

"How the hell am I supposed to stay out of it? Brantley nearly died on the spot when he saw you two kissing, and I had to intervene to remind him that he'd blow your cover if he said or did anything further. Now get your ass back to work and deal with this before everyone here knows and one of you loses your job over it," she adds, raising an eyebrow. She means me. I'd be the one who would lose my job. Fuck it all.

"Okay, okay. I'm sorry. Thank you for filling in the blanks. I'll do what I can."

Returning to my office, I suck in a deep breath and close the door behind me. I clear my throat to catch Brantley's attention. His eyes rise from behind his laptop and he's still in a bear of a mood.

Sandra A. Sigfusson

"I understand you saw me kissing Anson yesterday." Brantley doesn't respond or change the stare in his eyes. "He's Karmyn's brother and we've known each other for many years," I add, hoping that information will ease his mind.

"Do all your friend's brothers kiss you like you were long-lost lovers?" he snaps.

"No," I say with a hint of indignation attached to my reply. "It's a much bigger story than that. Anson and I were once engaged. He joined the army and we broke it off because of it. I didn't want to follow him around the world or give up on my career aspirations. We were heartbroken but we got over it," I say with confidence.

"He's not over it, Jess. And I'm not over seeing him handle you like that." There is still a bite in Brantley's words, and I understand how this must have looked. "Are you over it?" he asks, staring hard at me.

I approach his desk, place my palms on the edge and lean forward on my arms so that my next words can be spoken quietly.

"I was. But his sudden reappearance has brought up a lot of emotions that I thought were ancient history. I

The Creative Director

will always love Anson, but we're different people now," I say, trying to convince myself of the same.

Brantley leans back in his chair and drops his pen on the desk. He rubs his eyes with the heels of his palms and blows out a long breath. "I can't share you with anyone, Jess. You are either with me or not. The sooner you get this matter sorted the better."

I've lost my cool now. I never indicated that I was interested in getting back with Anson, only that my emotions about us have resurfaced. I can't help myself and strike back with, "Oh, I see. But, you'd allow me to make love to a woman so you could watch?"

His eyes narrow at me and his jaw tics. I think I've made him more angry than he was in the first place, which was not my intention. But it's too late to take my words back now.

"Make your decision as to who you plan to spend the night with for the rest of your life," he says. "I can't handle the idea that your ex-fiancé has suddenly dropped out of the fucking sky and has decided you and he can pick up where you left off. I won't have it, Jess. You have until tomorrow to give me your answer."

The fine hairs on the back of my neck rise at his sharp ultimatum. "I have until tomorrow to give you my answer? Really?" My body stiffens as I stand erect before him. "Is everything about you based on deadlines? Do you have any idea how hard this is on me?" I huff and return to my desk holding back every pooling tear that threatens to fall from my eyes.

"You already know what is in your heart. I'm giving you until tomorrow to get the balls up to make a decision. I know that sounds harsh, but that's how I feel about it. If I were not here in the office I'd be tossing my apartment apart like the Hulk right about now. That is how angry I am at witnessing another man kissing you."

Brantley stands from his desk and enters the washroom, shutting the door behind him. I'd not thought of Brantley as possessive or the jealous kind, but now I know without a doubt how important our relationship is to him.

I'm choked. Deciding that this is no place for me to be, I hurriedly collect my things and have a quick chat with Jason. I make up some story about meeting up with a potential new client that I had forgotten to add to my business calendar, then head home to search deep within myself for a reason why Anson still has this hold on me.

The Creative Director

Chapter 29: Know Thine Own Heart

As I'm driving home to my condo I try desperately not to cry, but the tears fall as sure as spring rain. I drag my exhausted butt up the stairs and flop down on my couch. I can't cry about it anymore. I have to figure this out fast. Brantley is right, regardless of the asshole he is being about it: I should know my own heart.

Later that evening I resolve to dig the box of letters from Anson out of my closet. The dust that floats up off the top of the box is a reminder of how many years it has been since I last considered the topic of Anson and me. I sweep the dust off with the palm of my hand and open the shoebox. Inside are nearly twenty letters, written in his horrid handwriting. Anson is good at many things, but legible handwriting was never his forte.

The first letter on the pile is the most recent. I had stopped replying to his letters long before this one arrived. He dragged out this long-distance love affair far longer than I was willing to, and that thought gives me pause. I unfold the letter and set the envelope it came in to the side.

Sandra A. Sigfusson

> *Dear Jess. I don't know that I can continue to write to you if you insist on not returning my letters. I phoned for you but your roommate said you were out and she'd pass on the message. Either she didn't tell you I was calling you or you are ignoring me.*
>
> *I still can't see why we had to separate when I joined the army. You are my world, but I need to do this. I've wanted to be in the army for as long as I can remember. I hope when I'm established in my career and can spend more time coming back home that you'll still be interested in seeing me. I love you, Jess, and I know you love me. Please write back. Love, Anson.*

I had stopped replying to his letters because to me it was over. I couldn't fathom stringing our relationship on for however many years it would take for him to come to his senses.

Folding the letter back inside the envelope and returning it to the box, I close the lid and set the box on my dresser. I need to call Anson and arrange to have a

The Creative Director

long conversation with him face to face. This is a much bigger decision than I bargained for.

I find my cell phone still tucked in the side pocket of my purse. I don't have Anson's cell number and I have to call Karmyn first to get it. It's seven in the evening when my call connects with her. She and I talk for only a few minutes before I hang up and attempt my call to Anson. While I'm dialing his number I hear my doorbell ring out from the hallway. Another ring from the doorbell and three rapid knocks follow as I approach the door. "Who is it?" I ask.

"Anson. Let me in, Jess. We need to talk about us."

I'm shocked that he's at my door, and I have to fuss a bit with my clothes and hair before I let him in. I wonder if Karmyn knew he'd be coming here and didn't tell me. I don't know how else he'd know where I lived. I wasn't prepared to have him here tonight. In my mind I had planned to arrange a time to meet and have my questions sorted in my head and prepared – not be thrown into the lion's den this minute. I unlatch the locks, open the door and stare blankly at him. He's so damned handsome. He leans on one of his big shoulders against my door jamb, holding his ballcap in his hands. Anson's face is serious as we stare at each other. "Are you letting me inside or are we having this conversation on the doorstep?" he asks.

I nod. "Come in," I say. Anson steps inside and quickly removes his shoes. I wave my hand in the direction of my living room as a gesture for him to seat himself. Following behind him I get a faint whiff of his natural scent which has always driven me wild. I think his body is even thicker and more defined than it was when we broke up. He never stopped loving being in top physical fitness.

I seat myself across the coffee table from him. "So, in November you're leaving the army to start a private practice as a civilian?" I ask.

"Yes," he replies with a nod.

"Why?"

"I want to have my own private practice," he says. "And now that I've found you again, I'm more certain than ever of that decision, Jess."

"What makes you assume that you and I can be together again?"

The Creative Director

"Jess," he says as he leans forward across the table to reach for my hands. "I've never loved anyone the way I loved you. I mean the way I have always loved you, and still do. Please give me another chance to make us work," he asks sincerely. His eyes search mine for the positive response he's asking for. I'm still puzzled as to why he'd leave his beloved army. He's crazy. We both are for even considering trying to be together again.

"I know that sounds unbelievable and shocking after so long," he says, "but when I heard about the fire at the vineyard my first thought was that my family needed me. Seconds later I realized that more than that, I needed you. I've been lying to myself all this time. I thought I could get past our breakup and live my life as I envisioned, as a psychologist in the army. But not one woman that I dated came close to what you and I had. That means something, Jess." He pounds his chest with his fist over his heart.

His truths are also mine, I realize, as my heart twists. "I never stopped loving you, Anson. Maybe that is why none of my relationships ever lasted more than a few weeks. They weren't you," I manage to say without breaking down into tears.

I clasp Anson's outstretched hands in mine. His eyes glass over before he stands to round the coffee table and hold me. Our embrace is otherworldly. I feel like my

Sandra A. Sigfusson

life has come full circle, but I'm still choked up inside. The mere thought of telling Brantley that I'm going to give Anson a chance to fix what was broken between us when he left for the army tugs so hard at me that I have to sit down before my weakened legs fold beneath me.

"Is that a yes, Jess? Will you let me show you how much I missed you and love you?" he asks.

I release Anson from our hug and ask him to sit back down. I wipe a wayward tear that's slipping down my cheek with the back of my hand and sniffle. "Do you remember me telling you yesterday that I was seeing someone?"

"Yes. Does this mean that you're not going to give us another try?" he asks, his voice cracking, his eyes still glassy.

I search Anson's face and confusion grips me. I realize that Brantley and I have only been seeing each other as a couple for a few weeks. What Anson and I had was the real deal. We were together for nearly six years, but I was too young and impatient to see what I gave up with him at that time. Maybe this time it's different. Maybe this is the right time for me and Anson.

The Creative Director

"No. That isn't what I'm saying. But you have to give me time to sort that out. Brantley and I have been together for a few weeks and I care very deeply for him. Had you not returned I'd have no reason to leave him."

My heart feels like it's going to explode. Without warning I break out into the deepest sobs I've had in as long as I can remember. I'm more confused now than I've ever been in my life. I love Brantley, I really do. But the flame of the candle I hold for Anson still burns brightly, and I've loved him for what feels like forever. There is no right decision here. Clear as mud.

As I try to collect myself and stop this crying fit, Anson tries to hold me again but I press his advances away. "Anson, you need to go home. I have a lot of things to think about and I can't have you or Brantley here to mess with how I'm going to deal with you both." Rubbing my cheeks of the dampness and sniffling again, I step away to my kitchen and lean against my countertop.

Anson looks hurt by my words, but he's going to have to suck it up until I'm ready to commit to him fully again. "I need time, Anson. Please go and I'll call you when I'm, when I'm … FUCK!" I scream. I've never felt more emotionally tortured than I do in this moment.

Anson nods at me. He's getting the picture now and knows that I need my space and time. Approaching me in the kitchen he presses a sweet kiss upon my cheek, squeezes my hand and moves to the door to put on his shoes. Turning back to look at me – still standing there wiping tears from my eyes – he nods again and slips through the door.

I break down again the moment Anson leaves. This is a mess I never expected to ever be in and wouldn't wish on anyone.

I had never considered what the consequences would be should Brantley's and my relationship take a turn for the worse. Would I lose my job? Would he be able to continue to work with me regardless of our breakup? Would my quality of work suffer from having to be side by side with him in the same office after such a torrid affair? I don't think either of us really considered what problems could arise when we became lovers. Perhaps this is the very reason he's never before dated a coworker.

Brantley and I were never supposed to turn our one night of passion into a relationship. While we were working side by side I kept my distance, pushed thoughts of his amazing lovemaking out of my head, and was doing well to stave off my desires for him. But he seduced me in the office. He took away my ability to

The Creative Director

stand clear on my side of our necessary boundaries. Are he and I simply making love to each other for comfort and convenience, or is there really something more there? To my heart there *is* more, yet I can't be sure he feels the same way. All I know for certain is that his level of jealousy is high when it comes to me. His biting words and his ultimatum spoke loud and clear on that point.

Tears continue to fall, and my breathing hitches over and over again while I attempt to resolve this issue in my head.

Sandra A. Sigfusson

Chapter 30: Torn Between Two Lovers

If I slept for more than five minutes last night I'd be surprised. I feel ill and broken. I can't go into the office like this. The tug-of-war between professionalism and my broken heart is killing me. Glancing over to my alarm clock I realize it's nearly seven-thirty. My alarm went off at six o'clock but I haven't had the energy to rise from my bed and deal with the day ahead of me. I absolutely cannot adult today. I reach for my phone and call Carol to let her know I'm taking a sick day.

At nearly ten o'clock, when I finally manage to pull myself out of bed, my cell phone rings from my side table. It's an office number and I have to assume it's Carol checking in on me – it is something she would do – unless it's Jason with a question about one of our clients' projects.

"Hello," I answer as brightly as I can manage.

A heavy sigh greets me through the receiver. "So, this is your answer?" Brantley asks. "Not showing up to the office so you don't have to face the music?"

The Creative Director

His words are not harshly spoken, but the impact is palpable. "Brantley, we have to talk," I say.

"What is there to talk about, Jess? You've made up your mind and I have to live with the consequences," he says, then sighs in defeat before disconnecting our call.

"Brantley," I shout, but he's ended the call abruptly in his usual short manner. I shatter again. How is it possible to love two men equally? Or is it that I've never fully dealt with losing Anson, and that explains why I've not been able to handle dating anyone for more than a few weeks?

Until Brantley. He's different. He is the first man I've ever felt real love for since Anson. Why did Anson have to come back into my life at this very moment?

While I mull over this crazy situation I feel the sudden urge to throw up. Racing to my bathroom I fold before the porcelain bowl and unceremoniously toss up what's left of last night's dinner.

Fuck. I've got food poisoning. Either that or I've gotten so upset that I'm making myself sick. After a few more gags the urge to throw up has passed. I struggle to stand steady, feeling spent. The only thing that's going to make me feel human is to shower and try to eat some dry toast.

Sandra A. Sigfusson

Hours later, I'm still so exhausted I can barely move without feeling nauseated. I contacted Karmyn by text and she told me she hasn't been ill, so I chalk my sickness up to my emotional distress. I also tried to call Brantley three times but he refused to take my calls. I can only imagine how angry he is with me.

The downpour of rain outside mimics how I feel inside. I'm too nauseated to drink my sorrows away, so I return to bed. I have to be better tomorrow, and I refuse to let this situation interfere with my job for more than one day.

The Creative Director

Chapter 31: Just One Week

I somehow overcame my exhaustion last night and awoke feeling less stressed. I'm eager to get to work and face my love life, fucked up as it is, head on. I thought to pull out the red shoes that give me so much confidence but remembered that they're the ones Brantley likes so much and opted not to put those guns in his face today. I have no idea how he's going to react to me, but what's done is done.

Arriving ten minutes before eight o'clock, I'm relieved to be here in the office before Brantley is. By nine o'clock there is still no sign of him, and I have to wonder if he's playing hooky today to avoid me. I dial up Carol's desk to inquire.

"Hi Carol. Do you know when Brantley is expected today?"

"Hi Jess. He's on a business trip to L.A. for three days. You can call him on his cell if you need him," she says brightly.

"Right. Perfect. Thanks."

Jason enters my office and smiles wide. "Glad to see you back, Jess. I missed you yesterday. I've got about ten things we should cover this morning. Are you free now?" he asks.

"Yes, of course. Fire away," I say, trying to be lighthearted.

Jason rattles off the list of things he wants me to advise him on. I pick them out in order of importance. Grabbing the first folder, I quickly review the ad copy. "It looks fine to me, so send it over to the client for a final proofing. What's next?" I ask.

Jason shows me two model photos and asks me which model I think would look best for the print ads for Ellen Peek lip gloss.

"Model two, I think. Her lips are plump and pouty but not fake looking. We're only photographing her lips, so the rest of her appearance is of no consequence."

We get through his stack of immediate issues before noon and I offer to buy him lunch from the cafeteria in the lobby.

"No, thanks," he says. "I have leftovers from my mom's birthday party. Any other time, though." He stacks his folders neatly in his arms and smiles softly at me. "Did you have the stomach flu yesterday?"

The Creative Director

"No. I thought it might be food poisoning. I'm good now, though."

"Shit. Well, I've had that before. Glad you're fine now," he says, then heads back to his desk.

I decide to stretch my legs and go for a walk since I don't have a lunch date. Yesterday it rained all day and today is bright and sunny, so I shouldn't waste the opportunity. The boardwalk near our office building is always a good place to stroll. After enjoying a small bowl of clam chowder at the deli, I notice an ice cream truck parked along the boardwalk. I'll take the spare change in my purse and put it to delicious use. While I'm standing in line I overhear a conversation between two younger women in the lineup behind me. I glance briefly at them and grin.

"If you two can't make it work, then don't force the issue," the frumpy one with hot pink sunglasses states. She's right. Forcing anything is often not the best solution.

"But there are times when pushing is worth it too," the redhead in jet black winged sunglasses argues. She is technically right as well.

"Just give up, Francis. He's not worth it. I've never seen a guy with so many issues in my life," the first one replies.

"Those aren't issues," Francis chides. "He's just eccentric."

I giggle at their conversation then tune out as my eyes roam over the crowded street. I'm looking to my left down the sidewalk when the ice cream vendor tries to catch my attention. "Miss. Are you ready to order?"

I stop my temporary daydreaming and re-enter the real world. "Sorry, yes. A double scoop of Neapolitan in a waffle cone, please," I say and smile. While my ice cream cone is being prepared I dig deep inside my purse for that spare change weighing down my bag, and a strong hand holds my wrist as its owner places a ten-dollar bill on the edge of the cashier's counter. I tip my head up from my purse to see that Anson is paying for my ice cream.

"Make that two orders of the Neapolitan, please," he says.

"What are you doing here?" I ask, surprised by his sudden presence.

"I was stalking you and thought it might be best if I let you in on my secret," he chuckles.

The Creative Director

"Stalking, hey? Is that what they teach you in military school?"

"Maybe. Or it could be we follow ice-cream trucks around New York City looking for infidels and spies." Anson smiles and passes me my cone from the vendor.

"And to what do I owe the pleasure of your stalking? Did I do something wrong?"

I take one long stroke of ice cream with my tongue and smile at the cool combination of three flavors delighting my taste buds while we walk toward an open bench.

"Yes, ma'am. You stopped returning my letters."

"Well, I lost my pen and one of the dogs in my uncle's veterinary clinic ate my notebook," I offer, trying to be lighthearted.

"Do you think I'm trying to be funny, Jess?" Anson asks.

"Why do you do that?" I sit down on the open bench and look up at him as he stands in front of me.

His brows furrow. "Do what?"

"You change your tone sometimes, and I can't tell if you're getting angry with me or not. It's a bit disconcerting."

"Did you talk to Bradley?" he asks, changing the subject.

"Brantley. And yes."

"How did the old chap take it?"

"Are you making fun of his English accent? That's kind of childish, Anson. We're not twenty anymore," I say, returning his frown.

"Sorry. I *was* trying to be funny, but I guess that was a cheap shot. So, how did Brantley take it?"

"The conversation was short, but then Brantley isn't into long sentences. He bowed out like a gentleman, somehow understanding what you and I are to each other. Honestly, I thought he'd put up a bit more of a fight." My heart breaks a little at that realization. Brantley was almost cold and calculating. Is it possible that I feel more for him than he does me? And, would Brantley have just ended up being another short-term relationship in my long history of two-week-long hookups that Anson so casually reminded me of the other night?

The Creative Director

Anson sits down beside me and rests a hand on my knee. "A gentleman, hey? You sound like you have a lot of respect for him."

"I do. And, he *is* a gentleman. He can also be quite the asshole when he wants to be, but once you get past his hard edges you find he's really quite sweet."

"Are you trying to make me like him? Because I won't," Anson says, and I frown again.

"You don't have to like him to appreciate what he gave up for you," I scold.

Anson thinks about that for a moment then nods. "Fine, I'll give him that."

"Why are you here?"

"I wanted to see you. I stopped at your office and they told me you were downstairs getting lunch. When I didn't see you there I was about to call you, then spotted you at the ice cream truck." Anson attempts to collect the melting ice cream dripping down the side of his cone while I smile at him. He always had a playful side to him that I adored and watching him lick his ice cream like a frantic child not wanting to miss a lick is amusing.

"Can you do me a favor?" I ask.

"Yes ma'am. Whatever you want."

"First, stop saying yes ma'am. I already have a hate-on for the army, and every time you say that to me it reminds me of why we broke up. Second, I need you to let me be for about a week."

Anson swallows a large section of the top of his ice cream and stares out toward the crowd passing along the boardwalk. "A week, hey. Why a week?"

"Because I need time to get over losing Brantley. I know that sounds crazy, but you have to remember that he and I weren't just lovers but we also work together. It's going to be hard for us to adjust."

"Can I inject a bit of wisdom here?" he asks as he tosses his unfinished cone into the waste container beside our bench.

"Sure, why not?" I say. I cross my legs while I fix my gaze upon Anson. He's not a stupid man and so I believe he's got something truly wise to share with me. He takes a deep breath before responding.

"You should quit working there and find a different place to do your ad agency business."

I nearly choke on the last bit of cone I had bitten off. I swallow hard and wipe the edge of my lips with my

The Creative Director

napkin. "I am not under any circumstances quitting a job I've worked my ass off to get. I've only been there just over four months, Anson!"

"Hear me out, please. I think that working beside Brantley after this would be too much for you to handle."

"I think what you are really saying is that it is too much for *you* to handle, Anson. I'm a professional. He's a professional. We don't let shit like this ruin our jobs." I'm pissed off now. Anson is pressing me to leave my job because he's worried I'll go back to Brantley. "Listen, Anson. Give me a week, will you? I'm not asking, I'm telling you. I need time to sort this situation out properly," I say. "You are the one who swooped in out of the blue, so you have to let me settle in at my pace."

Anson goes back to looking at the crowded boardwalk before he replies. "Okay, Jess." He leans forward and plants a worriedly passionate kiss on my lips. "I'll see you in a week," he says, then rises and walks away from me without a glance back. He stuffs his hands inside the pouch pocket of his hoodie and disappears down the staircase to the subway trains. I can't tell if my request pissed him off or not, but the point is moot. If he wants me to abandon a man I've fallen in love with to rekindle a love I thought was long gone, then he's going to have to play by my rules.

Sandra A. Sigfusson

Chapter 32: Unfinished Business

When I arrive back to my office I see a large bouquet of red roses set inside a stunning vase upon my desk. I have to assume they are from Anson, since I know he was at my office looking for me earlier. I'll forgive him his haste in wanting me to jump right in where we left off eight years ago if I'm getting flowers like this. I guess Army Boy still has a romantic bone in his big, hard, tattooed body.

The scent of roses has long been one of my favorites, and I can't stop myself from sticking my nose inside a few of the blooms and breathing deep. Roses have a calming effect on me. Nestled between two blooms I find the little envelope attached to the flowers and pull the card out to read it.

Please reconsider, Jess. You mean more to me than anyone ever has. Love, Brantley

I read the card for a second time, feeling shocked that the blooms are from Brantley. I'd assumed that our conversation about Anson's sudden reappearance, and

The Creative Director

Brantley's swift bow-out when he pressed me on who I was going to choose, was the end. Brantley doesn't hang on for anyone if he's been rejected – at least that is how I assumed this would go.

 I plunk my ass in my office chair and gaze at the beautiful blooms, tapping the notecard against my lips to ponder this situation while my chest begins its familiar ache. I know why Brantley chose the deep-red ones. This color is as much about love as it is about my red shoes. At that thought I smile. I pluck one of the blooms from the vase and give it to Carol for her to enjoy at her desk. She too is a fan of red roses.

 Trying to stay focused for the balance of the day proves to be more difficult than I imagined it would be. I sent Brantley a text to thank him for the beautiful roses but he didn't reply. I'm not sure what kind of reply I expected, but if he's busy in L.A. with his client then I shouldn't expect too much.

 At five o'clock, when everyone in the office is winding down and heading home, my phone pings with a text.

 Brantley: *I'm home this evening if you want to talk.*

 Me: *Carol said you'd be gone for three days. Did your plans change?*

Sandra A. Sigfusson

Brantley: *No. I thought it best to work from home.*

Me: *Is there anything here I can do for you?*

Brantley: *You can come back to me, Jess.*

I'm shocked that he wants to talk, even after his note in the roses demonstrated that he wasn't giving up on us as easily as I first thought. When he gave me the one-day ultimatum to decide who I wanted to share my bed with, I assumed that he wouldn't bend on the decision. This change of heart I never expected. Nor did I expect the roses. When I told Anson that I needed a week to get myself in order, I thought I was letting Brantley cool his heels and adjust to seeing me every day in the office after our breakup.

I don't know if I can handle having another face-to-face conversation with Brantley about us. If it were only business we were discussing, I'm certain we could be professional enough to muddle through it. But he's right. At the very least I owe him a longer conversation.

Me: *I can come by your place around seven.*

Once I've arrived home I change my clothes to something more comfortable. I have a pair of well-worn light blue jeans and a white linen casual button-up shirt that I love,

The Creative Director

which will help me feel comfortable in the summer's evening heat. Deciding to walk the eleven blocks to Brantley's place, I slip on my white tennis shoes. The weather is so great, and the walk will give me time to clear my head.

Approaching Brantley's building I find him sitting on the stairs with his elbows resting on his knees, his hands clasped together and his head tipped down. He too has donned a pair of jeans and a white t-shirt – a look I've not seen him in. I never picture Brantley in my mind as anything but naked or in a business suit, so this is completely new information for my brain.

I don't know if I should smile at him when I approach or keep my expression somber. When I'm just steps away from the stairs, he lifts his head and catches a glimpse of me, and a tentative smile eases over his lips. I cannot help but smile back. Brantley rises and descends the stairs to stand before me. Just then I wanted him to kiss me. God, how I wanted him to kiss me. Instead he takes my hand and pulls me to walk with him. I don't hesitate.

We walk the first block together at a leisurely pace, hand in hand, in silence. Brantley speaks first. "We are similar creatures, you and I," he says. His hand squeezes mine after those words. I nod but don't say anything. "My biggest issue with Anson is his sudden appearance and his impatient desire to have you dive straight back in on a relationship that, as I understand it, was eight years ago. Do you see where my mind is at, Jess?"

"Yes I do. And this is why I needed to discuss this with you. But you threw me an ultimatum with a ridiculously short time limit, and it left me wondering if you truly cared for me as much as Anson says he does. It's not that I don't understand you, because I do. I know you tend to deal with things quickly, abruptly sometimes, but with matters of the heart I'd have expected you to be a little less impulsive," I say.

My hand gets squeezed again while he mulls over my last comment.

"I don't think you realize how important you've become to me. Perhaps it wasn't until I saw you being kissed so passionately by another that the concept of losing you hit me so hard. Nobody has ever ripped at my heart that way before. I'll not deny I could have dealt with it better, but deep emotions such as those are not an everyday thing for me," he says. Brantley's eyes focus on the ground before us, and I don't know if it's because he can't look me in the eye or is just choosing not to for whatever reason. But then the words I'd never expected

The Creative Director

are spoken as his eyes lift to meet mine. "I'm in love with you, Jess."

The crowd along the sidewalk thickens, and we pause beside a tree to let the large group pass by. I'm dumbstruck by his confession. "How can you say that to me now?" I lean against the tree and close my eyes while I think about how powerful his last words are. Why did he have to pick now to tell me he's in love with me? I open my eyes, now glassy from trying not to lose my composure.

This situation is far more difficult than I anticipated. Taking in a deep breath, I say, "I understand you were upset over seeing him kiss me, but I also never expected to feel like a commodity to you. You gave me an ultimatum before I fully understood how deep your feelings for me were. It felt like a business deal – take it or leave it, because I won't offer you this again. If we're being honest with each other, your reaction to Anson made the decision easier for me, and it's why I questioned whether you cared for me as much as I do you. And with Anson, regardless of the years that have passed, we are unfinished business."

We don't continue our walk after the crowd thins. I want Brantley to look me in the eyes for the rest of this conversation. He nods in acceptance of how I perceived his initial reaction to Anson's sudden appearance in our lives. I was sure Brantley didn't feel the same for me as I do for him. Until the roses and his request to talk it over. And now he's admitted that he's in love with me.

When he realizes I'm not going to continue walking, his next question catches me by surprise. "Have you slept with him since his return?"

I can't help my reaction. This entire situation suddenly feels comical. I laugh but immediately regret it. His question is legit, and the only time I've felt the urge to make love with Anson since his reappearance was when I was drunk off my ass at his parents' house. *Should that mean something to me?*

"You think the question is funny?" Brantley asks as his brows knit together in frustration.

"No. I guess I was shocked by it. I haven't slept with Anson. I saw him earlier today and told him I needed a week apart from him to deal with how you and I were going to manage our work situation. Anson suggested that I quit and find work elsewhere, but I'm not willing to quit my job. I told him you and I are professionals and that we'd deal with it in that way. We can do this, right?" I ask.

The Creative Director

Brantley lets his fingers slip away from mine, then he stuffs his hands inside his jean pockets and stares out beyond me standing before him. He's mulling again, and I have to let him sort out what we've discussed. His analytical mind is wrestling with his heart, and I can see it in his face. That beautiful face. Both Brantley and Anson are handsome men, but in such different ways. Anson is rugged, broad-shouldered, heavy set and imposing in his stature. Brantley is fit, trim, tall and elegant, his features aristocratic in comparison to Anson's. These two could not be more opposite in every way. This makes me wonder why I'd fall for both of them when they are so remarkably different. Have my tastes in men changed? Have I grown out of Anson's good-old-boy appeal?

I intrude on Brantley's mulling with another question since he doesn't seem able to answer the last one. "Is the question of whether I've slept with Anson the one you needed answered most?" I ask. "If I were staying with you, would that have been an ultimate deal-breaker?"

His jaw tics. "No, but it would bother me to no end if you had. I could barely stand to see you kiss another, so how do you suppose the thought of you fucking him would make me feel?" he says, his words spoken with a jealous bite. Brantley's jaw tightens again. He puts one hand to his chin and scrubs the light growth of hair around his jaw while he looks down at the ground beneath us. I've never seen him so vulnerable. It's touching and makes my heart twist surprisingly hard. What have I done to this man? I'm back to questioning every decision I've made in the past twenty-four hours. For fuck's sake, he confessed to being in love with me.

I reach to touch Brantley's face but he clasps my wrist before I do, just inches from his chin. Holding my wrist firmly, the pressure nearing the edge of an angry hold, he stares deep into my eyes for a few beats before his lips find mine ready and willing to connect. The kiss is heartbreaking. He means to let me know that this is my last chance to change my mind, and to me this kiss is goodbye. I can't in all good conscience flip back and forth between them. I've made my decision and I have to be true to it, crushing as this incredibly testing moment is.

We release from the kiss and I attempt to speak, but Brantley has made it clear that no other words are going to soothe the situation. "I'll see you at the office, Jess," he says softly, then strides away from me. I turn to watch him walk away as my heart shatters inside of me. I feel so alone, so vulnerable standing in the middle of a New York sidewalk holding the cuff of my linen shirt to my nose as my chest heaves and my eyes well with a

The Creative Director

flood of tears. The question that repeats itself over and over in my head while Brantley fades into the distance is, "What have I done?"

Sandra A. Sigfusson

Chapter 33: Have I Lost My God-Damned Mind?

As confusing and wonderful as it was to be kissed so intensely in the middle of this busy New York street by Brantley, that moment and that conversation have solved nothing for me. I wanted this coming week to be a resolution to our affair. I knew that Brantley was a true professional who would manage his emotions, his work and his relationship with me, given a few days. I also believed that I could do the same, although a week would barely be enough for me to fully commit to that end.

Why did I want to make love to Brantley that afternoon? I'd given up just the day before on the thought of us being lovers. But I can't have it both ways, and I can't blow up Brantley's world without suffering some form of consequence. My punishment is my aching heart and the pain I have to acknowledge in Brantley's heart.

Instead of thinking Anson has more to offer me than Brantley, I know now that both of them have deep-seated love for me. The bigger question is, how is my current world going to work with Anson's? He's decided to leave the army and we can be together every day, but

The Creative Director

he's still an army man through and through. If the military ever needed him for anything he'd leave me in a heartbeat to defend his country. That was always my biggest fear with him, and I'm now reliving the moment when I decided that I couldn't be his wife. Now, just as before, the thought of losing him in war or even in a training accident stabs at me like a knife through my chest.

The week of absence from Anson passes more quickly than I anticipated. Few words are exchanged in the office between Brantley and myself, for obvious reasons. He seems to have the ability to set aside our relationship in a way I'm not capable of. Or perhaps he's simply a much better actor than I am.

While I'm sorting through piles of files, copy materials, phone message slips and model photographs, my cell phone rings. I drop my rummaging and answer the call with a briskness in my voice. "This is Jess."

"It's been a week, Jess. I need to see you," Anson says abruptly.

"Oh, Christ. Yes, it has," I say as I glance at my wall calendar. "Where did the time go?"

"Can I come to your place tonight? When are you finished at work?" he asks.

Sandra A. Sigfusson

"Yes. Fine. Say six o'clock?"

"Can I bring you dinner?" Anson asks.

I hesitate at his last question. I feel awkward talking to Anson while Brantley is a mere ten feet away from me. I feel like I'm cheating on my lover. This is so ridiculous. "Sure. Or we can order pizza or something, okay?" I ask. My mind is not clear, and at this point I'd agree to anything Anson said to end this phone call as quickly as possible.

"Yeah, that works for me. See you at six, babe."

Our conversation seemed strained. I'm guessing Anson is chomping at the bit to be with me completely, and perhaps he's nervous about us now that we've been apart for a week, fearing I've changed my mind. I'm certain that he'll not want to discuss Brantley on any level and that he'll likely want to make love.

My increased pace of breathing brought on by my sudden anxiety overcomes me. I reach for my coffee mug but it's empty. My eyes rise to where the coffee machine is, and I know that I have to walk past Brantley to refill my mug. I can't be any nearer to him than I am now. The scent of him will only bring on memories of how incredible he is in bed and how much I miss his touch.

The Creative Director

I opt to use the washroom instead. I can take a sip of water from the basin and collect myself behind a closed door before anyone else is the wiser about my sudden change in mood.

Jason enters the office just as I'm walking toward the washroom. I see him and raise my hand. "I'll just be a few minutes. I'll come to you when I'm done." Jason nods and retreats to his desk with his paperwork.

It doesn't take me long to relax once I've had a sip of water and reassured myself that I'm fine. There are still a few hours left for me to get some work done before I meet with Anson. But now, as I stand here gripping the edges of the pedestal basin looking at my reflection in the silver-trimmed mirror, I am reminded of the glorious sex Brantley and I shared in this very spot. *Fuck me!* I scream silently at myself. I'm going to have to use the main office bathroom for a while, as this room is simply too much of a reminder of Brantley hammering himself unabashedly into me while I came gloriously around him.

When I've returned to my desk I try not to look over to Brantley, but I can't help myself. I don't think he sees me watching him. *Is this what I truly want? To let go of this amazing man for one I've not been with for years. Have I lost my goddamned mind?*

Sandra A. Sigfusson

I haven't talked to Karmyn about all of this because she'd be completely Camp Anson. I can't expect her to comprehend how much Brantley means to me when she knows my history with Anson like it were her own. We are about to rekindle what Anson and I had – the crazy beautiful love we shared that brought us to the point of deciding to marry all those years ago. And I'm sure Karmyn will be beside herself with happiness for us both.

When Anson arrives to my apartment he's all hands and lips. I don't fight him on it, as I know he's been waiting patiently for this moment to have me all to himself. We kiss deeply at the front door. He hasn't removed his shoes or his hoodie before we find ourselves making out like teenagers on my couch. Our make-out session lasts for close to fifteen minutes, and it surprises me that I'm not completely naked and being made love to by Anson at this point. We stop briefly to collect ourselves. Anson's smile is huge as we adjust our clothes and begin to talk about what to order for dinner. Is it strange that I am feeling like a teenager, or does Anson bring out that side of me?

The Creative Director

Anson pulls out his phone to call for pizza delivery. While he's busy ordering food I go to my fridge to bring out his favorite beer and pour myself a glass of wine. We sit next to each other on the couch again, with my hair disheveled after our attempt to suck each other's faces off. I smile and then break out in a fit of laughter. Anson joins in and a blush covers his face in the sweetest way. My big army man is blushing and it's adorable.

"How long before the pizza arrives?" I ask.

"Forty minutes, they said. That is just enough time to show you how much I've missed you this week," he says matter-of-factly.

We fall into each other's arms again. Another hard kiss crushes my lips, and then I'm lifted like a feather in his arms and taken to my bedroom.

Anson pulls away quickly at my clothes, and before I know it I'm standing completely bare before him. He wrestles with his own clothes to disrobe just as quickly. A chill surrounds me and I don't know if it's excitement or if the room is actually cold. The tattoos that I caught a glimpse of last week on his arms are now on full display, and my eyes roam the patterns and letters inked so boldly on his massive biceps and forearms.

My fingers trace one of the more ornate images. It appears to be roses intertwined with numbers in some sort of heavy gothic font. "Do you like my tattoos?" he asks softly.

"I don't know. I've never seen you with ink, and I'm trying to sort out what some of these images mean to you." Anson pulls me into his chest and a line of kisses follows the column of my neck. The tattoo I was touching a second ago is staring me in my face as my cheek is flush against his chest in our embrace. I finally figure out what the numbers mean, and I lean back away from him to look up into his eyes. "Is that my birthdate?" I ask, shocked at what I'm seeing.

"Yes," he says, then kisses my forehead.

My voice cracks as I question him about it. "Why would you have my birthday numbers tattooed on your body, Anson? We haven't been a couple for eight years!"

"When we broke off our engagement I was devastated. That was an argument and a moment in our history that I'd never want to repeat. A week later me and a couple of buddies had a few too many beers before we ended up at the tattoo parlor I frequent. Anyway, I had the artist add your birthdate there, then a few days later I had him try to cover it up with a flourish pattern that he could build upon later."

The Creative Director

"Wow. That's kind of crazy, don't you think?" I ask, still dumbstruck by what I'm seeing. "As a psychologist, what would you say to yourself after doing this?"

Anson chuckles, smiles wide and kisses my head again. "I'd have kicked myself in the ass. The next day I realized how stupid it was, no offence. I knew what the numbers represented, but you're the only one who has seen the numbers intertwined in the flourish and knows my secret. That makes me happy," he says and chuckles lightly.

Anson picks me up again and lays me on the bed. He's as strong as an ox and built nearly the same as one. I know what to expect next as the memories of all the times we've made love in the past come rushing back to me. Sex for us was never a gentle affair, as we seemed to bring out the animal in each other. Anson does everything hard and fast, which is why I never doubted that he'd be so well suited for the army, as much as I hated to admit it. But there are glimmers of tenderness now that weren't there when we were younger, and I'm liking this new mature side of him.

Our eyes meet and a slow, beautiful smile fills his face. I smile back at him, and then his mouth is kissing mine with deep desire behind every move of his lips and tongue. My center stands at full attention now. He's got me right where he wants me – aroused, impatient, ready to reconnect with this powerful man again for the first time in a very long time. And holy hell, how could I have forgotten how impressive his cock is?

My hand reaches for him, and oddly I briefly compare the sensation of Anson's cock in my palm to Brantley's. What the hell is wrong with me? I've made my bed and now I'm literally lying in it with the man I chose to spend my time with, to devote my life to. I can't be comparing Anson to anyone, least of all the very man I gave up for him.

Guilt must have slipped in, as the next words to come out of my mouth shock me. "I need you to fuck me hard, Anson," I say.

"When did you get so bossy, baby?" he murmurs in my ear. A wolfish grin rides the edges of his lips and he chuckles at me. "Don't let me stop you from taking command. If you want it hard I'll give you hard," he says.

Anson leans back on his knees as he straddles me and holds his ridiculously big cock firmly in his hand. "Tell me how much you've missed this, Jess," he says in a deep tone. "Because I've fucking missed you," he adds.

The Creative Director

It is all coming back to me now in a flash flood of memories. "I shouldn't have to tell you, Anson. You should know that I missed you. I wouldn't be here with you if I didn't," I reply. "I want you inside of me and I want you to take me like you own me," I say and stare hard into his eyes.

Anson pumps his fist rapidly over his shaft a few times then leans over my body to insert his primed cock deep within me. His moans echo through my room and inside my head. I thrust my hips high to encourage him to go hard with me. I feel like I need to be punished for something. I'm suddenly angry with myself, and I've never been so mad that I just wanted someone to fuck me hard, ridding me of my bad thoughts or bad behavior. But I do now. I don't deserve the pleasure – only the pain.

I focus my attention on Anson's face while trying to forgive myself. My hands find their way around his body, sweeping over deeply defined muscles, inked skin, his smooth-as-a-baby's-ass chest and the ripples of his abdomen. He's gorgeous. He's more beautiful than I remember – more defined, more mature, more of a man in the same way that I am more of a woman now.

We continue to punish each other with heavy thrusts, grunting and sweating our way through our first lovemaking in so long. My climax threatens to reach before his does, and my guilt over how badly I feel for

Sandra A. Sigfusson

Brantley surfs on the wave of my orgasm's arrival. I don't deserve to be satisfied by an orgasm. My heart clenches in a mix of pleasure and heartbreak.

"I'm close," I say before I grunt in Anson's ear again as his next thrust pushes me closer to the edge.

"I'm right there with you, babe," he says and moans loudly as his punishing pounding reaches its peak and he comes hard through heavy breaths. I shudder beneath him, exhausted. I want to cry now, but I choke back hard on my emotions and force a smile while my fingernails rake through his short-cropped hair.

"That was awesome, baby," he breathes over my lips, placing a chaste kiss on them.

I nod and force a smile. "Yeah, amazing," I say softly while I catch my own breath.

Anson collapses beside me on my bed and I'm once again choking back my intense desire to cry. I'm not over losing Brantley, and I'm questioning everything about my decision to be with Anson again. I think I need to see a therapist, and the ironic situation of fucking one while needing one is laughable. What did I expect of myself? Did I really believe I could just flip a switch and be perfectly fine making love to another man only days

The Creative Director

after letting Brantley go, without feeling like I've betrayed him? And I feel betrayed, too. I betrayed myself in that I know I have a better moral code than this. One week apart from Anson to settle in my head that I was doing the right thing wasn't enough time. I'm not a robot. And I'm not as ready to commit to Anson as I thought I was. This scares the living shit out of me.

I try to shake the feelings I'm having out of my system. This is not the time or the place to be beating myself up over the turn of events this past week. And yet I have nobody to blame but myself. "Are you happy?" I ask.

"Yes! I couldn't be any fucking happier than I am now," he says. Anson rolls over to his side, nesting his head into the crux of his bulging, inked bicep to gaze at me. "Are you happy?"

I nod, mustering the best version of a smile I can. "Yes. It's great to have you here in my bed with me again. I'd never imagined us together like this, knowing that our lives had gone in such opposite directions."

Anson's hand cups my cheek and a sweet kiss is placed upon my lips. This is a tenderness I never saw in him when we were younger. This is maturity that has come from his experience with other women. I can't help but appreciate this new side to him. "We have a new and

Sandra A. Sigfusson

improved version of ourselves to explore," he says, then rolls over to lie flat on his back, closing his eyes.

I rise from the bed, draping the top sheet loosely around me as I head to the bathroom. As I drag the length of sheet behind me through the bathroom door, I look back at Anson who has his eyes closed, his left arm above his head. He is spent.

"The pizza should be here soon," I say. "Maybe we should get dressed and set the table."

"Sure, baby," he responds without opening his eyes.

Dropping the bedsheet at my feet, I heave forward toward the basin with the urge to throw up. I'm making myself sick again with my heavy, whirling emotions controlling me. I can't let myself get overwhelmed now. *"I'm with Anson. I'm with Anson, I'm with Anson,"* I say repeatedly in a whisper, hoping my chant will relax me.

My stomach settles as I begin to slowly calm down. I can hear through the bathroom door that Anson is putting his clothes back on. The clicking of his belt buckle and the sound of his heavy footsteps fading away from the bedroom let me know he's waiting for me to re-dress and join him.

The Creative Director

Sucking in a deep calming breath, I go back to the task of cleaning myself up. I freshen my makeup and then gather the bedsheet up off the bathroom floor. "You've had your emotional breakdown now, and it's over," I say quietly to myself. "Get in there and pick up on your relationship like we've never been apart." Just then, the doorbell rings.

Sandra A. Sigfusson

Chapter 34 – Brantley: Lace Knickers

This is pure madness but I have nobody but myself to blame. Shagging a woman I work with was always on my absolute Do Not Do list. At the moment I don't know who I'm more angry with – myself or Jess. Our indiscretion at the hotel room should never have amounted to a relationship, least of all love. I told myself she'd be the death of me, and now that day has arrived.

I've walked so far that the sun is about to set and my feet ache. I raise my hand in the air to hail a taxi, knowing that wandering aimlessly for this past hour has taken me too far to walk back. Once I've slipped inside the taxi that stopped for me I'm immediately reminded of the first time Jess and I rode in a taxi together. She was angry with me and rightly so. Yet I did very much enjoy toying with her from the get-go.

I now realize why I walked as far as I did. Had I not I'd have returned to my flat and torn the entire place apart like a child in a tantrum. I swear she brings out the best and the worst in me. Damned woman. Yet, I do adore her taking the piss out of me. Most people,

The Creative Director

particularly women, run and hide from my sharp tongue and rather demanding nature, but not Jess.

"Where to?" the taxi driver asks.

"1132 Trillium Street, please," I say. The taxi lurches forward to enter the flow of traffic while I try to recall if I've even got my wallet with me. I pat around my body and confirm it's in the back pocket of my jeans, then turn my gaze back outside the smudged window, wondering what the hell I'm going to do now with my life. But here is the funny thing: my life was perfectly fine without a love interest, so why do I suddenly feel like I've lost all direction?

I don't recall ever losing a woman to another man. I've never been knocked to the curb. I'm the one who sends them off when I've grown tired of the relationship. "Bugger," I mutter, and the driver stares at me in the rearview mirror. "Not you," I say apologetically.

I may as well have fallen asleep, as I don't recall the last twenty minutes of the drive home. Pulling my wallet out of my back pocket, I hand the driver the first bill I retrieve from it and let him keep the change.

Entering my flat I can't say what feels more vacant – my heart or my head. Trying to keep myself occupied, I attempt to straighten up the bedroom and find a pair of Jess's lace knickers beneath the bedframe. It

Sandra A. Sigfusson

seems ironic, considering I always reminded her to never wear them when she came to see me. Bloody hell. Standing here holding her knickers in my hand, wanting desperately to smell them, makes me wonder how I'm possibly going to handle working with her.

The soft silky fibers slip easily between my fingers as I raise the pale pink garment up to my nose. Her scent is intoxicating and I find myself getting hard from the smell of her sweet pussy, striking down my resolve to be strong. "I can't do this," I say aloud, shaking my head. "I cannot continue to torture myself like this." But I do. I take one long inhale while I unbuckle my belt, dropping my denims where I stand. My rigid cock fills my right hand as I hold the delicate lace garment between my teeth and begin to stroke myself hard and fast. As frustration, desire, anger and pleasure race through my blood vessels, my orgasm scorches through me in record time. This is the last time I'll let her control me.

The smart thing to do now is to put her knickers in an envelope and leave them inside her desk drawer. Out of spite I want to rub my ejaculate all over them before I return them, but it isn't Jess that I despise in this instant – it's Anson.

The Creative Director

I'll return to the office tomorrow, a day earlier than I am expected. I'll not run away from the problem I created. And if I manage to get an hour's worth of sleep tonight that would be brilliant, but I doubt it's possible.

The morning arrives as quickly as I predicted and I feel like shite. The mirror before me reflects the dead tired loser I've become. I decide not to bother shaving. I'll grow a bit of stubble for a few days and see where that takes me. Is change really as good as a rest? Only time will tell.

I'm arriving later than I typically do, and Carol is surprised to see me at all since I lied to her about my three-day trip to L.A.

"Were you not supposed to be back in tomorrow?" she asks.

"It is tomorrow," I say, attempting to confuse her, but she knows me too well to fall for my redirect. "Tomorrow is yesterday's today," I say as I pass through my office door.

"Today is yesterday's tomorrow," she calls back.

Jess is seated at her desk, eyes glued to her laptop screen. She is as acutely aware of my presence as I am of hers, and I wrestle with the idea of politely saying good morning in order to cut the tension. I remind myself to suck it up and be kind. I'm the one who couldn't get her out of my head after our hotel sex night then pressured Jess into having another shag in the office loo. She did not instigate. I cannot blame her for what became of us. "Good morning, Jess," I say quietly. I keep my back turned to her as I locate a clean mug to make a cup of coffee.

"Good morning, Brantley," she says, with a tentative smile. "Did you not already have your morning specialty coffee in your hand from the shop downstairs when you came in?" she asks.

"Shit, yes. I don't know where my mind is this morning." The specialty latte coffee I purchased before coming upstairs is on the counter directly beside me as I attempt to make another cup with the office coffee machine. Perhaps I shouldn't have come in today either.

"I'll take the coffee you just made," she says.

I nod and take my latte with me to my desk then flip open my laptop. "Right. Is there anything that went on here in the past few days that I need to know about?" I ask.

"No. Anything that popped up was dealt with by either myself or Jason," she says.

The Creative Director

Jess rises from her chair and approaches me to retrieve the fresh cup of coffee from the machine. My eyes close as she passes behind me. Then I'm reminded of the envelope with her panties sealed inside stashed somewhere in my briefcase. I'll need to insert it in her desk drawer while she's in the loo or away from her desk. Briefly, I ask myself if I do want to return them, but I have to rid my flat of anything that might remind me of her when I'm home.

As Jess stirs a bit of cream into her coffee mug, she asks me a question that had not crossed my mind since we ended our affair. "Are you still interested in helping me with the Beaumont Winery situation, or would it be too difficult for you to participate now?" she asks softly, hesitantly. "I'll understand if you've changed your mind."

"If you need help with something, then I'm not opposed to assisting, however I'd rather leave the bulk of the task in your hands," I say, trying not to be too sharp with my tone. "I think what we decided on for an approach is solid. It's now just a matter of you executing those ideas," I add.

"Okay, thanks," she says, then returns to her desk.

The remainder of the morning passes predominantly in silence. I'm certain she feels as awkward as I do, all things considered. When Jason approaches me after his lunch break, I find I'm still my regular self, the cutting asshole who treats others as though they are lesser creatures than I. This has to change.

"Jason. I've made a decision to try to be less hasty with the staff. If you catch me being, you know, me, please use a single word to remind me I've stepped over the line."

Jason's stare at me is of pure shock. "Sure," he says, appearing a bit nervous. "What word do you want me to use?"

I see Jess's eyes rise away from her laptop screen and focus on me. "What word comes to your mind first when I inadvertently insult you?" I ask.

Jason laughs nervously and straightens his already-stellar posture. "Do you really want to know or is this a rhetorical question?"

I can't help but laugh. "Not rhetorical, Jason. Be serious with me," I urge.

Jason starts counting off his list of options on his fingertips, with his left palm open as he pulls down on

The Creative Director

each digit in sequence. "Asshole, prick, ball-basher, fucking asshole," he says laughing, then covers his mouth trying to stay his outburst. Jess breaks out in a fit of those lovely giggles of hers, and I raise my hand while nodding my head up and down in acceptance and agreement.

"Right, well, you can probably stop there. Only one word is necessary," I chuckle. "Let's stick with prick and if you feel like I've stepped over the line you are welcome to use it on me, but only loud enough for me to hear."

"Wow," Jason says, his eyes wide at my comment. "This is like Christmas came early!"

Jess continues to giggle uncontrollably, and her laughter hits me right where I hurt the most – in my chest where my broken heart resides.

"Okay, enough fucking around. Shall we all go back to doing business?" I chirp.

Jason nods, and says, "Prick," under his breath as he exits our office.

Sandra A. Sigfusson

Chapter 35: La Famille

The deep connection between Anson and I builds as the following days pass. I don't think either of us realized how much has gone on in our lives in eight years. Sitting on the back patio by the pool at George and Gabrielle's house, Anson and I talk endlessly about his army buddies and the bullshit stuff they've pulled when on leave. He admitted to having a bit of an unexpected baby scare from one of his short-lived girlfriends, and I was shocked to hear him tell the story.

"Did she miscarry?" I ask.

"No. She lied about the pregnancy to get me to go back with her. I dodged a bullet with that one," he says. "I've done a lot of really fucked-up stupid shit in the last little while." I watch his face while he tells me his stories, and I can see that most of it, he regrets. "Guys who don't have girlfriends can be real assholes, you know?"

"You have a wild side, Anson. You always have," I muse. I rise from my chair and sit my bum between Anson's legs on the lounger. I lean back onto his chest and relish his big inked arms wrapping around my frame.

The Creative Director

"We can be wild together now," he whispers in my ear.

I smile wide and giggle. "Okay. You lead and I'll follow, just like we used to," I say.

Gabrielle comes outside with another fresh beer for Anson and a chilled glass of white wine for me. "You don't have to bring us our drinks, Gabrielle," I say. "We're perfectly capable of serving ourselves."

"I know, Jess. You look so comfortable and seeing you two together again is the best thing to happen since the fire," she says. I nod. I'm happy she and George are happy for us.

Since Anson has to head back to the base at the end of this week, I've agreed to sleep here at the Beaumonts' guest house until his departure. The love we've made to each other nearly every night this week cements my decision to be with him. And my long-standing feelings for him have never truly faded. He's not the kind of lover Brantley is, and few men in my life have come close, but we have plenty of time to refine it.

On our last evening together, we've retired to the guest house and crawled into the bed to cuddle.

"Babe, how am I supposed to leave you after this?" he asks.

Sandra A. Sigfusson

I prop myself up on my elbow beside him and smooth my hand over his bare chest. "I don't know, Anson. It's going to be tough on both of us, but I think your body knows how to show me what I'll be missing," I say as a cheeky smile eases over my lips. "And all I can say is that staying in the guest house with you is a relief, considering how loud you are when you make love to me," I tease.

"Ha, that's funny, Jess. I think you're the one who needs to have a sock put in your mouth when you come," he says, laughing at me.

I walk my fingers up the center of his chest to the edges of his lips, then slip my fingers inside his mouth. "Are you going to make me scream your name again?"

He bites my fingers and then sucks hard on them.

"Ouch!" I say and giggle. "I want you to be sucking something other than my fingers," I murmur.

"Oh, yeah? And what would that be?" he murmurs back.

"I think we can both get what we want at the same time. I thought sixty-nine was your favorite number?"

The Creative Director

"Oh, yes it is, babe. Yes. It. Is."

Anson and I will be separated for a few weeks before I can see him again. I've made plans to fly out to his base for a long weekend next month.

We drive to the airport holding hands and chatting about the future. After our goodbye kisses and hugs, I get a sense of relief that he's gone. We've been smothering each other a little bit for the past week, trying so hard to catch up on our respective lives. When we see each other again it won't be as intense a time. We will be more relaxed and focused on our future together. Which makes me wonder if he still has the engagement ring I returned to him?

When I arrive to my apartment I realize how much I missed my own space. I only returned here once in the past week to pick up clothes to wear to the office. Anson gave me one of his army duffle bags to put my dirty laundry in, and as I unload my clothes I find a letter tucked inside the bag. Anson has written me a note, and I smile as I open the envelope to read it.

Babe,

These past days with you back in my arms have been a dream come true. I don't think

Sandra A. Sigfusson

you realize how long I've waited to kiss you and make love to you again. It was a leap of faith that returning home to help Mom and Dad after the fire would result in you coming back to me. Behave yourself while I'm gone. Miss you already. Love Anson.

So, Mr. Tough Guy still likes to write me love letters. I shake my head and smile wide. I wonder if his army buddies know how much of a pussy Anson really is when it comes to women. I also wonder who else Anson might have written love letters to, or if I'm the only one he's ever done this for. I did notice that his handwriting has improved, although only slightly. Instead of putting his most recent letter in the shoebox still sitting on my dresser, I opt to place it in the drawer of my side table.

I relax while my laundry is being washed, deciding to retrieve the book I attempted to start before the news of the fire interrupted my whole life. That fire turned everything upside down in more ways than one.

I have my cell phone beside me on the coffee table while I get comfortable on my couch to start reading. I read the first few chapters then look over at the phone. I read a few more pages then glance at my phone

The Creative Director

again. "Why am I concerned about my phone?" I mutter to myself.

I guess I'm so used to seeing texts from Brantley that I've become a bit lost without his messages. I should text Anson to find out if his plane has landed and he's back on base. My thoughts about Anson override my desire to keep reading or messaging with Brantley.

Me: *Did you make to base safely?*

A reply from Anson doesn't come immediately. The washing machine stops running and that is my cue to switch the garments over to the dryer. While I'm setting the dryer to sixty minutes' drying time I hear my phone ping from the living room.

Anson: *I arrived fine. I feel lost without you. Did you get my letter?*

Me: *I miss you too and I did read your sweet letter. Thank you.*

Anson: *It's going to be a tough few weeks thinking about you every night from the bottom half of the country.*

Me: *You'll be fine. I'll be fine. Make it up to me when I see you next month.*

Anson: *Roger that, Babe. I'll call you tomorrow.*

Sandra A. Sigfusson

Me: *Good night, Anson. xxx*

The following night Anson and I are able to have a long phone conversation. He's concerned that I'll not be able to keep my promise to work with Brantley and not fall back into his arms in his absence.

"Anson, you have to understand something," I plead.

"Understand what, Jess? I'm frustrated not knowing if I'm going to lose you again. Being apart from you now that I have you back in my life is stressing me out."

"I get that, Anson. But Brantley and I never intended to become lovers. We work together. It was a drunken business trip and we were both lonely when it all started. One thing led to another and we found comfort in each other. We both knew there were risks associated with us working together and dating. And in that, we now understand how irresponsible it was for us to date a colleague. Do you see that?" I ask.

I can almost hear the wheels spinning in Anson's head throughout our phone connection. He's a jealous

The Creative Director

guy and headstrong, just like Brantley is. But I can't make him less worried about me working with Brantley after all that he and I have been through. There is no winning here, but this is the place we're in, and we'll have to figure it out as we go along. "Answer me," I say softly.

"You have to quit working there, Jess. It is the only way I'm going to feel okay with you when we are apart."

I hear the tension in his voice. His words are tearing away at my insides, but I have to stay firm in my belief that I can set Brantley aside on a romantic level, do my job and move on with my life in Anson's arms and only his arms.

"I want to believe you, Jess. I really do. Please think about it, will you, babe? Just think about it," he says.

I nod even though I know he can't see me. "I should get some sleep. I've got a busy day ahead of me tomorrow, and I'm presenting the financials to a potential investor for the winery at one o'clock."

I hear his deep breaths across the distance between us. "Okay, Jess. Sleep tight and I'll call you tomorrow."

Sandra A. Sigfusson

"Sure, Anson. I'll fill you in on how the meeting went tomorrow night, okay? Love you." I say before hanging up.

Chapter 36: Knickers, Part Two

I have a one o'clock meeting with Geoffrey Cardiff, a potential investor for the Beaumont winery. He has several interests in the wine industry, which is why Brantley approached him to invest in replanting the Beaumont vineyard. Since he's a contact of Brantley's who knew he and I were dating, I don't broach the subject of Brantley and I parting ways on a personal level, as I'm nervous that might sway Geoffrey to rethink his interests. As petty as that sounds, I don't know this man well enough to understand if something of that nature would sway him one way or the other. Geoffrey wants to invest two million, and I couldn't be happier to shake the man's hand when the meeting is over.

Returning to my office I find my email inbox bursting at the seams. I get straight into answering as many as I can, forgoing a fresh coffee or one of the lovely oatmeal-cranberry muffins Carol brought to the office. As I rummage through my desk drawers looking for a stick of gum or a candy, I see an envelope with my name on it in Brantley's handwriting.

As I pull the envelope out of the drawer, my brows knit and I wonder how long it was sitting there before I noticed it. I tear away at the top corner wondering what would be so bulky inside and realize it is a pair of my panties. "Shit!" I say loudly, then stuff the panties back inside the envelope and shove it inside my drawer.

I text Brantley since he's out at a meeting: *Why would you bring my panties back to me in the office?*

He responds quicker than I expected.

Brantley: *Because they belong to you. I don't imagine you'll be going commando anymore.*

Me: *Do you think this is funny?*

Brantley: *Not in the least, Jess. Would you rather I'd tossed them in the bin?*

Me: *No, I guess not. But what if Jason found them in my desk while looking for something?*

Brantley: *He'd likely have been as aroused as I was. Is that all? I'm busy.*

I don't bother replying. I mutter to myself, "He'd likely have been as aroused as I was," in my bad English accent. "Prick," I mutter further while retrieving the panties and stuffing them inside my purse.

The Creative Director

Chapter 37: The Rift

As I talk to Anson daily at his post in Texas, his anxiety over my workplace situation continues to be a bone of contention. Thus far Brantley and I have been able to be perfectly respectable of each other in our business dealings. We occasionally catch each other with a glimpse across the room and quick, courteous grins flash between us.

I know Brantley is hurting as much as I am. He's different in the office now – obvious in his attempts to keep as much physical distance as possible between us. But knowing why he can't be near me tugs at me, as I enjoy and desire his company even without the physical contact.

I'm thankful our clients' Christmas campaigns are coming along as planned. I've coordinated with Brantley on a few of the clients in my portfolio because he knows them much better than I do. I'll have to follow his lead when the Christmas season is over and track the sales records in January for the accounts I manage. And, I'm happy to be busy so that my focus isn't on how much I miss Brantley as a friend.

Sandra A. Sigfusson

The only luncheon we've been on together was at the invitation of Grady, to celebrate Brantley's birthday. It's what Grady does for all his executive staff, and he'll do the same when my birthday arrives in mid-December. I expected our luncheon to be awkward since Grady never knew Brantley and I were previously dating, and we pulled through by focusing all of our attention on Grady's conversations. Another Academy Award for my acting skills is on its way.

By the time two weeks has passed since Anson left for Houston, I've secured three million dollars of investment money for the Beaumont winery replanting project. The other million George projected in his budget will have to be borrowed against the land value to cover operating costs for the next four years. George will keep the staff down to a bare minimum and remain on-site daily to personally oversee the growth of new plantings.

As I'm sitting at home in my kitchen waiting for my kettle to boil for a cup of tea, my phone rings and I'm happy to see it's Anson calling. But a frustrated sigh begins the conversation. Tonight's phone call with Anson quickly becomes more of an argument than a healthy chat between long-distance lovers.

The Creative Director

"Jess, I need you to come out here to see me. Fake a meeting with a potential client or something and get your ass down here," he says.

"Well, hello to you too," I say.

"Sorry, Babe. Hello, and I miss you. Please come out to Texas for me this weekend," he asks softly.

"And, who do you suppose is going to believe I'm entertaining a client from Texas for Digame in New York?" I ask.

"Fuck. I don't know. There has to be a client in your company that has a branch office in Texas somewhere."

"There is, but that's Brantley's client, not mine," I reply, being short with Anson.

"Take an extra day off then. Make it a three-day weekend. Work with me here, Jess." I can hear how frustrated Anson is, but taking off now while things at work are so busy isn't possible.

"Anson, I've been working Saturdays just to keep up with my current client demands. I want to see you. You know I do, but the time isn't right. Please stop pressuring me. I feel like all the guilt of you working in

Sandra A. Sigfusson

Texas is on me. It shouldn't be, and it's not fair that you make me feel that way," I say.

"What isn't fair is you still working side by side with your ex in the same office, while I have no idea what is going on over there," he charges. My back gets up instantly. We've rehashed this issue twenty times by now. I want to say *fuck you* and hang up on him, but that won't solve anything. And it sounds to me like he's had a few beers before calling me.

I lose my cool but attempt not to shout through my phone. "You know what else isn't fair?" I ask, then answer without waiting for his reply. "It isn't fair that you've disrupted my perfectly good life by dropping out of the sky. We were over eight years ago, Anson. If you can't deal with how my life is now, then this is never going to work. We are back to square one. Is this what you want? To piss me off so much that I walk away, again?"

"NO! God, no, Jess," he yells back.

The shocking silence after our shouting match is broken only by my tears. I'm under so much stress at work, and with my constant guilt at being in the same room as Brantley every day – pretending that I don't love

The Creative Director

him anymore – and my frustrations at trying to appease Anson, things have come to a head. My phone slowly slips from my hand, dropping to the shag carpet area rug at my feet in my living room, and I succumb to my physical and mental exhaustion by breaking down and sobbing uncontrollably. Maybe Anson is right. I may have to quit working at Digame.

From below me I can hear the faint words of Anson. He's trying to soothe me and he can't. Not from Texas. I need him here and he needs me there. And now we're screaming at each other like children fighting over the same toy. "Dammit," I yell across the room.

Collecting myself and rubbing the tears off my cheek with my sleeve, I retrieve my phone from the floor. My breath hitches while I calm down and I can hear Anson swearing and talking to himself in the background. "Please, don't let her do this to me again," he begs. I'm guessing he's looking up at the ceiling and addressing whatever higher power may be listening. But I know his prayers are not going to be answered tonight.

"Anson. Anson can you hear me?" I ask loudly.

A heavy sigh replies back to me. "Yes, babe. I'm here. I'm not going anywhere and neither are you. I can't fucking handle you not being near me. And I've tried so hard, but I'm struggling to deal with the thought of you working there with your ex. This is seriously fucking with my head, Jess." Another heavy sigh comes, then he speaks to me again. "Please call the ad agencies in Houston that I noted down for you in my last email. You are a fantastic marketing specialist and they'd all be thankful to have someone like you on board."

I shake my head. "I'm at the top of my game here in New York, Anson. Do you have any idea how hard it is for a woman to get in the door at my level? Nobody in Houston knows who I am, and if I leave a Creative Director position within six months of starting at Digame I'm going to look like a complete flake. I can't risk it, Anson. I've worked too hard to be where I am today."

Collapsing on the couch and holding back another outburst of tears, I realize there is no middle ground with us. I calm down again and speak softly. "You said you were leaving the army to start your own practice, Anson. In my mind that meant you were coming here to New York, not me coming to Texas. If for one minute I thought otherwise I'd have never agreed to start a relationship with you again."

A long silence passes before he replies. "I know. But doing that fucks up my situation here."

The Creative Director

This is new information. I sit up and furrow my brow. "How?"

"Because it's been recommended that I stay here and set up my practice in Houston. I've already been counseling ten patients who I've made great progress with, and leaving them in the hands of someone else may set them back by weeks, even months. You don't understand how messed up some of these soldiers are from their experiences. Anything that changes with them, especially a sudden change in who they're getting treatment from, could be catastrophic to their already-fragile mental states. This is what I'm dealing with, Jess," he says emphatically.

My heart breaks in a thousand pieces. That's it, then. We're done. I stand, pace the living room and throw my arm up in the air in exasperation. There is no way in hell I'm stepping back in my career for anyone. He can't just swoop in like an eagle on gilded wings of love and devotion, pluck me from the ground and take my heart with him. How did I let this happen? How fucking stupid am I to let my heart lead my head after all I've worked for to get where I am?

Then an idea hits me that might solve the problem of our mutual bull-headedness. "Could you not work with a new psychologist in tandem with yourself for a few weeks with your existing clients, and ease them in on getting used to the new doctor?" I ask. I cross my fingers on my free hand and close my eyes. This is the only solution I can come up with. I stop pacing while I wait for his reply.

"Jess, I know what you're thinking, but there aren't that many military staff like me trained specifically to deal with army veterans suffering from PTSD in the Houston area. It could take months to find the right person to hand over my patients to. That's just adding more time away from you."

I don't know what comes over me, but I acquiesce a little for him. "I'll make you a deal then. I'll entertain talking to the ad agencies in Houston if you'll entertain looking for a replacement doctor for your patients. If we both try, then neither of us can lose. Do you agree?" I ask, my voice anxious to hear his favorable reply. I can't believe I'm caving to him, but I'm going to wager it will be easier for him to find a replacement doctor than it will be for me to find an ad agency in Houston who's willing to take me on.

"Is that your Creative Director solution?" he chuckles. "It's not half bad, actually," he says, sounding surprised.

The Creative Director

"I'm going to assume you meant that as a compliment, army boy."

"Sergeant Beaumont to you," he teases, and I can't help but laugh.

"Sergeant pain in my ass," I say and Anson chuckles loudly at me.

"That I am. That I am, babe."

Chapter 38: The Mishap

I am dumbstruck by the first question Brantley asks me the next morning. No hello or good morning – just this one question the leaves me dead in the water for an answer.

"Has he asked you to marry him?"

I raise my head from my laptop, my blank stare lingering on Brantley's beautiful face. His cologne which drives me to distraction hangs in the air from when he passed my desk a minute earlier to reach his. I reply with a question: "Why do you ask?"

Brantley sets his morning specialty latte on his desk. As he opens up his laptop his answer comes. "I know the reason he wanted to get back together with you is partly because you two were once engaged. With that thought in mind, I expected you'd have his ring upon your finger by now, but I've not noticed you wearing one."

I nod in understanding. "We're dealing with a logistics issue. He wants me to move to Texas where his current PTSD patients are, and I don't want to leave New

The Creative Director

York or my position here at Digame." Shit! I let it slip that I might be leaving Digame. How could I have planted that seed without catching myself?

"That sounds more like a stalemate than a logistics problem," Brantley says under his breath, but I hear him regardless.

I can only hope Brantley didn't pick up on my possibly-leaving thing. I'm so mad at myself now. Just then Jason enters our office, smiling like he's the cat that swallowed the canary.

"Good morning," he chimes. "Is there anything new on the menu today, or can I go back to my desk and carry on with current projects?"

"Nothing new that I need to bother you with," I say.

Jason nods and spins on his heels to return to his desk. I'm guessing Jason felt the tension in the room and decided not to get involved. We've trained him well.

"Brantley, I would love to tell you all about it, as a friend, but along with our relationship, I also lost the confidant-and-friend privilege we had with each other."

His eyes lock on mine and he seems profoundly perplexed by my observation. "No, Jess. You haven't. If you need help with anything not related to Anson, you can talk to me and I will listen as a confidant. I think we've both dealt well with our other situation and can now move past it to remain friends."

His thought makes me smile and I feel the tension in my shoulders slip away. I'd never thought he'd be able to be comfortable enough with me after our split to still consider me a friend. I don't know of any guy who'd agree to stay friends with their ex-lover, but if he thinks he can handle this then I'm game. "Okay. You have a deal. But," I say, holding a finger in the air to make my point as clear as possible, "You *have* to stop wearing that cologne in the office. It's what got me into trouble with you in the first place, and it only reminds me of sex," I say, hoping that didn't come off as a tease.

A riotous laugh comes from Brantley and I am surprised at his reaction. "You have a deal, Jessica Adeline James. I'm getting tired of this scent anyway."

I pause at his remark then smile apprehensively. The truth is, no matter what scent Brantley wore I'm sure he'd still be attractive to me. The attraction will never fade, and that realization digs at me no matter how hard I try to suppress it.

The Creative Director

"To answer your initial question in more detail, I don't know that I'd say yes if he did ask me to marry him. Not just yet, anyway. I'd never have thought that eight years apart would have changed us so dramatically. He's still the Anson I knew back then, but we are in many ways very different people now. We've both matured substantially, yet the basic things about us that are deep-rooted from years ago still exist. Like any relationship, we are a work in progress."

"Right. I won't ask you about it again," he says. "And I'm not sure why I asked you in the first place. Perhaps a little part of me wants you to fail, and please don't fault me for that opinion." Brantley takes his coffee in his hand to sip it, but the plastic lid pops off and hot coffee spills down the entire front of his shirt, pants and jacket as well as across his desk.

"Bloody hell!" he yells as he leaps up from his desk chair looking shocked at the mess.

I jump up from my desk to help him by grabbing some paper towels from the kitchenette to sop up the spills on the desk and dab at his clothes. "Please stop that, Jess," he says as his hand stills my dabbing and his eyes meet mine in a rock-solid stare.

Standing so close to Brantley, touching him and treating him like he's still my lover, I pause. "Shit. I'm sorry. It was an instinctive reaction to help you." I cover my mouth with my hand and break out laughing at the realization that I'd been dabbing at the crotch of his pants.

"The desk, Jess. Focus on the desk, please," he says, frowning at me. He turns to head to the washroom while I hold back more laughter and dry off his desk before the hot liquid seeps in around his laptop.

"You find my accidental coffee mishap amusing?" he asks sharply from the washroom.

"No. That isn't what I was laughing at and you know it."

"Yes, well, now you'll have to give me five minutes for a correction to happen from the … uh, repercussions of your actions."

That only makes me laugh harder now. It shouldn't but it does. I manage to wipe down his desk and toss the soaked paper towels in the trash. I hear the door to the washroom close and return to my desk to go back to work, trying to get my giggles under control and not think about how much I loved Brantley's touch on my wrist.

The Creative Director

After a few minutes, Brantley exits the washroom and looks over to me. His white dress shirt, green silk tie and pants are covered in coffee stains. "Do you think it would be inappropriate to ask Jason to go to my flat for me to retrieve a new suit? I have a conference call in ten minutes that I cannot reschedule."

"No. I'm sure he's dying to see what an English prick's flat looks like," I say and giggle uncontrollably.

"Right. Well let's hope it's not a complete disappointment," he replies, frowning at me.

Brantley strides past me in his foul mood to locate Jason. They are back in two minutes, with Brantley handing Jason his apartment keys and giving instructions on where to locate his suits and ties. "And I trust you'll be back as soon as possible?" Brantley asks Jason. "I've got an in-house meeting at eleven o'clock and I'd rather not be wearing coffee-soaked clothes when the client arrives."

"Yup, no problem," Jason says then strides past my desk and winks at me. "I'll be back quick, Jess."

"Sure, thanks."

Sandra A. Sigfusson

Chapter 39: The Things We Do for Love

In order to appease Anson, I choose to work all day Sunday and book the following Friday off so I can fly down to Houston to visit with him next weekend. I'm doing the best I can to compromise on our short-term long-distance relationship.

    As I wander around my apartment after work, adjusting throw pillows and trying to locate the TV remote, I can't help but rehash my conversation with Brantley a few days ago. The comment Brantley made about me not wearing an engagement ring has been sitting in the back of my mind for several days, festering like an infected wound. Should it bother me that Anson hasn't discussed getting engaged again? It had not crossed my mind until Brantley suggested it. And, do I bring the subject up while I'm visiting Anson or let it be?

The Creative Director

I already know that if Anson suggested we reinstate our engagement I'd ask him to hold back until we were together full-time. I'm worried about jumping in too quickly. There is no denying that I love Anson, but we aren't the same people we were back then. I need reassurances that we can solve our problems before I take that next logical step. "I'd be that way with anyone, right?" I ask myself aloud.

On Sunday evening I call Anson to share my good news. The phone only rings twice before he answers. "Hi Anson. Have you got time to talk or are you in the middle of something?"

"Nah, I'm not busy. I've got all the time in the world for you, babe," he says and chuckles. "I thought you'd call earlier, but I was busy working on my truck this morning anyway so it doesn't matter."

"Is it fixed now?"

"Yeah. I replaced the spark plugs and the rear left taillight. Nothing major."

"So, I worked all day today to catch up on my open projects so I could take off Friday next weekend to come down to see you," I say excitedly.

"Don't tease me, Jess. Did you really do that for me?" he asks.

Sandra A. Sigfusson

"Yes. Why would I joke about that?"

"I thought you getting away was impossible, is all. But I love that you put in the extra time so you could get down here. You know how much I miss you. I've got some good news to share with you when you get here," he says.

"Can't you tell me now?" I press.

"Nah. I want to surprise you," he says softly.

"Oh. Okay." My first thought naturally goes to him presenting me with an engagement ring, and I feel my gut tighten at the thought of dealing with that prospect so quickly. Maybe it isn't what I think it is. Maybe he found another doctor to take over for his patients down there. That thought gets me excited. It would mean the world to me if we could both stay in New York and I wasn't pressured into leaving Digame for a job in Houston. I cross my fingers over my lap and start in on idle chitchat about my week.

Our talk slowly, somehow turns into a phone sex conversation. I've never done this before with anyone, and I find it quite arousing to think I can turn someone on so much through the phone that they'd masturbate. I

The Creative Director

guess everyone likes a little taboo in their lives to keep things hot between lovers.

"I should have taken some pictures of you naked when we were at my parents' guest house," he says with his voice low and sensual.

"Oh yeah. What kind of naked pictures?" I ask, trying to be equally sensual.

"Those amazing tits of yours for starters," he says, then growls and laughs.

"Would you like me to take a shot of them now for you?"

"Fuck yes! Don't keep me waiting," he says. I giggle, surprised at myself for offering that up.

"Okay. Give me a second here and I'll text it to you." Slinking off to my bathroom, I take off the silk nightshirt I've been bumming around in and hold my cell phone camera up in a landscape position. I adjust the distance between my body and my boobs, looking for the perfect shot, then snap one. I look at the image and decide it isn't well enough in focus, delete it and try again.

I'm still connected up with Anson through the phone, and he can hear me messing around trying to get the perfect shot. "What's taking so long, Jess?" he asks.

Sandra A. Sigfusson

"I want the picture to be perfect. Hang on a minute," I say.

"I don't need perfect, babe. I just need your tits in the frame. Never mind taking a picture. Put me on FaceTime and show me those girls of yours. Jump up and down a little while you're at it," he says.

"Are you being serious right now?" I ask, only half shocked at his request.

"Totally. And I want to watch you masturbate on FaceTime too," he says.

"I'm not masturbating on FaceTime, you perv!" I say and break out in a fit of giggles.

"You're no fun. Fine. Just show me your tits. I'm fucking rock-hard here and I want to come so badly while looking at your naked body."

"Fine," I say, and sigh. I connect through FaceTime and put the camera on me live in my bathroom, naked from the waist up. "Happy now?" I ask, and then bounce lightly on the balls of my feet so my tits jiggle a little. I feel so stupid doing this, but I know he's alone and nobody can see me.

The Creative Director

"Oh, fuck, yes," I hear him moan. "Rub your hands over them and pull on your nipples for me," he says.

I oblige and shockingly find myself getting highly aroused by his voice and commands. "Like this?" I ask softly while I fondle one breast, press it up against the other one, then tug on the nipple to lengthen its peak.

"Yeah, just like that, babe. Now show me your sweet pussy. I want to see you rubbing your clit and making yourself come for me."

"Nope. Not going there, Anson. Tits, yes. Pussy, hard no."

"Do you have any idea how fucking hard I am for you?" he moans.

"No. Show me," I say. Tit for tat. I've shown him mine and he can show me his. The second after my request, my cell phone screen is showing the full throbbing length of Anson's penis and his big hand slowly stroking it. Holy fuck, that's so sexy. I can't help myself and slide my leggings off, slipping my fingers down to my sex to start rubbing. I aim my cell phone at myself and my busy fingers. The instant Anson realizes I've succumbed to masturbating on FaceTime while he does the same, he blows his load.

Sandra A. Sigfusson

"Fuck me that's a sight for sore eyes," he moans. My fingers rub so fast now and I'm ready to climax at his words. This happened so fast. Out of seemingly nowhere I was diving right in to something only minutes ago I said I'd never do.

Where the hell did my backbone go? I've turned into a jellyfish as of late, and I don't know what to make of what is happening to me. My orgasm crashes through me, and I place my phone face-down on the countertop while I regain control of myself and slowly stop rubbing my clit.

"Jesus, what just happened?" I ask, catching my breath.

"You fucking came for me on FaceTime, Jess," he says, laughing.

"Shhh!" I say. "Can anyone hear you?"

"No, no. It's totally private here. Fuck that was awesome," he says, smiling from ear to ear.

I want to feel like it was awesome, but I feel a little ashamed of myself. This was totally out of my comfort zone. How did he get me so hot and willing to get myself off over the fucking phone? "God," I groan as

The Creative Director

I rinse off a washcloth and clean myself up at the bathroom basin.

I swear the Beaumont kids have some weird control over me. First I make love to Karmyn against my better judgment, and now I've done live phone sex with Anson. What could those two possibly ask of me next?

I pick my phone back up off the counter and see his satisfied grin fill my screen. "I love that you did that for me," he says softly. "Same time tomorrow night?" he asks, arching his brow and smiling like a sex-starved fool.

"No, Anson. Once was enough. Next weekend is only five days from now. I'm sure if you're that lonely you can entertain yourself behind closed doors," I say.

Anson chuckles and replies, "I just might. Now that I have video of you making yourself come I could get myself off anytime I want."

"That wasn't recorded video, Anson. That was in real time. You can't record that shit while you're live."

"Oh, yes I can, and yes I did."

The next thing I see on my screen is the video he took of me while I was in the bathroom. My movements, the soft moaning sounds I made while I climaxed, and then the loud exhale of my breath when I came all shock me. I'm pissed off and have about thirty swear words in my head ready to explode from my mouth.

"Erase that right this minute!"

"Hey, hey. Why are you so uptight? This is just you and me, Jess," he says, attempting to calm me.

"Delete it now!" I say as sternly as I can. I take a deep breath and repeat my request, but less harshly. "Delete it please, Anson. I'd be livid if anyone but you saw that video. You have to erase it, I'm begging you."

"Okay, okay," he replies reluctantly after a few beats of silence. "I don't understand why you're so upset about it, but if you want it gone, it's gone." A heavy sigh comes through the phone speaker, and I see him frowning on my screen as he taps to delete the video as I asked.

"Is it gone?"

"Yes, babe. I deleted the video. I'm sorry that pissed you off. You have to know my heart was in the right place. I want anything I can get my hands on to have some part of you close to me when we aren't able to be together," he says, attempting to calm me.

The Creative Director

"Thank you," I say, and breathe out a relaxing breath.

"Can I ask why it was such a big deal? You wouldn't have had a problem with this before. Why did this bother you now?"

"Because I'm not twenty-two years old, Anson. I don't get drunk every weekend and party half naked. I'm a professional businesswoman and I need to protect my reputation at every turn. What if you had lost your phone and someone posted that video online? What if you got drunk with your friends and showed them the video? I just don't like the possibilities existing if they don't have to," I say.

"You're right. I'm sorry if I upset you. You know I was thinking that it was just for me. For my eyes only."

"I know. And thanks for understanding," I say.

Sandra A. Sigfusson

Chapter 40: All Roads Lead to Forks

I'm feverish in my attempt to ensure I have everything in order at the office Thursday night before my flight Friday morning to Houston. Brantley looks over at me as I quickly scan my desk, looking for anything that I may have forgotten to address before I leave.

"Why are you so stressed? It's not like you're to meet the bloody Queen," he says, shaking his head at me. I glance over, narrow my eyes and give him a disapproving look.

"Ha, ha. You think you're so funny," I chirp back. I've been sarcastic a lot lately. The smart-mouthed tomboy in me has come out to play as of late, and I have to blame that on Anson. He's a fun-loving playboy with me and always has been. He's a good ol' boy-boy with big muscles and a big attitude. Although he may stand tall and proud and salute the American flag as a patriotic sergeant ready to defend his country, the minute nobody is looking he's a rough-and-tumble player with a lot of crazy ideas. I love that about him. He brought out the best and worst in me from day one. I can't count how many

The Creative Director

times I've been carted around the back yard or at a party somewhere, slung over his shoulder like a duffle bag, having my ass smacked while he smoked a cigar and guzzled another beer. So many memories flow through me now.

I pause over my final desk check and ponder if I'm still that same girl he fell in love with. Am I that tomboy deep down and it's Anson who brings that side of me out?

As I leave the office I make sure Carol knows I'm not in tomorrow and that I'll have my cell phone on to take any emergency calls. "Jason knows what's an emergency and what isn't with my portfolio," I remind her.

"Yes, Jess. Have a great weekend," she says and nods.

My flight appears to be on schedule as I confirm my flight number on the illuminated sign above my head inside JFK International Airport. I'll arrive in Houston at ten forty-five AM. I decide to text Anson while I wait in the boarding area.

Me: *Flight is on time. I expect you will be too.*

Anson: *Did you actually question my ability to be on time?*

Sandra A. Sigfusson

Me: *That would be sacrilegious, Sergeant Beaumont.*

Anson: *Damned straight Miss James.*

Me: *LOL.*

I didn't expect it – although I should have – but Anson greets me by throwing me over his shoulder and carting me out of the airport arrivals lounge while my face turns a deep shade of red. How embarrassing. But, he did show up in full uniform and so it probably looked charming to people around us.

"Put me down, you big ox!"

"Are you giving a sergeant an order, civilian?"

"Yes!" I state through gritted teeth.

"I outrank you on so many levels. Behave yourself or I'll have you thrown in the brig," he says then chuckles loudly.

"Not funny, Anson," I say, squirming from within his hold. Jesus, I thought he'd grown out of this tossing-me-over-his-shoulder thing. My short skirt is making me feel exposed to the public but I'm thankful I'm wearing panties. I try to reach behind me and tug down the skirt

The Creative Director

but the task proves impossible. I'm certain the whole airport can see right up my skirt. "For the love of God would you please put me down?" I beg.

"Fine. I want to kiss you anyway, and I can't do that with you draped over my shoulder." Anson gently eases me off him, and when my feet reach the ground I quickly adjust my skirt and hair. Before I've even finished his lips are tight upon mine in a deep, warm kiss. I wrap my arms around his thick neck and relish his passionate hello. Once our kiss is over, he hugs me so tight I can barely breathe.

"That's more like it," I murmur, and he chuckles at me again.

The house that Anson shares with an army friend of his named Craig is only a few miles away from the base. Craig doesn't hold a doctorate like Anson, but they rose up the ranks together and have been nearly inseparable since Anson joined the army.

Anson holds the front door open for me to enter, and I see Craig sitting on the couch reading a novel. "Hi," I say and smile brightly at Craig.

"Hello. You must be Jess," he replies as he stands to shake my hand.

Sandra A. Sigfusson

"Yes," I say, then stand there nervously, not knowing where to go or what to do with myself. "Do you read a lot of novels?" I ask, trying to start a casual conversation while Anson wheels my bag down the hall.

"I prefer science fiction action books, but this one was recommended by a buddy. He said he's read it three times and loved it, so I thought I'd find out what he thought was so great about it," he says.

"And, how is it so far?"

"Not bad. But I still prefer science fiction elements over classic war novels," he says, nodding. "Do you like to read?"

"I read a lot of ad copy and magazine articles in my job. I don't have much time to read books for pleasure, but if I do pick one up it's usually from a reader's online list of recommendations or from friends. I don't have a specific genre that I gravitate to. I'm open to anything that will make me escape the real world for an hour or two," I say.

Craig nods, and seconds later Anson returns to wrap his arm around my waist and kiss me. "I believe Craig has something he has to do for the next hour, right Craig?" Anson says.

The Creative Director

I elbow Anson. "Isn't that a bit obvious?" I say, furrowing my brows at Anson.

"I was just leaving, Jess," Craig says and smiles wide. He shakes my hand again and exits the house without another word.

"That was rude, Anson," I chide.

"House rules. When his girl is here I'm scarce. When my girl is here, that's his cue to beat it," he chuckles. Anson lifts me off my feet and carries me down the hall to his bedroom. I don't have the chance to visually explore his private space before I'm being nearly suffocated by his deep kisses and roaming hands. I can't help but laugh at how quickly Anson wants to get down to business with me. I stop his kissing and hold his handsome face between my open palms.

"Are you sure we won't be disturbed?" I ask.

"Yes. Nobody is in the house or expected in the house for at least the next hour. Now let me get your clothes off. I need to make love to you and I can't wait any longer," he says as his eyes widen and a big-ass smile is thrown my way. I nod and smile back while I help him remove my skirt and blouse.

In a few quick moments we are naked and sliding deep inside the bed sheets of his neat-as-a-pin, bare

Sandra A. Sigfusson

bones, clinical-looking bedroom. The nearly all-white sterile environment feels cold and impersonal to me, and I try to keep my eyes closed while we make love to each other. As a heady heat of desire fills my sex, the little squeak in his bedsprings makes me laugh uncontrollably, which in turn makes Anson laugh. We nearly don't finish reaching our orgasms because of our inability to keep our laughter under control. I feel like I haven't laughed that hard in quite some time, and it's as good a release as my orgasm. All my apprehensions about coming to Texas have slipped away and I feel relaxed again. I'm happy that I've made Anson happy by making an effort to come to see him. He is almost kid-like in his excitement, and that feeling is rubbing off on me.

We have so much to catch up on. These weeks apart have been hard on both of us. Our lovemaking sessions are as intense as they always were, but this is the Anson I remember and loved so long ago. He has a way with people, regardless of his rough-and-tumble first impression. It all makes sense to me now. I'm delighted he's found a calling to help others, as he's always been a great listener – surprisingly wise beyond his years – as well as a real softy deep down.

The Creative Director

When I heard from Karmyn that Anson was becoming a psychologist I was shocked at first, but knowing his deep affection for his uncle Ben who suffers from PTSD, his decision to go in that direction professionally makes sense. I'm sure Anson is quite good at making his patients feel at ease. He's always had a way of making people talk about themselves without them realizing they are spilling their guts. Not many people have that gift.

Spent, happy, and wondering what the heck it was that Anson said he wanted to surprise me with, I climb up to lie atop his thick naked body, fold my arms over his chest and rest my chin on my arms. I gaze longingly into his eyes and wait for him to say something.

"What are you looking at me like that for?" he asks, curious. A beautiful sweet grin graces his handsome face and I smile back.

I trace my fingertip around the pattern of one of the tattoos on his chest as I ask, "You said you had a surprise for me and I want to know what it is."

"Later, babe. I just want to lay here with you until Craig comes back." Anson strokes his fingers through my messed-up long hair and smiles at me again. "You're still as beautiful as the day I fell in love with you," he says.

Sandra A. Sigfusson

"I think you are more handsome than you were when we were younger," I say.

He slides my long bangs away from my eyes, a single finger tracing the outline of my forehead. "I love how powerful you've become. I think it's amazing that you've made Creative Director already. You're only thirty-two this year. That's really impressive, Jess."

"Why, thank you, sir. I appreciate your vote of confidence. Does my wielding of woman power turn you on?" I ask playfully and lick my lips.

"You have no idea," he growls before leaning forward and biting at my bottom lip. I return his love bite and then we're back at it again, turning the small double bedsheets inside out, making loud noises and giggling as we pleasure each other. I opt to be on top this time, as his massive frame nearly crushes me when I'm underneath him. But this position doesn't last long. Anson flips me over in one smooth move and once again I am beneath him. Tender kisses grace my shoulders, breasts and belly as he makes his way down my goose bump-coated body. I want to weave my fingers through his hair but the short army cut doesn't allow me this pleasure.

The Creative Director

"How many times do you think we can do this before Craig comes back?" Anson asks as his nose rubs along the ticklish space between my hips.

"Oh, God. You're planning to wear me out, aren't you?" I say and giggle. "If I can make it through three times with you in one hour without being too sore to walk straight, I think we'll be good."

"Duly noted," he says before his face dives down into the sheets to suck on my clit and finger-fuck me. That's it, I say to myself. I'm definitely going to be walking bowlegged tomorrow.

"Oh, sweet Jesus," I moan as my body responds instantly to his hands and mouth playing my sex like a finely tuned instrument.

"When did you decide to shave your pussy?" he asks after he finishes his outstanding snorkeling mission between my legs.

I breathe out a loud sigh as I calm down from my orgasm. "Oh, I don't know. About two or three years ago. And it's waxed, not shaved."

"But why?" he asks with curious brows knitting together.

Sandra A. Sigfusson

"I went to a waxing salon with Karmyn one afternoon to try it out and I kept it up. I feel cleaner without hair." I rise up on my elbows and look him in the eyes. "You don't like it?"

"It's okay, I guess. I'm not used to it." Anson rubs his chin for a second while examining my hairlessness. He's clearly struggling to decide if he likes it or not.

"So, none of your other girlfriends had waxed pussies?" I ask now that I'm curious.

"One or two might have had fancy landing strips, but no. Most have been *au naturel*," he admits.

"You'll get used to it. I promise," I say as I tug at his arms for him to climb up my body and kiss me. Anson nods as our lips touch and our eyes close, enjoying this sweet tender moment.

Just an hour later we hear the front door of the house open and Craig call out, "Is everybody decent?" then follow his question with a chuckle.

"No, but I think I've burned her out so it's all good," Anson yells back.

The Creative Director

"Good man. I'd have expected nothing less," Craig calls back and then both of them crack up on opposite sides of Anson's bedroom door. "I'm hungry. Are you two interested in going out for lunch?"

Anson turns to me as he's dressing and smiles. "There's a great restaurant down the road. You up for going to eat?" he asks.

I nod and slip out of the covers to collect my clothes. "Sure. Let's go eat."

Anson calls through the bedroom door. "Yeah. We'll be ready in ten."

The restaurant is a classic family diner that appears to be frequented by many other army personnel. The place is buzzing with conversation and the typical sounds of a busy restaurant. I engage in more topics of interest with Craig while Anson's hand gently rests on my leg under the table.

"You know, your asshole boyfriend has been talking about you since the day we met. I was beginning to think that you were his imaginary friend and not a real person," Craig says, teasing. Anson kicks Craig under the table and Craig kicks him back.

"Are we still in high school here, boys? Are you going to drape your arm around my shoulder and cop a feel while we eat lunch?" I tease Anson.

Craig chuckles. "You know your boy Anson well."

"Yes, well, we've got a long history," I say. "I'm not so sure I'd like a repeat of any of the crazy shit we did back then, but we've got some serious catching up to do."

"So I've heard," Craig muses before he gulps back nearly half his beer in one drink.

"What exactly did you tell him about us?" I quiz Anson. My forehead crinkles with concern that Craig knows more about me than I would have divulged on my own.

"Every tantalizing detail," Anson whispers in my ear and smiles wide.

"Awesome," I reply before I roll my eyes at them both.

After our lunch, Anson takes me on a driving tour of Houston's most impressive locales. I'd not realized how

The Creative Director

big a city Houston was until the airplane circled around it before landing at the airport. It's nearing seven o'clock when we arrive back to the house and rest our weary feet atop the coffee table from our positions on the couch.

"What should we do tomorrow?" I ask.

"Sex, eat, sex, eat, sex, eat, sleep," Anson says before leaning forward to kiss me, and then chuckles.

I can't help but laugh. "Okay, Mr. Hardon. What do you say we don't have quite that much sex and insert a little conversation in that plan of yours?"

"Fine," he sighs and laughs at me again. "What should we talk about?"

"How about you tell me about the surprise you have for me? All this mystery is driving me nuts."

Anson fidgets a bit with his feet atop the coffee table. "How did your investigation into finding a position here in Houston go?" he asks. I get the feeling he's trying to change the subject, but this is a conversation we should have this weekend while we're in the same place.

"I contacted five of the bigger-named agencies here. None of them have open positions for a Creative Director, so that was fruitless," I say. I fix my gaze on Anson and wait to see what he says about it.

His face goes slack and he cricks his neck left to right as if to stretch it. "Shit. I thought for sure that someone with your credentials could be at least considered," he says.

"And what about you? Did you find anyone to replace you here in Houston?"

Anson squeezes his eyes shut and then pops them back open. I'm not sure what that was about, but I'm guessing it's not the good news I was hoping for. "There are two people who have the right experience to replace me. One is a woman who only works with female patients, and the other is an older doctor who hasn't replied to my inquiry yet. Not promising on my end either." He blows out an audible breath and tries to avoid looking at me.

I want to scream. I try to gather myself and stay calm. "Anson, one of us has to give here. Let me ask you this. I want you to be perfectly honest or this entire situation is pointless." I sit sideways on the couch, tucking my right leg under my bum and holding his right hand in mine. "I want us to solve this issue quickly and to the benefit of both of us, as much as possible."

The Creative Director

I take in a deep breath before posing my burning question. "When you said you were leaving the army, did you mean that? Did you understand what you were giving up to be with me?"

His gaze is soft and I can see he's hesitating to express his thoughts. I'll wait all day if it means I get an honest answer. My gut instinct is telling me that his words about leaving the army don't hold as much weight as I thought they did. He has built a solid career here, under the supervision, guidance and support of his beloved army. Why would he drop all of that for me? I'm the girl that let him go because he wanted to join the army in the first place. Does his love for me really mean more to him than what he's spent the last eight years honing? In my heart I know the answer, as much as I don't want to hear it from him.

"Babe, I love you more than anything," he says. His eyes blink several times after his words are spoken and I wonder if he's trying to hold back emotions. My hand gets squeezed between both of his big warm palms and he leans in for a tender kiss.

Now I'm getting emotional too. "What are you trying to say to me, Anson?" I whisper.

"I'm trying to say that I can't leave Texas. And I'm not certain I can leave the army either. This is my

Sandra A. Sigfusson

life, Jess. I've worked incredibly hard to be where I am. I already have patients who rely on me to give them the treatments they need, that they deserve as past and present army personnel. If you could only see what these people have seen, live what they have lived through, you'd understand my need to stay by their side while they get better. Some of these people will never recover. That's how important my work is here. If you move to Texas to be with me, we can get married, raise a family, you can eventually find a job you love with an agency or even start your own agency," he says.

I try to withdraw my hands from him but he holds them firm. He's not letting me go until I've heard every word he's said. Until I've fully comprehended how important being in Texas and staying with the army is to him.

Change a leopard's spots; that is what I'm trying to do to him. I can't believe I've let myself get so wrapped up in our rekindling of our devotion to each other that I failed to understand that his needs and his life will always take precedent. What angers me the most is that he made me a promise. He pulled me back in under the guise that he could do his work anywhere, leaving me under the distinct impression that I didn't need to make

The Creative Director

changes to my career in order for us to be together again. Was I wrong to assume that? Was I assuming, or did he not make it perfectly clear it was his intention to leave Texas for New York? I don't know anymore. Everything we've said to each other up to this point is now shrouded in a fog.

"This is our crossroads," I say and wipe away the saline dripping from my nose with the back of my hand. My eyes are swollen with impending tears, my heart pounding in the saddest of rhythms – my world exploding in front of me.

"Why won't you come here, Jess?" he pleads. "I can't understand why you won't give Houston a chance to show you all she has to offer. It's not just me here. We can create whatever world you want. The perfect job, a beautiful home, a place to raise our kids." His words are spoken with a desperate need for me to agree with him. This is what he envisions for us. I can't look at him now. I just can't.

My eyes cinch tight and I shake my head as my tears fall. I sniffle again and try with all my might to accept what Anson is offering. Many women would jump at the chance to have that life. But it's not me. I'm a New Yorker through and through. I love the stupid cold winters, the sweltering hot summers, the ridiculous traffic and the crazy people wandering the streets at all hours of

Sandra A. Sigfusson

the day and night. I love my job, the people I work with, my clients and my family. I heave in a deep breath, hoping my next words won't make me totally lose my composure or crush his beautiful heart.

"I love my life in New York, Anson. I can't move here to Texas." I wave my hands in a circle above my head. "This isn't for me, and I have to be true to myself first. Do you understand that?" I ask. Our crossroads is now a fork in the road. "I have two choices but only one of them makes sense to me, Anson."

Anson withdraws his hold on my hands, shakes his head and looks up at the ceiling. I fully expected him to completely lose it on me now. I thought he'd be raging at me for taking this journey with him and then putting up a roadblock that neither of us can seem to get over, but he remains surprisingly calm.

After a few moments of mulling over my words he says, "I thought the idea of you and I marrying and raising a family was what you really wanted at the end of the day, Jess. I know you have a career that you worked hard to get, but I truly believed that what you do can be done here with me in Texas. I believed that if I got you here it would be easier to convince you that this is the perfect place for both of us. I can see now that you are as

The Creative Director

pigheaded about your career as I am." He pauses to look me in the eyes and hold my hands again. "But moreover, you're not willing to take any chances, and that surprises me more than anything. You were always willing to take chances. That was one of the things I loved about you, Jess." His hand reaches up to my face as he gently palms my cheek. The warmth and tenderness of his touch nearly kills me in this moment as I lean into his big, warm hand. "What changed?" he asks.

I can't help but smile through my tears, knowingly at myself. I have changed, but it was an evolution over time. I grew up to learn there is a difference between taking chances and making educated decisions. I know what chances I'm willing to take regarding my career and moving to Texas for Anson isn't one of them. If I could've gone back in time, maybe I would have reconsidered breaking off our engagement and gone to school wherever was closest to Anson. But I was so angry with him for joining the army without considering how that would affect us, I couldn't see what I was giving up by leaving him. I truly believed that if I put my foot down he'd change his mind. I should have known that putting my foot down once again wouldn't garner the results I needed this time, either.

Before I can answer he takes another chance to state his case. "What I was counting on was your willingness to take the leap of faith for me. Correction. For us, Jess. My surprise for you was that I've put an offer on a house for us," he says. His eyes stay locked on mine, waiting for me to react. I press my cheek harder inside his broad palm and hitch a breath as I wrap my hands around his wrist. I twist my face to kiss his palm before slowly removing his hand from my cheek.

My tears continue to fall as I climb up on Anson's lap and drape my arms over his shoulders. He wraps his big arms around my hips and squeezes me in tighter against him. I tilt my forehead to touch his and close my still-weeping eyes. "You should have fought harder for me back then," I whisper. "And I shouldn't have been so blinded by my anger that I let you go. We'd be in a different place now if we had behaved differently – if we'd have been able to predict our future. I'd have been happy to buy a house with you and raise a family, but not now." I suck in a shallow, jagged breath. "I can't blame you for this anymore, Anson. And now we're suffering the consequences of what we could have been."

My tears continue to soak my cheeks. Warm, wet kisses press gently upon my lips as we realize we've come to our end. Anson is weeping with me now. I've never seen him cry before.

The Creative Director

Our kisses are bittersweet and so filled with love it's crushing. As the tender kisses stop, I rest my open palms over his bulging pecs and I know for certain this bridge we've been standing at either end of has fallen down. If I loved him as much as I'd thought I did, I would follow him to the end of the earth and never question where he took me. But not now. I don't want to be blaming him if my career suffered for following his dream, and I know I would.

"Anson," I whisper.

"Yes, baby," he whispers back while drawing his thumb over my damp cheek.

"Make love to me."

Not another word is spoken. Our lips crush over each other before Anson lifts me up from the couch and into his arms, carrying me to his bedroom.

What I want from him now is the Anson I left behind when we were twenty-somethings. I want the unbridled passionate sex we shared, the roll in the hay with my big, handsome guy who once rocked my world like no other. I want this last time we are ever together like this to be Fourth-of-July-fireworks spectacular. And in the morning when we wake, we'll have come to terms with the fact we can't make a forever life together happen. This is no longer just about our love but also about long-term compatibility. I've changed too much, and he hasn't changed enough.

    Is it unfair for me to ask him to make love to me when I've destroyed his vision of our future? He knows deep down that I am letting him go, and he is having to let me go. No anger, no regrets, just pure, unabashed passion. The amount of hunger in our lovemaking tells me he understands. Maybe this is what we were missing; this opportunity to properly say goodbye to each other that we never took eight years ago. We know this is our last hurrah without having to say the words aloud.

    As heartbreaking as it is for Anson and I to agree we'll never be the couple we envisioned, I am relieved to have sorted out my future. We sleep together, spooned in his small bed, savoring every second of this last night together.

    When morning comes, Anson makes me a hearty Texas-style breakfast and we talk about everything but us. Discussing us is not an option any longer.

    I book a taxi from his house to the airport because I don't want to make a scene of crying in public. Our last hug is so tight, our last goodbye devastating. He loads my bag in the trunk of the taxi, and holds the back-seat door

The Creative Director

open for me to climb in. Before I can get myself seated inside, Anson grabs my arm, plants another crazy passionate kiss on my lips and touches his forehead to mine. "Nobody loves you more than I do, Jess," he says. I nod, give him one last chaste kiss, and slip inside the taxi, holding every welling tear until the taxi drives away.

There will always be a space in my heart for Anson. That deep-rooted emotion stood the test of time, and I know this because eight years apart didn't change how we felt, even if it did change who we are.

I silently cry as my plane leaves the tarmac in Houston. I know for certain that what transpired between Anson and me last night was the right decision, but it will take me some time to fully let him go.

Sandra A. Sigfusson

Chapter 41: Putting One Red Stiletto in Front of The Other

I needed time to focus on myself now, but my work, which has been poorly managed since my return trip from Houston last week, has also suffered. Although my clients haven't been privy to my absent-mindedness thanks to the amazing work of Jason, I cannot let my professionalism slide for another day.

I need New York. I am New York, and I refuse to change for anyone. These are the words I repeat in a mantra every morning when I rise. It may be my fierce independence that will keep me from finding my true Mr. Right, but I'm okay with being single for a while longer now that I've completely come to terms with myself and what I want and need.

Anson will always be a major part of my life. We will forever be connected through my love of his sister Karmyn, and his parents, George and Gabrielle.

The latest update on the Beaumont vineyard is that everything regarding the upgrades and replanting is on track as per our anticipated schedule. The architects

The Creative Director

and designers Gabrielle hired to restyle the tasting room and gift shop and add the new Phoenix Fire Grill Bistro to the old gift shop area are already hard at work. Construction work should be completed by the end of November, which will give ample time to prepare for a Christmas launch of the restaurant. The Beaumonts are planning a massive friends-and-family Christmas party there, and I'm excited to be a part of this celebration. Moreover, I'm proud of the work I did to take this tragic event and turn it into something worth celebrating.

As Christmas approaches, Jason and I are swamped by the clients working on seasonal promotions. Brantley has been surprisingly calm and collected during this busy time, but I imagine the helping hand of a temporary assistant for him and his clients has been one of the reasons for his calmness.

I have not mentioned anything to anyone in the office about breaking up with Anson. I don't need to drag others down with me. It is hard enough to know that my relationship with Karmyn is strained over this turn of events, and all I can hope for is that she will come around to seeing my side of the story soon. It is a tangled web that connects me and the Beaumont family. Everyone needs time to heal; however, I am feeling a bit shunned as of late.

Sandra A. Sigfusson

Grady has booked his favorite restaurant for my birthday this coming Tuesday evening. He's promised to bring his wife along for the dinner date and I'm glad to be finally meeting her. Brantley tells me she's quite the stunner and based on the photograph of her on Grady's desk, I'd have to agree.

On Tuesday morning I arrive to find a beautiful display of red roses upon my desk. They are a gift from everyone in the office for my birthday, but I know this was Carol's doing and I must remember to thank her sometime today.

Brantley and I hunker down at our respective desks, sorting through the last of the details for our clients' seasonal promotions. We sigh loudly in unison, then dart a glance at each other and break out laughing. We are spent. I'm tired of drinking coffee and nibbling on rice crisps stashed in my desk drawer. I need a good meal to boost my energy and it's well past noon.

"Do you have plans for lunch today?" I ask after our laughter subsides.

"No. I was just about to order in. Do you have plans?" he asks.

The Creative Director

"Nope, not a one. Do you want to go downstairs to the bistro and have a bite with me?"

Brantley nods and a quick smile graces his face. "Yes. It's been a while since we had a proper meal together," he says. "I know we'll be seeing each other tonight for your birthday dinner with Grady and his wife, but I need to stretch my legs and I'd be happy to buy you lunch today."

I nod and stand to adjust my skirt and grab my purse. "Ready when you are."

The bistro downstairs changes their menus frequently, so it's always a surprise when the menu arrives at the table. "I had a hankering for clam chowder," I say, "but it's off the menu this week." Now I'm perplexed as to what I want and scan the new items quickly for anything that might grab my attention. "Oh, they have steamed mussels. I'll have that and the garden salad," I chime happily.

Brantley raises his eyes from staring at his menu and smiles at me. "You are much more chipper than you were last week. Good to see you come out of your shell," he says.

I smile hesitantly at him. I'm not sure this is the best time to tell him I've broken it off with Anson. I don't want to think about Anson today, on my birthday. I want to think happy thoughts and look forward, not back. "Last week was a bit of a struggle, I'll admit," I offer casually.

"Anything in particular that had you so glum, or do you not care to divulge it to me, as your friend?" he asks. Brantley closes his menu and sips from his water glass in his oh-so-elegant way. Just then my cell phone rings and I flip it over on the table top to see who's calling.

"Shit. It's my mom," I say and glance up quickly at Brantley.

"Take it. I don't mind," he says.

I breathe out and then suck in a deep breath before answering the call. "Hi, Mom."

"Happy Birthday, Jessica!" she says, loud enough for nearly every table next to us to hear. I pull the phone away from my ear a bit. She's drunk and tends to talk loudly when she is. I cringe a bit and Brantley's eyes focus on me while he intently waits to see and hear my mother's next loud thoughts. "When are you coming to see us? I have a gift for you, baby girl!"

I cringe again and now Brantley's brows are raised as he looks a bit curiously at me. The waiter comes

The Creative Director

and takes our orders from Brantley, and I nod at them both while passing my menu to the waiter. "I can come by next week, Mom. How's Dad?" I ask as quietly as I can. I can feel several eyes on me now and I wish I hadn't answered the call in this very public setting.

"Your dad is your dad. You know that. How about you come by on Sunday?" she says, still basically yelling into the phone. Brantley tries not to smile at me, but I know he wants to laugh at how embarrassed I look at the moment.

"Yes. Sunday it is, Mom. I'm kind of busy at the moment. Can we save our chitchat for Sunday afternoon?" I ask.

"Sure, honey. And bring one of those bottles of wine from the Beaumonts, will you? I know you have a few of them just lying around your apartment."

"Yes, Mom. I'll be sure to bring wine." My facial expression and my posture – holding my phone three inches away from my head – must be amusing, as Brantley is now trying desperately not to break out into that boisterous sexy laughter of his that nobody but me seems to know exists. I smile at him and he loses it. I try not to laugh with him as I repeat to my mom that I have to go.

"Alright, baby girl. See you Sunday!" she chimes loudly.

"Okay, Mom. Bye for now." I hang up the call and burst out laughing with Brantley.

"Your mum is deaf?" he asks, and seems surprised that I'd not said anything to him before.

"No. I wish that were the problem. She and my dad are alcoholics, and not a day goes by without them being drunk. They lost everything many years ago and live in a trailer on a small plot of land not far from the Beaumonts' ranch. I bought it for them so they had a safe place to live," I say then sigh.

Brantley nods in understanding. "Are they well otherwise?" he asks, genuinely concerned.

"Not really. They've been drinkers for most of my life and Dad is also a heavy smoker, so his lungs are a mess. Mom is very frail and always has been. Neither of them can work due to health issues, and so I send them money every month to supplement their pensions. They had me in their mid-forties and I'm their only child," I tell him.

The Creative Director

He nods and thinks for a minute before asking another question. "Is that why you're so close with Karmyn's family?"

"Yes. Dad once worked for George for a few years after he was laid off from the accounting firm, but as his health declined and the drinking became a daily event, George had to let him go. I don't blame George for it. He wasn't doing his job, and no matter what I tried I couldn't get my dad to stop drinking, or my mom for that matter. They are peas in a pod, those two. It's a good thing they still love each other," I say and then try to smile, but that attempt is lame. "Don't get me wrong. My parents are good people but just a bit broken, and it bothers me that I can't fix them."

I try to change the subject and redirect to Brantley's mom's cancer issues. "How is your mom doing?"

The waiter arrives with our meals, and I lean back to let him place my bowl of steamed mussels and my garden salad in front of me.

"Mum is good. The last round of chemo seemed to arrest the spread of her cancer and the latest scans indicate that the original tumor is shrinking," he says as he places his napkin over his lap and slips the bottom of his tie between two buttons on his dress shirt. I smile at his little routine and he grins at me. "But enough about all that. Happy Birthday, love," he says and raises his water glass to toast to me turning the big three-o.

"Aw, thank you Brantley," I say and offer him a kissy face from across the table. I think I made him flush a little and he chuckles at me.

"Does Anson know you make kissy faces to your coworkers?" he muses.

I choke a bit on my bite of salad and wipe my lips with my napkin. "No," is all I can manage to reply.

The Creative Director

Chapter 42: The Heart Never Lies

It has been a full month since Anson and I parted ways. I've dedicated every spare minute of my time to my work, and it has been mentally cleansing being preoccupied with my clients' needs and not having to think about him.

I take a minute to reset my eyes from staring too long at my computer screen. I blink rapidly for ten seconds to moisturize my eyes, then rise from my desk to refill my coffee mug.

Brantley's at his desk, and I'm standing behind him now at the coffee maker in the kitchenette. "Can we have dinner together some time this weekend?" I ask.

Brantley turns in his chair and pauses for me to turn to look at him. "Any specific reason?" he asks. He leans back in his chair and I notice that the telltale squeak is gone.

"You had your chair oiled?" I ask and smirk.

"Yes. Is this the first time you've noticed? I did it a week ago. It was driving my office mate crazy, and since she's already a bit of a mad mouse I thought it best not to continue irritating her," he says and chuckles.

"Where did this kinder, gentler Brantley come from?" I tease and make a shocked face at him. "You seem like you're in a good mood. Do you have news to share with me?"

"Nothing too exciting. All my clients are perfectly happy at the moment and that doesn't happen often. And, the new year is fast approaching."

I nod. "Dinner to talk about whatever you want," I say. "Just casual."

His brow rises and he nods. "Fine. Where do you want to go for dinner?"

"Your place? Order in? Go for a walk in the snow after dinner?" I suggest, then wonder why I offered that.

"Why not at a restaurant?" he asks as he flips his deep-orange silk tie in his fingers and looks back up at me.

"Because I don't want to be interrupted by waiters and loud-mouthed patrons when we talk," I say.

The Creative Director

"Okay," he says slowly. "And what would Anson say about you sharing dinner with me at my flat?"

I blow out a long breath. "That is no longer a problem. We couldn't solve the logistics issue. We ended our relationship for good about a month ago and it was a mutual decision."

Brantley stares at me with what appears to be shock, and then his expression softens. In a gentle tone he says, "Naturally, I should tell you I'm sorry, but you know how I feel about that situation." He stares harder at me as if to attempt to read my mind. "Saturday night I'm free. Come round at four-thirty and we'll decide together what we should order to eat."

Nodding, I head back to my desk. I didn't want to elaborate on the subject of Anson, because nothing more needs to be shared. I assume that Brantley and I will remain friends and nothing else. I think this will be a pleasant evening with him because, regardless of our previous role as lovers, he and I have so much in common and we chat easily in private company. We've proven we can take whatever comes our way personally and professionally with grace. I need to reinstate his friendship now on a deeper level without concern for upsetting anyone, and I want to attempt that in a place away from work and other distractions.

Sandra A. Sigfusson

I highly doubt Brantley would entertain the idea of us reestablishing our physical relationship. He appears to have moved forward in that aspect and I have to respect him for it. If he asked me to make love to him I would in a heartbeat, but my hopes of it ever happening have been dashed by my own hand.

I've fucked up on so many levels here. I had the kind of love women around the world want – dream about. I had that love from two amazing men, and I lost both of them in a matter of weeks. Resting my forehead on the palm of my hand at my desk I think to myself, "Stupid, stupid girl."

As for friendship, I have Karmyn and she is a sister to me, not just my dearest friend. We've been shying away from each other as of late because of my ordeal with Anson, and that breaks my heart too. But she'll forgive me over time, and after a month I should think she'd be resolved to seeing it would never work between me and her brother. Her focus is on the vineyard, and her Oklahoma sommelier boyfriend Caleb, who seems to have woven himself nicely inside the Beaumont family. I think I need to give her another nudge, as I miss her so much.

The Creative Director

I worried that by Saturday evening I'd be nervous about going to Brantley's apartment. I want desperately to tell Brantley that I'm open to going back to being his lover but making assumptions about anything has been my downfall more than once. If that interests him I'll let him make that decision, and the first move.

I enter his apartment carrying a bottle of wine that neither of us has ever tasted, or so I hope. "A gift for my host," I say as I raise the bottle in my hand to show Brantley.

Brantley reaches to take the bottle from me and leans in toward my face. He stops himself and asks me, "Is it appropriate for me to kiss you?"

"Yes," I say and his gentle kiss on my flushed cheek warms my heart. I wanted a real kiss upon my lips, but he seems a bit nervous to have me here. "Did you think about what to order, or were you waiting for me to add my two cents?" I ask.

"Waiting for you, Pet," he says. "Shit, I guess I shouldn't call you that." His brows furrow as he silently chides himself, and I smile.

"I don't mind if you don't," I say. I stand behind him while he pours the wine into two long-stemmed glasses and turns to hand me one. He has changed his cologne to something a little less woodsy, but it still smells amazing on him.

Brantley raises his glass to mine. "To lasting friendships and brilliant ad campaigns," he says as a toast. Our glasses clink together and we both take a sip of our wine. "It's lovely," he says as he gazes upon me with those blue-pools-of-heaven eyes.

I clear my throat and nod. "Yes, it is rather nice." My smile is subtle and I'm suddenly feeling nervous. I let out a soft sigh and turn my eyes toward his living room. "Sit with me," I say. I walk toward the living room and seat myself on the couch. Brantley follows and sits beside me with about two feet of space between us.

After resting his glass upon the coffee table he leans forward, resting his forearms on his thighs and clasping his hands together. He lowers his head for a moment before raising it again and turning his head so his eyes meet mine. "You have something on your mind. Spit it out," he says softly.

"I do have something on my mind." Sucking in a deep breath I spill my news. "As I mentioned, Anson and I couldn't sort out our career issues to either of our satisfactions, and thus our relationship came to a full end.

The Creative Director

He's going to set up his clinical psychologist practice in Houston, Texas. I can't and won't follow him there. New York is my home."

"Why wouldn't you go with him? There are plenty of ad agencies in Texas, excellent ad agencies, in fact. I know this because I'd researched many of them before I agreed to work at Digame."

"That doesn't surprise me," I say and flash Brantley a quick smile. "I did contact several agencies but none were hiring CD's. Anson couldn't find a doctor to take over for his patients, so that was the stalemate situation – me not able to move to Texas and him not being able to, or rather, not willing to leave." I raise my wine glass to my lips and breathe in the bouquet before taking my next sip.

Brantley moves slightly on the couch to look more directly at me. "I was worried that you'd be leaving Digame soon. I hated the idea of you moving away, but I came to respect whatever decisions you made – reluctantly, obviously, although you hadn't shared many of them with me until recently."

Brantley is still perplexed at my news, and it's hard to tell if this is a good thing or a bad thing. He told me when Anson suddenly appeared that I'd know my own heart. The truth is that deep down I did, but I ignored

Sandra A. Sigfusson

it. I should never have left Brantley for Anson, but it's easy to say now that I have all the hindsight in the world.

I've fucked with this man's heart with my rash decision and I feel terrible about how it all transpired. I need Brantley back. Desperately. Sitting next to him here in his apartment, sipping wine and chatting, I feel so comfortable. My heart truly does belong to him and this is the emotion that rules me now. In the past two weeks of soul searching I've discovered that this is ultimately why I couldn't follow Anson to Houston. Regardless of my attempts otherwise, my heart belonged to Brantley.

Should I ask him if he still feels as much for me as I do him? What if he rejects the idea of us getting back together? How would I handle it? I couldn't blame him if he rejected me. This is do-or-die time. I know I thought it best to let him be the one to make a move back to being lovers, but I can't stand not being in his arms while we sit beside each other like this. Unless I tell him I want him, I'll never know how deep his love for me goes, or if he has it in his heart to forgive me. I know I cannot be crushed any more than I already am.

I rest my hand on the couch, palm up between us, and look down at it. "I want your hand in my hand," I

The Creative Director

say. "If you'll agree to forgive me for walking away from what we had together."

I slowly raise my eyes to meet his. Brantley hesitates briefly before I feel his warm hand slowly weaving its fingers in mine. He squeezes gently but I'm still not certain that he's willing to take me back. If he has resolved to letting me go, this may be permanent and I've absolutely lost them both. I take in a deep breath and my heart flutters at the possibility he has forgiven me.

The hesitation and seemingly long time before he replies grips me. "I've considered this situation for quite some time, Jess."

I nod and squeeze his hand back.

His eyes are not as soft on me as they were a moment ago. I've thrown our casual night together into a serious place within the first half hour of my arrival. I had to let him know that I regret, deeply regret, choosing Anson over him.

Brantley's eyes narrow before he speaks. I know this look is a warning that he's about to make a serious statement. "I'll not play games." He pauses for a beat, and I have to remind myself to breathe while he tells me how he feels. "I love you. I want you more than you'll ever know," he says softly, but his jaw tics and that worries me. My heart stills at his words.

Sandra A. Sigfusson

"It was my actions that threw us into a relationship neither of us were looking for. I also understand that I hold some fault in letting you go so easily. What we had was still new, still raw, but I fell for you so swiftly that it took me by surprise. But," he says, holding up his finger in the air between us, "I've never given any woman a second chance, Jess. When it's done, it's done. You know I'm black and white about everything – my work, my life choices, and romance. I don't think it wise for us to continue dating, predominantly because of our work situation. It's not a good plan, and I think we both can agree on that point. You know how I feel about work relationships and I fault myself, not you, for where we ended up."

I take a deep breath at the thought that he has been thinking about us for the entire time we were apart. His honesty and surprising understanding of what happened between us remind me that he is not an unreasonable man, but second chances with him are not an option. Truthfully, I'd have expected nothing less from Brantley. He's always been clear on where he stands in everything he does.

It takes everything in me to reply. "My past is firmly behind me. I've realized that looking backward is

The Creative Director

of no benefit other than to learn from my mistakes. And this is what has happened. My biggest mistake was letting a man I once loved tear me away from the man I'm in love with. I thought I was mature enough to know where my loyalties should lie, and yet I betrayed you without understanding how wrong it would be."

My breaths are heavy and my chest feels tight. I *have* lost them both. I feel as though I'm trapped inside a room with two doors, and neither of them will open. His hand squeezes mine again and then he releases his grip, rises before me briefly, and returns to his kitchen to refill his wine glass. I sit in silence while he does this. Deep silence. I can't be here anymore. I must leave now before Brantley sees me crumble.

Without looking back behind the couch, where Brantley stands refilling his wine glass, I rise to my feet and move toward the door where my boots, coat and purse lie waiting for me. I continue to stay focused on the task of putting on my boots and grabbing my belongings while Brantley remains silent, watching me.

"I'll see you at the office," I say as I open his apartment door, slipping away into the darkness of the hall leading to the building's main exit. I struggle to decide if I want to leave this heartbreaking scene in a sprint or a saunter. My hands wrestle with my coat as I try to slip my arms inside the sleeves while I walk briskly to the exit door. Do I want to give Brantley time to miraculously change his mind and call out to me before I've left his building, or do I want to run for dear life to the safety of my own fucked-up world? My confused thoughts are broken by the sound of his voice.

"Jessica."

I stop in the middle of pushing through the heavy glass exit door, but I don't turn back to look at him. I stand frozen anticipating his next words.

"Jessica, I'm sorry," he says, just loud enough for me to hear.

I don't acknowledge his apology with a look or a vocal reaction, instead pressing harder on the glass door and exiting onto the busy street. I will not let him see me fall apart. I start walking and pass three brownstones before I completely lose all self-control. I run down the sidewalk back to my apartment at full speed while I kick myself for thinking that Brantley would be willing to take me back. How foolish am I? How ridiculous did I look pouring my heart out to him while he waited for the opportunity to crush me like I did him? I don't know what I'll die of first tonight, my broken heart or my shattered ego.

The Creative Director

*Chapter 43: Big Girl Panties
Are Ugly*

I was thankful to have several client meetings outside of the office over the next two days. I communicated with Jason by phone calls and texts. I even had Jason drop off any presentation materials I needed for my meetings to my home, so I wouldn't need to spend a single minute in the office.

When I did finally return to my desk I felt like I had my head on straight. The idea of putting on a pair of big-girl panties and growing the fuck up left a sour taste in my mouth, but life isn't all cotton candy and lollipops. I'm a top-end executive in an all-man's world and I need to stay focused on my career, now, more than ever. I've given up on love for the unforeseeable future. Brantley and I had managed to deal with this nearly identical situation before when I left him for Anson, and we can do this again. No more hiding. My chin is high, my aspirations still intact, and my goal is to keep my clients as well-tended-to as humanly possible.

There were only a few awkward moments in the first week, much to my relief. Then on Thursday Brantley and I physically bumped into each other while standing in the kitchenette. "Pardon me," he uttered quietly and I

Sandra A. Sigfusson

tried not to laugh at him. I bit my tongue and nodded instead, then promptly returned to my desk.

On Friday morning I receive a phone call from a college friend who is coming to New York for a three-day getaway. His flight from Seattle will arrive at six-thirty this evening, and I offer to pick him up and take him for dinner. Leslie McKinnon and I shared three classes together and spent many hours studying in the same library space or in the coffee shop on the campus grounds. I knew he was gay the moment I laid eyes on him and it never bothered me. I don't now and never will define people by their sexual orientation.

Leslie quickly became my male version of Karmyn during my college years. I could not be more thrilled to see him again, and my excitement at hearing his voice on my phone echoes throughout the room. Brantley's eyes follow me as I walk around our office space chatting happily with Leslie and making arrangements for him to stay at my place during his visit. I smile at Brantley as I hang up my call.

"A friend of yours is coming to visit?" he asks.

"Yes, my best friend in college is flying in tonight. I haven't seen Leslie since we both graduated."

The Creative Director

"Does she work in marketing as well?"

"Hmm, Leslie is a guy and yes, he works for an up-and-coming marketing company in Seattle as their head of research," I say, smiling wide. "I feel like I haven't seen him in forever. This is going to be a fantastic weekend!" I do a little jig in my chair behind my desk.

Brantley goes back to his paperwork but shrugs his left shoulder as if attempting to stretch it. His face grimaces from the pain he's in. I watch curiously as he repeats the shoulder roll then attempts to massage it on his own over his clothing.

Rising from my desk, coffee mug in hand, I slip behind him to rinse and refill my mug with cold water. "Did you injure yourself?" I ask.

"Yes. I was rearranging furniture and lost my balance while moving the telly stand. I got my foot caught in the edge of the area rug and I fell backward, hitting my shoulder on the corner of the side table. It wasn't terribly bad last night, but today the pain has increased. I'll be fine tomorrow."

"Let me have a look at it," I say, setting my mug down on the countertop and approaching him.

"It's fine, Jess. Just a little tender when I move the shoulder too quickly."

"No. It's not fine." I reach to remove his jacket and his hand stills mine while I hold the lapel.

"What *are* you doing?"

"Removing your jacket so I can see what you've done to yourself."

"Stop fussing. I'm not a child."

"Have you looked at it in the mirror?" I press.

"Woman, please. Let me be, will you?" Brantley shrugs his shoulder at me, winces again, and I step back a pace and glare at him.

"Take the damned jacket off, Brantley. Follow me to the washroom and show me your shoulder. I'm not taking no for an answer and I'm not treating you like a child. You are behaving like a child," I retort and frown at him.

His eyes meet mine and his jaw twitches. "Fine. But only because the longer I sit here the more the pain increases. I should see if Carol has pain relievers in her office." He stands and pushes his chair away with his other arm, and I follow him to the washroom. Brantley winces again as he removes his jacket and hands it to me.

The Creative Director

I fold it neatly over my left arm while he loosens his tie and unbuttons his shirt to reveal his shoulder to me. His face is stern as he looks at my reflection in the mirror, but I ignore his resting asshole face and close the door behind me.

Once his shirt has been pulled back to reveal his shoulder, I try not to gasp at how big and black the bruise is. "Brantley! Holy shit that's huge!"

Brantley twists his body to look at the back side of his shoulder and smirks. "I've always wanted to hear those words from you," he says and tries gallantly not to roar with laughter. I want to smack his shoulder, but instead I reach for a spare towel and run cold water on it. I frown at him and press gently with the cold wet towel over his bruise.

"You think your accidental mishap is funny?" I say, attempting to speak in Brantley's accent. He smirks at me and shakes his head. "I don't know what you've hit under the skin to make it so black, but you really should see a doctor just in case you've done more than just bruise it. This is truly nasty."

I take Brantley's free hand and cross it over his body to hold the cold towel in place. "I'll get some ice and have Jason contact your doctor for an appointment."

He nods and I leave him to raid the ice tray in the freezer. Over my shoulder I call out to Jason, and he appears in the doorway within seconds. "Make a doctor appointment for Brantley, will you? Any time slot today is fine." Jason nods and heads back to his desk.

Brantley comes out of the washroom still holding the towel, and I take it from him to fold the ice cubes inside the towel then reapply it to the bruise. "Hold that there for as long as you can," I instruct and he nods.

Just then Carol pops inside the office. "What happened?"

"Brantley injured himself last night and now it's bothering him, so I'm trying to lower the swelling," I say.

Carol approaches to view Brantley's shoulder and says exactly what I said to him in the washroom. "Holy shit that's huge!"

Neither Brantley nor I can control ourselves and we break out laughing. Carol laughs gingerly with us, unsure as to what is so funny. Jason comes back in to report that Brantley can see his doctor in forty minutes. "Should I drive you, or do you want me to call a cab?" he asks.

The Creative Director

"A taxi is sufficient," Brantley replies. "You are all making far too big a fuss about it. Go back to your work and I'll manage re-dressing in a minute." He looks at me, looks at Carol, and then nods his head toward the office door indicating we should leave him alone. I step back and grab my water-filled coffee mug then return to my desk.

Three hours later Brantley returns to the office. "Well?" I say. "What happened?"

"It is a nasty bruise and nothing more. I was sent for x-rays and there are no broken bones. It is merely tissue damage," he reassures me.

I nod and go back to my business at hand. I liked tending to him much more than I should have. Just being able to touch his skin, and that little private laugh we shared, warmed my heart. I redirect my thoughts to my dinner with Leslie tonight and press on with my paperwork.

Leslie and I go for dinner Friday evening, drink all night before passing out, then share a great breakfast in my kitchen the next morning. Later Saturday afternoon we go shopping, taking selfies of our stroll through Central Park, and then Leslie treats me to a carriage ride with the Clydesdale horses. I post all my pictures of our

Sandra A. Sigfusson

adventures online before we settle on going back to my apartment to decide what to do about dinner. My favorite shot is the one where Leslie kissed my cheek unexpectedly before the shutter snapped us. More wine flows, as do the laughs and discussions of where we see our lives in five years. We are both career driven. I mention that my long-term goal is to have my own ad agency, and Leslie thinks I'd be a great boss.

"What would you call your agency?" he asks while scanning the sushi restaurant menu attached to my fridge.

"Something simple like *The James Agency*. Unless I had a partner – then I'd have to do what the lawyers do and combine the names."

"That sounds classy, Jess," he replies and kisses me gently on my cheek. "I'm spent now. What's on the TV worth watching?"

"Pick whatever you want. I'm just going to vegetate here on the couch," I say.

"Fine. I'll order sushi first then pick out a movie," he says. We'll enjoy a quiet evening together before Leslie has to go back to Seattle in the morning.

The Creative Director

*Chapter 44: A Shift in Space
and Time*

The following Monday morning I'm still suffering the repercussions of drinking far too much alcohol in the past two days with Leslie. Brantley's shoulder doesn't appear to be bothering him anymore, and I watch him scurry around the kitchenette preparing to leave for a meeting. His Nortex Energy client upstairs wants to run more print ads, so he's agreed to meet with them briefly to arrange an updated contract.

The time passes faster than I anticipated, and I nod at Jason as he packs up his desk to leave for the day. The office is quiet now and as usual, Brantley and I are the only stragglers left, plugging away at our clients' projects. I hear Brantley clear his throat and it grabs my attention. "We appear to be here again after the dinner hour," he says. "Are you hungry? Shall I order something in for the both of us?"

"Sure. What do you feel like eating?"

"Italian? Baked lasagna?"

Sandra A. Sigfusson

"Yes. I'm up for that," I say, nodding. Brantley places the order on his cell phone and I go back to checking the list of ad placements Jason arranged for the Ellen Peek Lip Gloss account. Now that all the Christmas and New Year's campaigns have been arranged, we're focusing on Valentine's Day promos. Which reminds me that I have to coordinate Brantley's sister's novel and the new Beaumont Phoenix Wine combo package with Karmyn before the end of January.

While we wait for the delivery of our meal, Brantley begins to chat with me. I thought about asking him about his shoulder, but I know better than to fuss over him. "It appears you had a rather eventful weekend with that Leslie character," he says.

I nod and smile. "He's an absolute riot and I adore him."

"Yes, quite," Brantley mumbles and I'm taken aback by his little comment.

"He and I discussed our futures and I mentioned that at some point I'd like to run my own agency." I close the folder I've been viewing and stack it neatly atop the other client files that are doing promos for Valentine's Day. I flick my gaze over to Brantley before I rise to go

The Creative Director

use the washroom. When I return to the kitchenette, I take out two plates and some cutlery from the cupboard to prepare for the food delivery. Brantley stands directly behind me, so close that I can feel his breaths against the back of my neck. I ease a step sideways so he can reach the countertop. I'm acutely aware of how hard it is having him stand so close to me.

"I saw a few of your photos from the past weekend on Twitter," he says.

"Oh. I didn't know you used Twitter that often. I know we follow each other, but I've not noticed you posting anything recently." I turn around to lean my bum against the counter's edge and fold my arms across my chest while Brantley grabs a couple of napkins from the dispenser and places one on each of the plates I set aside.

"Are you and Leslie seeing each other?" he asks, without turning his gaze to me.

I shrug. "Well, so far it was just a whirlwind couple of days together." I smile to myself as I'm getting the distinct impression that Brantley is jealous of my fun-filled weekend with another man. I don't dare tell him at this juncture that Leslie bats for the other team. I try not to giggle and have to place my fingers under my nose to prevent myself from laughing.

Sandra A. Sigfusson

Brantley's head turns slowly to the left to look at me, and I look back at him, still attempting to stay my giggles. "I see," he says, and then he swallows hard. I turn my face to look out over his desk and the door to our office space. Without warning Brantley steps in front of me, planting his lips upon mine in a deep, hungry kiss. His hands grip my shoulders to hold me in place. Our kiss deepens as my surprise fades and I fall heavily into this moment.

I came to agree that another office fling with him was out of the question. Still, I've fantasized about him doing this very thing to me more times than I care to admit. Him suddenly taking me by surprise, kissing me hard and pressing his body tight against mine is a vision in my head nearly daily.

I fucking love this man more than any man I've ever known. I separate my lips from his and begin yammering on about how much I've missed his lips on me.

My words are cut short by another kiss, warm and gentle this time. "Stop talking, Jess. You've said what you needed to say and I'm trying to tell you that you haven't lost me. I've learned so much about myself in recent days. I don't love you because you let me take you

The Creative Director

to my bed, Pet. I love you because you are truly special to me. This is how I know that what I feel for you is real and unshakable. Don't go out on another date with Leslie. Be with me and only me, please."

As his eyes search mine for the favorable reply he's in need of from me. I lean in for another taste of his beautiful mouth telling me that I could do him no wrong. But I have and I did. I'm bewildered by his sudden change of heart. Between sweet, tender, powerful kisses I ask, "Are you sure about this? What changed your mind?"

"This time apart was a test of our love for each other. I've come to realize my black-and-white view of life should be less so. You've taught me that, Jess." Brantley's fingers skim across my forehead before he plants a kiss on the tip of my nose. "Don't ever leave me again, Pet. I'd rather die than consider a world without you in it." He smiles and holds my chin in his hand. Our mouths touch in the sweetest of kisses. The tenderness of this moment makes me want to cry, and I fight to keep my emotional breakdown in check.

With my chest heaving from deep breaths and those words of love from him, our bodies scorch with desire. He continues to kiss the side of my neck in a seductive trail while my heart melts and I fight not to go limp in his embrace.

Sandra A. Sigfusson

"When the order arrives can we take it to my flat and eat it there?" he asks as his lips caress the sweet spot below my ear. I nod vigorously.

Upon arriving to Brantley's place we drop the food bags on the floor and start to undress ourselves. Our coats fall at our feet, our boots get yanked off, and he leads me to his living room by the hand. I don't want to make love with Brantley on his couch. I want to be in his bed, able to feel, move and endow him with as much pleasure as he can handle. This moment is about him.

"Take me to your bedroom," I breathe while his teeth tug at my earlobes. Brantley nods and smiles wide. I follow his lead. Brantley's bedroom feels warm and comforting, as if I were at home. He shuts his bedroom door, and I ponder his decision to secure us from the rest of his apartment before realizing that his gesture creates a quiet intimacy. It is as if a closed door transports us to another world.

We step closer to each other, reaching out to entwine our fingers together against our chests while our eyes lock on each other's. A wave of warmth coats my skin. His fingers hold all the power, squeezing gently,

The Creative Director

telling me I'm the only one he wants and needs. I reciprocate that squeeze, drawing my face closer to his waiting lips.

We touch, mouth on mouth, opening our lips, our swirling tongues sending waves of arousal through me, head to toe then pooling in my center. My eyelids become heavy as my brain focuses only on this kiss and what it is doing to me.

The light clicking sounds our lips make as each tender kiss is released are the only sounds I hear over our breaths. I'm sensing the increased heat building between my legs, the desire and anticipation of his thumb pressing just there, exploring and searching for the source of my arousal, now throbbing like my heart in my chest. I exhale a soft sigh while I reach to undo his pants.

Our hands move slowly, appreciating the sensations of fabric in our fingers. We pull one piece of clothing off each other in turns. My sweater slips off first, slowly over my head and arms, and I reciprocate, removing his shirt. A tender touch of his fingers follows the edges of my collar bones, then sweeps in a light tickle down my arms before he reaches to undo my dress pants' buttons and fly. His kiss is deeper now, hungrier.

Our tender touching continues as each piece of clothing pools at our feet. My hands sweep up his chest before I curl my fingers up around the nape of his neck and lock my eyes to his. Our physical and mental connection in this moment says more about how much we love each other than words could ever express.

Bare of clothes, our bodies press firmly against each other. His skin is warm, his swollen cock firmly pressing at my belly, his hands gripping my bum in this heavenly skin-on-skin embrace. A warm, wet tongue travels up the side of my neck before he gives me a gentle suck of the skin below my earlobe.

"Lay back on the bed for me, love," he murmurs.

Taking two steps backward, my legs feel the edges of the mattress while his arms gently lay me down atop the thick gray duvet cover. My eyes follow his eyes while he soaks up every inch of me, as though he's deciding which part of my nakedness appeals to him most.

I part my legs, toes still touching the ground at the foot of the mattress, breaths deepening in anticipation. Brantley stands between them, bending over me and planting his arms on either side of my torso to grace my breasts and belly with small bites and nips. He travels down my body, slowly easing his way in a trail toward

The Creative Director

my throbbing sex as I weave my fingers through his hair in anticipation of this slow, sensual tease. I moan and reach to hold his cock in my hand, needing to feel the hot firmness and silky skin of him within my palm, but he denies me.

"Not yet, Pet," he whispers over me. My reaction is to arch my back and writhe beneath him. My clit is so rigid, swollen, ready to be coaxed, and I'm not sure I can handle waiting any longer to be satisfied.

Brantley eases his hand over my mound then slowly inserts two fingers inside of me. "Deeper," I beg.

"Patience," he whispers. "There is so much more of you I need to taste first."

His mouth finds mine again, parched and in need. Brantley lies beside me propped up on his elbow, kissing me, twisting his tongue in my mouth while his fingers plunge slowly in and out of me. My heart beats a little faster as the intensity of the sensation continues to rise. His fingers stop plunging to roam the folds of my sex in search of my swollen clit. I'm so slick, coated in my own arousal from his teasing. He finds what he's looking for and uses the pad of his thumb in quick circular movements. I'm almost too stimulated to come at this point.

"Are you going to fuck me before or after I suck your beautiful big cock?" I ask.

"I haven't fully decided how I'm going to let you play this out with me," he says, as a wolfish grin eases over his sexy mouth.

Sliding down off the bed, Brantley kneels before my spread legs and kisses my mound. A slippery hot tongue slides over my parted lips and I quiver. I'm still desperate to hold his cock in my hand and massage his balls. I wrestle with the duvet cover gripped in my fingers at either side of me. This is heaven, this sweet torture thwarting my ability to lie still. And just when I think I can't handle how much pleasure I'm receiving he plunges three fingers back inside of me.

"Brantley," I breathe. I'm panting now and my breaths come with sounds of light cries and whimpers of pleasure between them.

"Yes," he replies while his fingers continue to drive a little faster, a little deeper.

"I want to come with you inside me."

"Do you?" he teases, and I moan the word *yes* for him.

The Creative Director

Releasing his fingers from me, he takes one long, delicious last lick and sucks gently on my clit for a few beats. That was all it took for me to come hard and fast. He climbs up over me as I shake out of my euphoric state, and at last I can reach for him, grip him, stroke him like I want so badly to do.

"That's it, love," he says with his mouth hovering over mine. We kiss harder now while I stroke him long and snug in my palms. He forgoes further kisses while focusing on the pleasure of my hands wrapped around him, his eyes closed and his breaths heavy through his parted lips. I twist my wrists while I pump, attempting to intensify the sensation, but in all truth I just want him in my mouth.

Brantley's breaths deepen as he lowers his head close to mine. My tongue finds the outer ridges of his ear and I breathe hot breaths into it before tugging on his earlobe with my teeth. "Are you going to come for me like this or inside of me?" I ask in a whisper.

His breaths become more labored. As much as I'm aching to have him inside of me, I don't want to stop pleasuring him with my hands if he's close to his release. I don't wait for his answer, as I think he's too far gone to speak to me. His hooded eyes, soft grunting and tight jaw tell me all I need to know. Suddenly stilling my hands and staring deep in my eyes, he says, "I want to fuck your breasts."

I nod and wait for him to slip up into position over my chest. I can't help myself, raising my head to roll my tongue over his crown and suck. I reach for his balls and massage them within my palms. Brantley moans, and it makes me so hot to hear him vocalize. He positions his cock between my breasts and I press them tight together around him. His breathing is still lightly labored when he starts to pump forward between them.

The visual is intensely erotic. Brantley cups his hands over mine and begins to pump faster between my breasts while he watches himself fulfill a fantasy. I squeeze my breasts tighter against his thrusts as I watch him closely. He comes swiftly. The hot ejaculate against my skin is not a sensation I'm familiar with, as no lover has blown his load over my body before. This was the most intimate of sexual pleasures that I've encountered.

"Thank you for that, Pet," he murmurs as he manages to slowly relax and open his eyes. "I don't imagine that was as pleasurable for you as it was for me."

I can't help but crack a smile as I stroke the back of my hand down his stubbled cheek. "It was a visual I'd

The Creative Director

never witnessed before and it was so erotic. A bit of lube would be recommended for next time, Sunshine," I suggest.

I hear a soft chuckle as he flops himself down on the sheets beside me. "I'd be quite grateful if you'd allow me to do that again, and I will gladly purchase a tube of lube for that occasion," he says then chuckles.

A tender kiss is placed on my lips as he rises to retrieve a warm washcloth to *tidy me up*, as he would say. When he returns, his hand sweeps gently across my neck and chest with the warm cloth. I point to a bit along the side of my neck. "You missed a spot," I whisper. A huge smile comes my way.

"Did I. Well, I must rectify that immediately," he says and gives me one of his cheeky winks followed by a light chuckle.

"Rectify? That word always reminds me of the word rectum. Why do two words that start with the same first four letters mean completely different things?" I say, curious.

Brantley's beautiful, hearty laughter fills the room. "You have a uniquely keen sense of observation and humor." After his laughter subsides and he's expertly cleared my body of his ejaculate, Brantley places the cloth on the side table.

Sandra A. Sigfusson

Climbing back between the sheets to hold me, his eyes fix upon mine. "You are so very beautiful to me. Every inch of you, inside and out," he says. "I'm so in love with you, Jess. And it's not this amazing sex we share that makes me say this. It is everything about you, from your ability to make me smile when all I want to do is smash something to the gentle giggle you have that makes my heart sing when I hear it." He pauses for a moment to kiss me tenderly before he continues.

"I thought I'd lost you to a ghost from your past, from something I'd never be able to control or destroy. I didn't want to hurt you by interfering with what you needed to do, but it was killing me to step aside while you made the decisions that you felt were right for you."

The fingers of both my hands weave gently through his luscious locks of hair. I'm trying not to be overwhelmed by his words, but my resolve in this situation is too weak. I want to hold him and have him hold me so tight now. I let tears of joy fall upon my cheeks while we kiss with a sense of prolonged hunger welling inside us.

I was broken by my own doing, but his amazing kisses and confessions of love heal my self-inflicted

The Creative Director

wounds instantly. "We are one once again. Nothing can come between us now," I whisper.

Brantley's hand finds its way back down the edges of my hips then slips between my legs. He nudges me to open for him. We continue to kiss hungrily while he slips into me again with two fingers. The sensation rides through my body, and my kisses soften because I'm incapable of focusing on the building intensity coursing through me and kissing him at the same time. He continues to wind me up until I'm nearing the point of no return, and I beg him once again to come with me.

Both of us still lying on our sides, I wrap a leg over his hip and he enters me. We rock gently together, mouths wet and exploring with tangled tongues, savoring the closeness, the tenderness, the immense gratification our two bodies give each other. He rolls me to my back and fixes his beautiful eyes on mine. Pressing harder and faster now into each other I cup my breasts and press them together, tempting him to lick and suck on my nipples, and he does. This sends us both over the edge, crashing together through our releases. I shudder as my orgasm subsides and a tender, barely-there kiss graces my lips.

"Sunshine," I say.

"Hmm," he replies.

Sandra A. Sigfusson

"It's a shame that nobody but me seems to know this Brantley. The one who is so tender, loving, beautiful."

"It's you that brings this side out of me. I've never been in love before you. You hold the power to control me like no other. And I trust you, like no other. I want you here tight against my body, listening to your soft breaths while you rest with me. This is what I desire from you tonight and every night," he says.

I nod, close my eyes and rub my nose against his in lazy circles. The heart never lies, and I should have trusted mine without question.

The Creative Director

Chapter 45: Fessing Up

I've learned a lot of things about myself in these past six months. I've learned that I'm not as strong or as smart as I thought I was. Very humbling. The silver lining in all that has transpired is that nobody has faulted me for my mistakes.

I received a phone call on Tuesday afternoon from Karmyn. It seems she's finally forgiven me for breaking her brother's heart, twice. She failed to note that I'd broken my own heart twice at the same time, but I won't call her out on that.

As for the vineyard, the replanted fields are hibernating in a thick carpet of snow, and now we cross our fingers that the first harvests shows promise for saleable wines when the plants mature in four years. I remind Karmyn about the book-and-wine Valentine's Day packages as well.

At the suggestion of both Brantley and Grady, we've submitted our designs and ad campaigns for the Beaumont Winery to the Advertising Awards for Excellence Organization, which celebrates innovative ad campaigns for the previous year. I've already won one award from this prestigious organization, and it would be

Sandra A. Sigfusson

wonderful to put a second on my glass bookshelf at home. Another huge bonus to the winery situation is that Grady agreed to allow me to work on this campaign pro bono, saving the Beaumont family thousands in billables.

I glance at my watch and note that it's nearly ten thirty. Brantley and I have a meeting with Grady in his office in fifteen minutes. I take a quick visit to the washroom to check my appearance. I don't normally do this, but today is the day Brantley and I fess up to our relationship. As I exit the washroom I look over toward Brantley at his desk.

"What do you need, love," he says.

"It's almost time for our meeting. Are you as nervous as I am?"

"No. I'm aware he's going to be angered about it, but it's time. I think we've proven that we can work together and have a relationship without it compromising our ability to get the job done," he says.

I nod and smile quickly. I'm obviously more nervous than Brantley is. Brantley's desk phone rings with an inter-office call and my ears perk up.

The Creative Director

"Yes," Brantley says into the phone. There's a quick pause before Brantley replies "Yes" again. He hangs up his phone and looks over to me. "He's ready for us now."

I wait for Brantley to rise from his desk chair and then follow behind him, holding my chin up high. I don't know why I feel so worried about what Grady's reaction is going to be. Perhaps it's because I don't know Grady the way Brantley does.

The double doors to Grady's office open at the press of Brantley's hand, and he waits for me to lead the way inside. Grady stands and smiles brightly, gesturing for us to take our seats before him in his crisp, yellow, tufted armless Italian leather-and-chrome chairs. For a man who presents as a tad frumpy he has a surprisingly modern taste in decorating.

I ease myself into the right chair and adjust the folds of my flared skirt while Brantley sits to my left, sitting tall in his chair with that famous level of confidence. "Grady," Brantley says. "How has your week been?"

"Well, the wife has been a bit out of sorts lately since our son moved to San Francisco, but other than that all is well on the home front." A quick smile flashes over his soft features. He is well preserved for a man in his late

Sandra A. Sigfusson

sixties. "I'm assuming everything is in order in your department?" he asks. Grady flips his tie through his thick fingers like Brantley does, then rests his arms on his matching, armed version of the chairs we are seated in.

I nervously pipe in, "Yes. All good. Couldn't be better. Fantastic, even," I continue, until Brantley eases his hand across my lap and clasps my left hand. I stop spewing superlatives so Brantley can take over.

"Grady, Jess and I would like to talk to you about something of a personal nature. We've been seeing each other as a couple for" – Brantley pauses to consider how long we've been messing around with each other in our corporate bathroom after hours – "for about three months." Before Grady can react, Brantley continues. "We are both quite aware of your position on office relationships, but this is different. We're in love."

I feel my hand squeezed a little tighter after his last statement, and my eyes are wide and fixed on Grady as I await his wrath. Brantley exaggerated how long we've been together, omitting my stint with Anson, but at this juncture there is no point in mincing Brantley's words.

The Creative Director

Grady eyes up both of us, looking back and forth between us as if he were watching a tennis match, and I suck in a sharp breath. He clears his throat and flips his tie again. "Why did you wait so long to tell me this?" he asks. His voice is calm, so that also calms me.

Brantley looks at me and I look at him. Neither of us really has a proper answer for his question. We both reply at the same time, "I don't know." (both narrator audio on this)

Grady's eyes again go back and forth between us like we're tennis players, and I suck in a deep breath. "You understand that those rules are in place for a reason," he says firmly. We nod. I release Brantley from his hold on my hand and clasp my hands together over my lap. Grady seems to be pondering the situation for a few moments, then clears his throat again. "I appreciate you bringing this to my attention. Since you've been dating for a while and I've not seen any indication of a disturbance when it comes to your responsibilities here, I don't have a problem with your" – Grady waves his pointer finger in the air between us – "situation."

"Brilliant," Brantley says, then stands to exit the office. Why do I feel like we were confessing to bad behavior to a principal at high school? Oh, yeah. That is because we were. How old are we again? This really feels quite ridiculous. I think for Brantley this is purely a respect thing. Still, this big ordeal Brantley orchestrated about confessing our love affair to the boss seems a bit over the top. Now I feel stupid. Brantley and Grady both look at me.

"What?" I say.

"Did you have something else to add, or do you have business to discuss?" Brantley asks me.

"No. Do you?"

"No." We both look at Grady and he smiles softly and politely at us.

"Okay, then. Back to work," I say, and I let out a long breath and nervously pound my right fist into my left palm. We exit Grady's office quickly and don't say a word to each other as we return to our desks. Once Brantley is seated he looks over to me and smiles wide.

"That went as smoothly as I anticipated," he says.

Now I'm even more suspicious. "You bugger! You made it look like we were going to have to battle it out with him when you knew all along that he'd be fine with it," I charge.

The Creative Director

"Actually, I must confess," he says, chuckling to himself. "Grady already knew, as I'd had this discussion with him before you and I temporarily parted ways." Brantley scoots his chair over to the coffee machine and pops in a coffee pod.

"Are you kidding me right now?" I say and roll my eyes. "Damn you, Brantley. What the hell was that little meeting for, then?"

Brantley chuckles at me again and I feel the hairs on my back rise in frustration. "We were messing with you. It was meant to be funny, Pet. I can't scare you, I can't tickle you, and so now I've resorted to pranking you. It was too easy, really," he says and smirks. "You should have seen how nervous you were."

"You are a jackass, you know that?" I huff. After a few minutes, when my anger subsides and my embarrassment at being punked fades, I say, "Well, Carol is going to be happy she doesn't have to be our keeper of secrets anymore."

"I doubt that, love. Carol lives to hold people's secrets. Sadly, I think we've just pissed in her coffee," he says and laughs loudly like he only does in my company. Just then Jason pops his head inside our office door and looks at Brantley with a shocked expression. I don't think Jason has ever seen Brantley do anything but chuckle, so

Sandra A. Sigfusson

I'm a little surprised when Jason doesn't pull out his cell phone to record this historic moment.

Jason looks at me, still shocked. "Is he high?"

I break out laughing and shake my head. "Well, maybe a little," I tease and pinch my two fingers together.

The Creative Director

Chapter 46: That Secret Dies with Me

Brantley looks over at me while I'm viewing more artwork through my loupe. He laughs lightly and shakes his head at me.

"What?" I ask.

"Nothing, love. I just find your fascination with that damned loupe amusing. Should you not get your eyes checked?"

"I already told you once before that my eyes are fine. But maybe this loupe is becoming a bit of a crutch," I say as I lean back and set the loupe down on my desk. "I guess if I can't see a glaring error with my own natural eyes then nobody else will."

Brantley nods and slips his chair back to stand at his desk. "I have a quick meeting with Grady in five minutes." He removes his jacket, which he rarely does, then rolls up his dress shirt's sleeves before downing the balance of the coffee in his mug. He continues to be relaxed in the office, and I have to attribute that to our relationship. Many people, including Carol, have appreciated that he's settled down as of late.

Sandra A. Sigfusson

"How long will your meeting be, in case someone asks?"

"I'm not sure," he replies. "Maybe half an hour." I nod and watch him as he strides down the hall toward Grady's office.

I rise to refill my coffee mug, and as I pass Brantley's desk I note that he's left his jacket hanging over his chair. I glance around the office and through the glass-paneled wall to check if anyone can see me. As stealthily as I can, I knock the stapler to the floor, and while I'm retrieving it I reach inside the jacket, searching for Brantley's wallet. I'm certain he keeps it in his jacket and not his pants, so it should be right here in the lining's breast pocket. Even after all this time together I never bothered to dig deeper into the mystery of Brantley's first name, but today I'm going to get to the bottom of it.

Smoothing my hands over the jacket searching for a lump, I locate his wallet and slowly slip it out of the pocket. I can't believe I never thought to do this months ago at home when he was in the bathroom or something.

Again, I visually sweep my surroundings to check if anyone can see what I'm up to. Just as I have the wallet

The Creative Director

in my hands and I'm about to flip it open, Carol waltzes in and catches me red-handed.

Carol's eyes narrow at me and I smile. I wave her closer and she obliges me. "What are you doing?" she asks in a whisper.

"Do you want to know what Brantley's first name is as much as I do?" I whisper.

Carol nods and gives me a wry smile. "Okay, but do this quick," she whispers back as she scoots up closer beside me. Easing the bifold open, I find his driver's license and slide it up with my thumb to read his full name.

Carol peers over my shoulder to read it with me. In unison we both say, "Julian?"

I try not to crack up but I do, and rather loudly. Carol slaps my shoulder while I tuck the license back inside the billfold and slip it inside his jacket. "I knew it!" I say, louder than I should have.

"Knew what?" Carol asks.

"He and I had a conversation one day about him never using any name other than Brantley. He told me some cockamamie story about his mother messing up his birth documents and that his first and last name were both

Brantley. I never believed him, and now that I've had this little chance to snoop I know he was lying to me."

I try not to giggle but I do. Having had my back turned to the office door while I talked to Carol I didn't notice Jason standing there. He clears his throat and eyes up Carol and me.

"Just what the hell are you two up to in here?" he asks.

I spin around quickly. Jason can see that Carol and I have been up to no good. "Spill it," he says.

"I'll die before I reveal my secrets," I say confidently. Carol smacks my shoulder again with the back of her hand and starts to giggle. She strides forward to exit the room, trying not to bump her shoulder with Jason's. Once she's past him she cracks up again. I can still hear her laughing as she sits herself at her desk beside our receptionist, and it makes me laugh again as well.

"I'm guessing this is a girl thing and I'm not included," Jason says as he plunks two folders on my desk.

The Creative Director

"Yes, sorry Jason. I'll check those files in a few minutes."

I go back to my desk and open the folders Jason gave me. Everything seems fine, but I grab my loupe and review the image of the model more closely with it out of habit. Just then Brantley enters our office and chuckles at me. "Your new nickname is Loopy," he says.

"Ha, ha," I reply sarcastically and continue on with my close inspection. "Sure thing, Julian," I mumble quietly to myself.

Brantley stops just steps from his desk and spins to look at me. "What did you say?" he asks, brows pinched.

"Nothing. I was just wondering if that canned food company you're working with uses a *Julian* date on their labels," I say, but then bust out laughing so hard that I have to run to the washroom to prevent myself from peeing in my panties.

"Bollocks!" I hear him say from outside the washroom door. "How did you find out?" he demands.

"That secret dies with me," I say, then crack up again.

"Open this damned door, Jessie James!"

"Nope," I say loudly.

"Who else knows?" he asks quietly through the door seam at the jamb. I hear him rattle the handle and I laugh heartily at him again. I collect myself after a few more seconds and open the washroom door to find Brantley staring me down.

"Chill, J.B. I promise I won't tell anyone else," I say in a whisper, bite my bottom lip for a sexy effect, and adjust his tie. I get a quick kiss on the lips from him.

"I want to fuck you in this loo so badly right now," he whispers.

At the end of the business day, Brantley sends me a text, even though we're sitting ten feet away from each other at our respective office desks.

Brantley: *Are you coming home with me tonight?*

Me: *Yes, Julian. I'll go home first to change my clothes. What time?*

Brantley: *Stop using my first name! And be there by seven.*

The Creative Director

Brantley: *Are you coming commando? Don't answer that. I want to be surprised.*

Sandra A. Sigfusson

Chapter 47: The Nightly News

The spring weather hasn't been favorable. A few days have been warm and inviting for walks, but between my workload and the weather it has been difficult to get some good old-fashioned fresh air. Today is one of those rare sunny days worthy of taking a stroll at lunch, and hopefully Brantley will want to join me.

I saunter over to our office kitchenette to put my empty mug in the sink. Brantley is busy formulating an email to one of his clients, and I lean over his shoulder to read what he's typed.

"Can I steal you away for a walk?" I say. "I think we need to stretch our legs."

Brantley looks over his shoulder at me and nods. "Two minutes, love. I'll meet you in the lobby and I'll buy you lunch."

Bits of sun peek through the clouds intermittently during our walk, and I find myself thinking about going on a vacation to somewhere hot and sunny. As much as I

The Creative Director

love New York, she does wear on you after a while. As we stroll the boardwalk hand in hand, Brantley suggests we have dinner at Mandolin's Saturday evening. I nod in agreement, as I love that place. After half an hour of strolling, we find ourselves back at our office building and decide to grab a bite at the bistro in the lobby before going back to the office grind.

"Do you care to spend the night at my flat after dinner Saturday?" he asks as he wipes his lips gently with his napkin for the tenth time during our meal.

I nod and smile in agreement. "Ten," I say, and try not to break out into giggles.

"Ten what?" he asks, smiling at me.

"Dabs," I say.

"Dabs? Dabs of what, Pet?" he asks, now quite curious.

"Of your mouth with your napkin. I keep a running tally of it every time we share a meal. The highest number is twenty-two," I say and then crack up while I mimic his mouth-wiping with my own napkin.

Brantley smirks at me and chuckles. "I'm assuming that this amuses you rather than annoys?" he asks.

"Yes. It should annoy me but it doesn't. Perhaps I admire how worried you are about having bits of food stuck to your face. My proper Brantley," I say in my bad English accent and then giggle again.

"Fine. Tease me all you want, Loopy," he says and chuckles loudly at me.

I nod and raise my teacup in the air. "Touché, my British bedmate."

We continue to tease each other about our private lists of each other's odd habits until our bill arrives and Brantley pays for our meal. "That was a lovely lunch with you, Pet," he says and gives me a quick peck on the cheek before we return to the office.

Saturday evening Brantley picks me up in a hired car to take us to Mandolin's for our reservation. These cars are much nicer than a typical New York cab, and I feel very special tonight. The restaurant tucks us in at a table in the corner and we love the coziness of the setting. As expected our meal is sensational. This night could not have been more enjoyable.

The Creative Director

We arrive to Brantley's apartment and quickly pour ourselves some red wine and settle down comfortably on his couch. Brantley puts on the television and settles on a local station that caters to news and events in New York.

Oddly, Brantley keeps checking his watch, and I have to wonder what it is that has him so concerned about the time. "Are you expecting someone tonight?" I ask.

"No, love. What made you think I was to expect someone?"

"You keep checking your watch," I say, pointing at his wrist.

"Sorry. I had no idea I was doing so," he says, pretending to be casual while he adjusts the watch band. "I'll stop this instant," he says and smiles brightly at me.

My lips press to a hard line as I silently wonder what is going on in his head. I turn my attention back to the news reports and take another sip of my wine before setting it down on the coffee table. Brantley reaches his hand across the small space between us and weaves his fingers into mine, followed by a gentle squeeze. I love when he does this.

As a commercial break comes on, I hear the voice of someone familiar speaking. I feel like I'm doing a

Sandra A. Sigfusson

double take as I tune my ears intently to the sound coming from the TV and then look over at Brantley, feeling puzzled at how much the voice of the man speaking sounds like him:

> *It's not every day when the woman of your dreams walks into your life, grabs you by the you-know-whats and makes you smile in a way you never knew was possible.*

My hand gets another squeeze as the TV shows a man's legs walking through Central Park while doves scatter around him. The man carries a stunning bouquet of long-stemmed red roses at his side.

> *I don't need to tell you who she is, or who I am, for that matter, but I will tell you that this very public message of love is intended only for her. Miss James, would you do me the honor of accepting my proposal of marriage?*

The man, who I have now confirmed in my mind is Brantley, stops, and the camera slowly follows his hand holding the roses up the length of his body as he brings the bouquet in front of his chest. But the camera shot stops short of showing his face. The man seats himself on

The Creative Director a park bench, crosses his legs, flips his olive-green tie between his fingers, and rests the flowers across his lap. The voiceover continues.

Now, before you say anything, please listen to my top five reasons why I'm asking you to be my partner for life:

5. You are so beautiful to me, inside and out.

4. My heart quite literally smiles when you walk into the room.

3. You are brilliant in all aspects of the word.

2. I cannot imagine a life without you beside me, and

1. Because I'm truly and madly in love with you.

The camera refocuses on a dove that has suddenly taken flight from behind him, then follows the dove as it flies away while the screen fades dreamily to white. Then words appear over the white screen in the most beautiful script font I've ever seen: *Say Yes.*

I turn to face Brantley, my mouth completely agape and my eyes welling with tears. He squeezes my hand again and then produces a cherry-red velvet ring box.

"Will you?" he asks softly. "Marry me, Jess."

I'm lost for words at this beautiful proposal as my hand covers my still-gaping mouth. A tear falls down my cheek and I nod vigorously. Brantley eases the velvet box open to present me his engagement ring. Excitement and nervousness fill me. With shaking hands I reach to touch the exquisite princess-cut ring in the red velvet box and suck in a deep breath.

"Have I surprised you?" he asks.

My eyes flick up to meet his. I nod and smile wide. "Yes. Yes you have. And yes, I will marry you!"

Brantley removes the ring from the box. He stills my shaking hand to slip the engagement ring upon my finger. I search his eyes while my heart races at the excitement of the moment and our undeniable happiness.

My smile could likely light up half of New York City as Brantley tugs me in tight to his chest to kiss me. He slowly falls back into the cushions of the couch with me tightly wrapped in his loving arms as our tender, heartfelt kiss seals the deal. It has been a bittersweet journey falling in love with this man, but I'd not change how we got to this moment for anything.

The Creative Director

With my forehead resting upon his, I take in a deep breath. "*Digame mi amor.* How much did it cost you to make and air that one-minute long, touching and romantic-as-hell proposal ad?"

Brantley's smile widens as his beautiful, rich laughter fills the room. He kisses me deeply before he replies, "That secret dies with me, Pet."

The End.

Sandra A. Sigfusson

About the Author

Sandra was born in Vancouver BC Canada. Her artistic nature led to an avid interest in art and photography from an early age, and that passion continues today. Her foray into the realm of writing romance novels started in July 2018 as a personal challenge to write a romantic made-for-television movie script in her spare time, but instead it became her first romance manuscript.

Other titles by Sandra A. Sigfusson include:

Avalon | Mr. Magnificent | Rain on a Tin Roof

The Playboy Next Door | The Voice From 808

Website: www.sandrasigfusson.com

The Creative Director

Reviews:

Avalon: "I thought I would pick it up and just read a few chapters, but once I got into it, I could not put it down. The lead character is a personal assistant to a well-known Hollywood actor, but really this is a love story with ups and downs just like real life. I found myself becoming very attached to the characters in the book and did not want it to end."

Mr. Magnificent: "Not my usual genre, but a romping good read! I really liked that the author did not follow the older style romance stories and took us on a journey with twists and plot development. Mr. M was not who I expected him to be and had to chuckle at myself on realizing my own naivete! As a fellow Canadian West Coast resident, enjoyed the recognizable references to Vancouver and the surrounding areas."

Sandra A. Sigfusson

Rain on a Tin Roof: "This is the 1st book I've read written by Sandra Sigfusson; she has done a great job at writing a good book; I can't wait to read more of her books. The story line caught my attention at the very beginning and kept me interested throughout the entire book. I loved the chemistry between the characters."

"A great five star read. Lots of chemistry. Plenty of steamy scenes. Enjoyed the back and forth banter between the characters. Characters were likeable and relatable. Highly recommend this book"

The Playboy Next Door: "Captivating, entertaining steamy romance story. The characters are intriguing. The well-developed story kept my attention throughout, enjoyed reading."

"The Playboy Next Door by Sandra A. Sigfusson is a new to me author that I hope to read more books by. A spicy read with likable characters, great character development and dialogue."

Manufactured by Amazon.ca
Bolton, ON